HARD TARGET

LAST CHANCE DOWNRANGE - BOOK 2

LISA PHILLIPS

TWO DOGS PUBLISHING, LLC.

eBook ISBN: 979-8-88552-125-3

Paperback ISBN: 979-8-88552-126-0

Larger Print Hardback ISBN: 979-8-88552-129-1

Published by: Two Dogs Publishing, LLC. Idaho, USA

Edited by: Christy Callahan, Professional Publishing Services

Cover Designed By: Ryan Schwarz

1

____

The blood might be gone, but Lyric Thompson could still see it. Despite the fact she had no black light or luminol, she knew where blood hid in this bathroom. Places where it had pooled in cracks of the tile and trickled toward corners.

It wasn't like she'd never cleaned up after a murder before.

Except that was years ago, in another life. One she'd swept under the rug of starting over and pretended—the way she couldn't do with this blood—that it didn't exist.

Lyric walked through the living area to the bathroom where a young man had been drained of blood in the tub. Even though crime cleanup had erased the murder scene, she still had the urge to tear the cabin down.

Or burn it to the ground.

She had experience with that, too. Even if it was her life that had been scorched to ash.

Every day she thanked God that He was in the business of making something out of nothing. After all, that was what they'd left her with.

Lyric sighed. The seven usable vacation cabins on her property formed a cul-de-sac. At the end, the lane stretched to the highway. The first structure visitors would come to was the office and the floor above, where she lived. Beyond that were the ring of cabins.

What did she need with an eighth cabin anyway? This place was not just the site of one murder but multiple crimes. Two teens had been held here years ago. Tortured until cops and federal agents came to their rescue. A man involved in that had killed a young guy right here, though he'd been another victim years ago, not the perpetrator. He'd gone and murdered a man in the bathtub just weeks ago—a guy who'd reportedly been obsessed with those original crimes.

Lyric leaned against the wall and looked around.

She'd read all about it on the newspaper website. The text, and what wasn't written—there between the lines.

"Knock, knock."

Addie. Lyric turned slowly. "Hey."

"I figured I'd startle you at least." Addie stepped into the cabin wearing new-looking jeans, a flowy slate-gray T-shirt tucked into her belt, and a short jacket. She had an FBI badge on that belt and her hair pulled back. The agent grinned. "Then again, considering Russ read me in this morning, I guess I know better now why I probably won't manage to startle you."

Lyric stepped away from the bathroom. "He read you in on what exactly?"

In the past month, Addie had been promoted to the supervising agent of a tiny satellite office of the FBI located downtown in Benson, Washington. Then she informed everyone that the FBI didn't have an official dress code.

Lyric's cabins were half an hour outside town. Which

was about as close as she wanted to be. But she heard word from town often. There was a new guard in Benson.

Addie's uncle, Russ Franklin, was a former US Marshal. His retirement gig consisted of mainly consulting and more recently heading up a branch of what was known as the Accountant's Office.

Lyric was a client.

"The whole thing." Addie swept out an arm. "At least what I have clearance for, anyway. Russ told me all of it."

She might think that, but Lyric figured Russ might not have given her much of it. Addie was a fed, so she could lend a hand. But being a cop meant she couldn't know *everything*.

Addie continued, "That the Accountant's Office provides new identities to people who can't get help from the government."

Lyric snorted.

"They never did you any favors?" Addie wore that "investigator" look all cops got when there were questions they wanted answers to.

"Just saying no doesn't quite cover how it went down." Which was all Lyric planned to say about that.

Addie winced. "I can't imagine. And I might know what your former career was, but I have no idea what you've been through."

No, she couldn't imagine. Still, Lyric liked the woman. If Lyric had a friend, she imagined they'd be a lot like Addie. Even if she'd never settle with the idea of having a cop for a friend. Instead of saying any of that, she shrugged. "Long time ago."

"How long have you been here, running these cabins?"

"Three years next month." That thought made her antsy enough she felt the need to step outside, feel the fresh air of being able to go wherever she wanted. Do whatever she wanted. She knew all too well what it felt like to be captive. Abandoned.

Freedom was more important than anything.

She motioned for Addie to follow and stepped outside.

"You haven't rented the cabin out since Austin was killed inside, have you?"

Lyric shook her head. "Bathroom needs a complete renovation. I'm still figuring it out."

"Well, the Accountant's Office is here. Whatever you need."

Lyric glanced over her shoulder.

"I'm serious." Addie grinned. "At least, that's what Russ said. I'm assuming he meant recommendations for local contractors as well."

Lyric smiled. "Everything was done for the most part when I showed up. Whoever owned the cabins or tried to make a go of them before me, had all the work done. They did all the renovations, then quit for whatever reason."

She'd planted flowers outside. Repainted everything in the cabins. Switched out cabinet handles and some fixtures. Bought furniture. Made the whole place hers.

The sign on the road said Second Chances. And that was the truth.

The Accountant's Office gave clients a shot at a new life —like the way witness protection did. However, with the witness security program, it was about keeping someone alive long enough to testify and then allowing them to live their lives. With the Accountant's Office clients got a new life, but the trade-off was that they were literally starting over from scratch. Usually because there was a price on their head.

"I have to admit," Addie said. "I am curious how you became Lyric Thompson, vacation rental owner."

"Not a story with a happy ending."

Maybe she would tell it. One day. Instead of just pretending none of it had happened. That she'd never been the person who knew how to clean up blood after a government-sanctioned hit.

Even the idea of doing that made Lyric want to pack her trunk and drive. Get out of here, go anywhere. She had carved herself free of the CIA. Made a life for herself where no one controlled her. She could go anywhere. Be whoever she wanted.

"You know what happened to me."

Lyric turned, drawn by the hope in Addie's voice. "So you think that should happen to anyone?"

Addie leaned against the porch rail of a cabin where a man had died, a porch she'd been shoved off by the killer. Lyric had been listening to music with her headphones on when Addie had landed on her back on the grass, dazed by shock. The FBI agent had pounded on her door to tell her the whole story.

That had better be the last time the police crawled all over her property. This was supposed to be a peaceful place where families and couples could relax. Where folks could come to get away from the busyness of life.

Addie stared at the parking lot, where a pickup truck covered in mud eased down the lane. "I think we should expect great things. But even still, prepare to be blown away."

"What's the point?" Lyric made her own future, and God had already given her everything she needed.

What more was there?

Lyric didn't know what to do with the yearning for more that happened sometimes. But she thought on it occasionally. Entertained the idea.

The pickup truck pulled over outside cabin three. All the

occupants piled out. Camouflage clothing, heavy boots. At least two open beer cans between the four of them. One guy stumbled to a knee climbing out, something the others seemed to find hilarious.

Two had beards. One of the clean-shaven guys had a bad hip. They all had an adequate knowledge of the weapons they'd been hunting with. One of them moved like he'd been trained—the military or martial arts.

He'd be the one she would take down first, while Addie contended with the others until Lyric could join in.

"Hey, baby." One of the open container guys wandered over, adjusting the front of his cargos.

Lyric heard a muttered, "Oh, this is gonna be good" from behind her, but didn't turn to see if Addie had put her badge away.

She left Addie on the porch and ambled down the steps to the gravel of the front walk. Addie hadn't been here long, so she didn't need to get mixed up in something. Lyric rolled her shoulders.

The one trying his luck sauntered over. "Hey, baby. Hey."

Nothing original to his material, then. His trained friend followed as backup rather than an attempt to cut off his friend.

"How was your day, fellas?" Lyric had carved a canyon between being personable as a fellow human and her position as the manager of this tiny resort.

"Pretty good." He sniffed and rubbed a thumb across his beard. "Wanna join us? We're celebrating."

Considering the limited number of guys she'd ever been attracted to, she could say for certain this guy wasn't one of them. There was one who she'd wanted to stick around, but he didn't.

Not that she entertained thoughts of him these days.

Much.

The trained guy motioned to the porch. "Your friend should come as well."

"We appreciate the offer." Lyric planted her feet, arms loose at her sides in a way that no one would mistake as readiness, but which was the definition. She'd been trained to within an inch of her life with the skills necessary to do her former job, and the ability to hide all that training under a persona meant to disarm a man. "But I have a lot of work to catch up on this evening."

Open-can guy glanced at Addie. "How about you, darlin'?"

Lyric turned to look over her shoulder in time to see Addie shift her jacket open to reveal the FBI badge on her belt. Lyric bit her lip to keep from grinning.

"Never mind." He spun around so fast he nearly toppled over.

His friend didn't bother trying to catch him. He just let the guy find his footing and head back to his cabin. The trained guy studied Addie, then Lyric.

"Anything I can help you with?" Lyric asked.

He lifted his chin. "Maybe later…darlin'."

His form wasn't anything to write home about, but the way he moved away made her surer he had some skill in the tone of those muscles. He knew how to handle himself.

But then, so did she.

And if things got hairy, the pistol she had holstered at the small of her back would help.

Depending on her outfit it might be a knife, pepper spray, or a stun gun. With these guys here until Saturday, it was her .22.

"Does that happen often?"

She glanced at Addie.

Before she could answer, the FBI agent said, "I'm guessing yes." She looked down Lyric, then back up. "Even though you do a decent job trying to hide it."

"I have no idea what you're talking about."

"Because you don't own a mirror?" Addie snorted. "You must've at least seen your reflection in a window at one point."

"I know what I look like."

"And that's why I figure we have a passable shot at being friends. Because you don't use it to your advantage, throwing around the way you look and all those curves—"

Lyric narrowed her eyes.

"That reaction is exactly why I consider you someone I can trust. Which in my world is hard to come by."

"Thanks?" Lyric didn't know what to say. She'd made her life what she wanted—needed—it to be. That was all this was. As for her appearance? It had nothing to do with the kind of person she was. Not anymore.

This resort of vacation cabins wasn't perfect, but it was hers free and clear. No one could take that away. She'd done this herself.

She stepped away from Addie. "I should get online, order a new bathtub for that cabin."

Addie wasn't fooled. "Sure. I'll stop by again soon."

"Great."

Addie laughed. "I'll call first."

"Thanks." Lyric smiled.

She could handle whatever Addie wanted to throw at her. If that was an invite to girls' night or the odd visit for some small talk.

In the meantime, she'd keep on living life on her terms. Free of anyone who thought they could tie her down.

Making beauty out of these ashes.

2

"Good work today."

Isaac Amrakov dumped the toolbox in the bed of his truck and turned, feeling the damp shirt on his back. The sun had begun to set behind the high rises of downtown, casting an orange glow across everything. Leaving shadows.

Isaac lifted his ball cap and settled it back in place. "Thanks."

Adam lifted his chin. "We're headed to The Terminal for a drink. The game will be on. Interested?"

"Sure." He'd been waiting for this invitation for two weeks. "I'll meet you guys there."

The others piled in their dirty pickups and pulled out of the parking lot. They were rehabbing an old medical clinic into an office for a lawyer, pulling out cabinets and replacing all the outdated plumbing. Repainting everything before they put down new floors.

Good work?

Isaac wasn't sure about that. He might have dyed hair and enough beard growth to obscure his features, but there was no way to hide the fact he'd been a fugitive only a few weeks ago. A panel of judges had cleared him of any wrongdoing—something he wasn't sure had been completely legit.

Between his mother and the Accountant's Office program, he'd been exonerated. A nuclear warhead had been stolen and the man responsible was dead, so what was there left to prosecute? He'd been arrested when he returned the suitcase nuke to the military so it would be safe. Didn't mean he felt like he deserved freedom. After all, he'd escaped federal prison.

Good work was being part of a team he respected, one that ran missions all over the world. The team of Chevalier Protection Specialists helped people. They solved problems and made the world a better place.

There was a team here in Benson called Vanguard Security Services. He'd tried to get an interview, even though the Accountant's Office wouldn't allow him to work any job related to his former career. Kind of like being enrolled in witness security.

He figured the team had been warned he might come by.

The receptionist hadn't even let him in the front door.

Isaac didn't get to be part of that world anymore, so how "good" could he be? Hiding out in Benson, Washington. He was doing manual labor at a perfectly respectable job, except that he was decently sure the rest of the crew were up to something spearheaded by their boss.

Isaac's instincts were all firing.

Getting invited to drinks was the best thing that had happened to him in weeks. But only because it might give him a shot at figuring out what they were up to. The entire crew had brand-new top-of-the-line trucks. They ate out for lunch and dinner practically every day, and the boss lived outside town at a lakeside mansion. Maybe they all had huge car loans, but no one had ever complained about money.

It made no sense.

Isaac pushed open the front door of The Terminal fifteen minutes later.

Wood paneling lined the walls. Chrome-rimmed barstools with red leather seats flanked the bar. Guests dined at tables with wood-backed chairs. The room was packed.

Rather than act desperate to hang out with his new work buddies, Isaac headed for the bar and ordered a drink from a twentysomething guy in a white T-shirt with tattoo sleeves on both arms.

He was just glad no one recognized him. The dark hair that replaced his previous blond helped, since he'd grown it long. Usually he stuffed a beanie over it. The beard was effective, but only made him think about his former team though he tried not to.

Isaac sipped the drink and fell into the character like someone drowning. He'd surfaced for a second and remembered who he truly was. Now it was time to dive back into the man he was supposed to be.

Someone bumped his arm, and the drink spilled over the rim of the glass onto his hand and the floor. He whipped around ready to berate whoever it was.

A woman spun around. "Oh no, I'm *so* sorry."

To her credit, she seemed genuinely apologetic. He lifted his chin. "Don't worry about it."

She took a second to look him over, then slid her elbow on the bar and lifted her chin. Her friend behind her turned away to someone else while the bumper said, "Hey, I can buy you another one?"

He shook his head. "No harm done."

She laid her hand on his arm. "What's your name?"

Someone came up beside him. Adam's friend Steve, given the smell of beans and cheese. "Hey, girl."

Isaac glanced at him. Did that really work?

He needed to get invited to sit with the group, then he only had to stick around long enough to figure out why two were antsy and the boss looked like he was waiting for something to happen. Whatever was going down, Isaac needed to know what it was.

The woman looked Steve up and down, clearly preferring Isaac—not that he cared since that wasn't why he was here. "Hey, yourself."

"I'm gonna go sit." Isaac didn't give either of them time to answer. He shoved Steve at the woman and headed for the table.

Isaac put his drink in front of Steve's chair and did the same move, acting before anyone could object. "Pretty sure he's gonna keep working the room until he gets a bite from some fish."

Adam slapped him on the back. "Better luck next time."

"So what's the score?" He could pretend to like the team for…whatever sport was playing. He looked at the screen. Ah, basketball. That would do. Baseball was just boring, even though Badger had watched it like a religion.

Isaac gritted his teeth. He needed to quit thinking about his former team, otherwise his life here wasn't going to work. That life was over.

Probably he needed therapy, which had been offered to him in all fairness. His gut reaction was to turn it down flat— a product of being raised by spies.

Talking about his problems wasn't something his father, or mother dearest, had encouraged. In fact, he rarely knew what mission they were on because her ability to disclose what was going on never seemed to have fully developed.

Yet another thing he needed to let go of.

Isaac didn't need to deal with the past. He just needed to figure out the present.

The future wasn't something he could afford to worry about, or he'd miss what was right in front of his face.

Like the fact the boss, Mitch Sanders, got a phone call an hour later.

Mitch shoved his hair back, gave one of the other guys a pointed look, and said, "Be back."

Most of the guys were five drinks in at this point. Isaac had finished the first while making the rounds, pretending he saw a girl he was into. He poured half the drink in a planter on the patio. He'd barely started the second, which the rest of them thought was his fourth.

"Gotta take a leak." He left the glass on the table but pocketed his phone to see what Mitch was up to.

Adam lifted two fingers, but no one cared when he sauntered away.

Isaac checked the hall was clear, then headed for the door marked EXIT. He pushed outside and passed a couple making out against the exterior wall. They didn't notice him.

He peered around the corner to the front door. The boss had moved away from the patio area to take his call close to the first row of cars. He waved one arm, agitated.

Isaac pulled the beanie from his back pocket and pulled it low over his hair so the end touched his eyebrows. He crossed from the corner and made a beeline for the first row of trucks. He ducked behind a Dodge and crouch-walked along the row of cars, ensuring he wasn't seen as he moved between vehicles in view of the bar.

The closer he got, the better he could hear Mitch's end of the conversation.

"…late. This is unbelievable."

Isaac leaned against the wheel of a Ram.

"Of course I still want the product. But you think I won't ask for a discount?" Pause. "You treat all your *customers* like this?" He let out a harsh laugh. "That's better. Yeah, we'll be there. So don't be late this time." Mitch let out a curse. His boots crunched the gravel on his way back toward the restaurant.

Isaac remained in his crouch. He needed a second to assimilate the information the way he'd been taught.

Drugs. Guns. Something more sinister. Didn't matter because it was in his nature to complete the mission.

Never mind that it hadn't been assigned to him. Isaac didn't do it out of the goodness of his heart—not when there was nothing good in there according to the Bible. It was simply who he was that he found a job and completed it. He worked the problem in front of him.

Whether it was construction…or an investigation he'd have to turn over to the police.

Or that new FBI office in town.

Russ's niece was a special agent. That meant Isaac could trust her, because no one related to Russ was going to be a waste of time. It just wasn't the way he was built. Kind of like Isaac's old team leader, Zander, and the fact he only surrounded himself with good people.

Which was why Isaac found himself unable to go back.

Leave it alone. It didn't matter what Isaac wanted. Life was the way it was, and there was nothing he could do about it— as much as he might want things to be otherwise.

He pulled the pack of cigarettes he didn't smoke out of his back pocket and lit one up. Took two puffs just to solidify the story of why he'd taken so long in the bathroom, then tossed it before heading inside. The taste made him sick to his stomach, but mission success had nothing to do with how he felt.

Comfort was hardly the point.

He kicked the chair out an inch and sat.

"That took a while." Adam smirked. "Everything come out okay?"

"I needed a smoke." The smell on his breath was the only thing that could solidify that story. The guys tried to joke, but the whole thing was so hollow it didn't engage him. He faked it well enough, though.

Until all the guys decided to head home.

Isaac got in his truck and tailed the boss across town, staying three cars behind them.

With Adam in his passenger seat, Mitch headed for an industrial complex across town, and Steve followed.

When he pulled around the corner of a shut-down warehouse, Isaac stashed his pickup on the far side of two storage sheds, switched his phone out for a burner he'd bought a week ago, and slid a gun in the back of his belt.

He sprinted around the far side of the warehouse, running flat out to get there in time. Then he pulled up short of the end of the building and peered around.

Nothing.

He sprinted to the next corner. The one that would show him the side where Mitch had parked.

Again he pulled up short. Glanced around.

The headlights of Mitch's truck lit up the five guys standing between two parked cars. His boss and the man he met stood close in the center, the others around them for backup. Two for Mitch, one for the other guy. Everyone was armed.

Someone brought a duffel from the back of the second vehicle and carried it over to Mitch.

Isaac pressed the camera button on his phone, capturing hundreds of photos. Faces. Movements. License plates. He took a couple of screenshots to show the time on his phone.

As soon as it was done, he made his way back to his truck.

Isaac wiped down the phone and the padded envelope he slid it into.

On the front he wrote *Special Agent Addie Franklin, FBI.*

He left the envelope on Russ's front porch on the way home.

3

———

Lyric tapped Delete on the voicemail. No matter that she probably should've saved it and shown Russ what she was up against. She didn't need help dealing with Allerton and Sons.

Like how she could take care of this bathroom by herself. Kind of.

Lyric had to figure out how she would get the old tub out of the bathroom. She'd picked out all the new fixtures and laid them in the cleared away living area. She planned to strip out the old stuff. Repaint. Put in the new.

A fresh start. One that she would do under her own steam if she had the strength to haul out a bathtub without scratching the floor all the way to the front door. And then how would she get it off the porch? Prayer could do the impossible, by the power of God, but not levitate a bathtub out of a cabin when what she should be doing was asking for help.

Lyric sighed. The voice mail message from Allerton had her head all mixed up.

We have a new number for you. Like all she cared about was the dollar amount? *One I'm sure you're interested in hearing. And we're sending a representative to you soon to talk. It's in your best interest to think about our offer, Ms. Thompson.*

Their best interest, maybe. Certainly not hers.

Some skeezy development company trying to buy her livelihood out from under her? Sure, they wanted to pay her more than she'd coughed up for the place. Still, it was hardly an offer that would induce her to jump on having cash and no home, or job.

As if she would trade what she'd built for money just so she could start all over somewhere else. *Lord, I don't want to do that when I believe You gave me this place to start over. I know You can move mountains. How about a bathtub?*

It didn't matter that she was tied here. Not when this was a great place to be tied to. The business had its pros and cons, but it was hers. She wanted to watch families enjoying themselves, relaxing together as they spent time away from their normal busy lives.

She'd had it that good as a child, but only for a short time.

Then it was over.

Pretending she still had parents and the best brother in the world wouldn't change her situation. She could offer her guests what she'd had during those few months to other people and know the world was better for it. That she was still making a difference in people's lives. Maybe not on a global scale so much anymore, but one person—one family —at a time. On her terms.

Even if she couldn't haul a bathtub alone.

Maybe that was something worth going to Russ with. He might be able to recommend a contractor in town, the way Addie had insinuated. Or a few people who could haul stuff, like those guys at the church who had a ministry helping people move.

Lyric sent him a quick text. He'd probably have info for her in the morning.

She closed the cabin for the night, pocketed the key, then walked the cul-de-sac to check on things. The bungee on one of the trash cans hung loose, so she fastened it. No one wanted to see the aftermath of raccoons—or bears—in the trash.

The cabin where the hunter guys were staying sat dark and quiet. Their truck was gone, so they'd most likely show up in the early hours of the morning and wake everyone up getting home. One of the neighbors had already complained, but Lyric tried to pick her battles.

Even if it was late, she was too antsy to try to wind down yet. Usually, she went for a run when she felt like this, but the night was too still. Instinct told her running on a night like tonight would turn out badly.

Or that was just her trying to justify the fact she'd already decided to get a milkshake.

Lyric didn't need to overthink that. She just grabbed her keys, locked her house, and drove toward Benson. The twenty-four-hour diner was a rest stop on the highway at the outskirts of town. A few cars in the parking lot. Couple of semis that were dark for the night, the occupants probably asleep.

She slid the pepper spray from her glove box into the back of her belt and tucked cash in her pocket. Phone in hand. She kept her head down, her attention on the screen as though distracted.

Anyone who saw her wouldn't think twice. They certainly wouldn't assume someone who allowed themselves to be this unaware had formerly been any kind of trained agent in the past.

That was the name of the game these days.

Lyric stowed the phone, entered the diner, found her favorite booth, and clocked everyone inside as she made her way there. One guy registered enough to move the needle. Sat at the opposite end of the counter, but he didn't have a view of her without turning completely around. She settled on the side where she'd see both him and the front door.

Then she slid over until her back was partially against the window and looked for the waitress.

Sasha was nowhere to be found. It seemed tonight the only waitress working was Clara. She brought the carafe with her, and Lyric knew it would be decaf. That was the deal.

Caffeine didn't affect her much, and she slept enough she wasn't incapacitated by exhaustion, but that was it. Still, she didn't need to ruin the small chance she had at getting any sleep at this time of night.

Since the alternative was therapy and sleeping pills, Lyric had decided to stick with decaf a while ago. And milkshakes.

"There's a new flavor. Peppermint chocolate chip." Clara flipped the mug and filled it.

"Serious?"

Clara winked, but no amusement lit her shadowed eyes. "You know it."

Lyric bit her lip.

Clara pulled a pen from her apron and wandered off.

Lyric slid over the paper napkin and clicked the end of the pen. She tried not to overthink about whatever was going on. She channeled the questions and energy into doodling, which started out as a rose, got lost, and ended up as a random assortment of blooms. She added a vase for it and a watering can, just because.

"Cute." Clara set the dripping milkshake in front of her.

"No cherry?"

Clara rolled her eyes. "I know, right? The delivery didn't get here yet. It's like, what is even the point, you know?" A minuscule amount of humor sparked in her expression.

Lyric chuckled. "I guess I'll have to muddle through it. Even though the situation is less than exemplary."

"Don't write a review online."

"Girl…"

"Yeah, yeah." Clara waved a hand. "I'm the best waitress you've ever known."

Lyric smiled around the straw. Clara didn't leave, so she swallowed and said, "Everything okay?"

The waitress glanced at the other customers in a cursory glance, then leaned against the seat opposite. "Sasha didn't show up tonight. Whatever that's about, I don't care with that girl. Some kind of drama. But Enrique is super mad. He wanted to leave early, and now he has to cover the register."

"Sorry." It wasn't fun to deal with an irate boss. Lyric understood that.

Clara shrugged. "I'll be back."

Lyric nodded and drank the milkshake, praying quietly for God to touch Clara's life. She watched the other customers and Clara's interaction with them. Enrique came back from his meal break and took a few minutes to berate the cook. Clara steered clear by refilling the coffee mug Lyric wasn't going to drink and cleaning a couple of tables. Chatting with another customer.

If Lyric had to guess, she'd say that the guy at the counter would begin the whole thing. But it was a toss-up between him and Enrique. The cook was deadweight, and the two guys would run for the door at the end.

Then again, it wasn't as if anything would actually

happen. Her life wasn't that interesting anymore, not even counting the young man who'd been killed in one of her cabins a few weeks back.

No one could know who she used to be, so she had to stay out of life here. As much as she might've wanted to intervene at one point, that wasn't her.

He'd killed Austin silently, but Lyric noticed when Addie showed up and had guessed another cop was on their way. She hadn't known the person in the cabin was a killer—or that Addie would get shoved.

The truth was, she'd seen the figure go inside, but it wasn't as though he'd had a Murderer sign on his back. Nor did she make a practice of snooping on her guests.

Right now she just needed to keep her eyes on the prize God had set before her. Continue building a bustling business, even if a location known as a crime hotbed wasn't the best for her online reputation. People who knew her and the local area continued to make bookings. Word got around.

Russ slid into the seat opposite her.

"Maybe I should just tear down that cabin."

He frowned. "I thought you were renovating again."

"Might not be worth it." Even if she had asked him for a recommendation. "I can return what I got from the hardware store. Maybe no one wants to stay in the death cabin."

Clara set a mug down in front of Russ and filled it. His lips twitched. Russ had been hit over the head a few weeks ago by the same killer who'd ended Austin's life and killed a series of other people.

"Or I should take the offer and sell. Even if the number is a joke."

Russ stalled the mug before he could take a drink. "Who's trying to buy the place?"

Lyric shrugged one shoulder. "Some developer."

He took a sip. Shook his head. "That's not okay. I'll do some digging, see what I can find out. Send me their information?"

"So they'll know I have your protection?" That would draw attention and make people wonder. No one would land on the Accountant's Office as a conclusion, but they didn't need the limelight either.

"A woman business owner, alone outside town?" Russ stared at her. "They should know I'm going to be all over making sure you're not unprotected."

"I thought that was why you helped me get the arsenal in my gun safe."

"That was just for fun."

Lyric chuckled. She sipped the straw. "You should get a milkshake. This flavor is really good."

"Addie said I have to watch my sugar intake." Russ made a face. "Then she goes and gets one with that friend of hers, and her fiancé."

"So they're engaged?"

Russ nodded.

"That's good."

"Sure. But it's not why I'm here." He took another drink. "I got your text."

"You came out here at this time of night because I asked for a contractor recommendation?"

He said nothing.

"You're going to have to explain what this silence is, because I've got nothing."

Russ was great about his role as coordinator with the Accountant's Office. He was point person for every client in town. Clearly something was going on.

"There's a guy…" Russ set his mug down. His attention remained on it as though it would hop up and dance across the table and he had to be ready. "He's been here a few weeks since he was cleared of wrongdoing. Settling in."

"All I need is someone to haul out a bathtub."

"Or he could do the work, and you can do all your other tasks without having the renovation eat up your time."

Lyric pressed her lips together. There had to be a catch. It was like standing on train tracks, watching headlights come at you from a distance. Big deal. Keep walking and get out of the way. "I think I'm not interested. Whoever he is."

"You get that I got a full history on you when you showed up here?"

That was par for the course. Complete disclosure. Lyric shrugged. "What about it?"

"This guy…"

"I already said no, so does it matter?" She motioned with her fingers. "Hand over your tip." She was going to leave now, before the train hit. Before everything she'd built got upended.

She was fine. She didn't need this—whatever it was.

Sure, part of her wondered who he was talking about. But that part was quickly swallowed up by a wave of panic. Things were good. Nothing needed to change.

"You're so sure you're right. There's nothing about your life that could be better?" Still, he handed her a fifty-dollar bill.

Lyric folded it in the fifty she had wrapped up in four ones and set the edge of the bills under her coffee mug. She slid out of the booth. "Goodbye, Russ."

4

It took a second to realize the buzz wasn't in his head. Isaac rolled over and reached for his phone. "Yep?" He didn't even bother to look at the screen.

"Isaac, honey?"

He clenched his abs and sat up. "Mrs. Hummet?"

She was pushing eighty-six and lived next door. Her grandson, a police officer Isaac had purposely never met—though that wouldn't last forever—usually took care of her. But he worked more than Isaac, and odd hours at that. Isaac was her point person if the guy was busy.

"I'm afraid…I need a little help." She sounded uncomfortable, but not in pain. He was glad she'd managed to get to her phone.

He was out of bed before she'd even finished. "I'll be there in two minutes. Is the front door unlocked?"

"No." He heard the disappointment in her tone. "And I can't get to it."

"Don't worry." He slid on a pair of basketball shorts and the closest T-shirt, even though it smelled funky. "I got it. One minute, okay?"

"Okay."

He knew she'd feel bad, like she needed to apologize. Isaac hung up instead of leaving her room to feel shame or guilt. He grabbed the lockpick kit he hadn't gotten rid of and slid his feet into brand-new running shoes the treadmill hadn't broken in yet.

This whole living in an apartment building thing just didn't sit right, but he hadn't had the chance—or the energy at the end of the day—to find a trail in the mountains outside town. Though, he'd heard there were plenty.

Until then he'd have to deal with feeling boxed in.

Isaac threaded his way down the hall at a jog and let himself into Mrs. Hummet's apartment. Her grandson the cop lived a few blocks away in a trendy condo complex but came by often, and she raved about him. "Edith?"

"Kitchen!"

Her hall was clear, the apartment an almost exact replica of his just flipped so it was a mirror image.

Glass covered the small square table in the center of the kitchen. "Whoa."

He found her by the sink, holding her arm. Blood seeped through her fingers. As soon as she saw him, her legs began to give out. Isaac caught her before she fell. He wrapped his arms around her middle, careful not to squeeze too hard, and settled her on a seat that didn't have glass all over it.

"Towels?"

"I was doing laundry. There aren't any in the drawer."

The laundry facility was in the building's basement. Isaac whipped off his shirt.

"Oh my."

He laughed. "You're good for my ego."

Her cheeks pinked.

He took her hand in his and slid her fingers away from

the slice. He let out a hiss, then pressed his shirt over it and applied pressure. "We should get you to the doctor for stitches."

Edith shook her head. The white pixie cut didn't move but her earrings swayed with the motion. "No doctor."

"There must be someone you see?"

"He's busy. Out of town." She shifted her lips, and the wrinkles around her mouth flexed. "We need to make do. No paperwork."

Russ had told Isaac the Accountant's Office coordinated the housing he'd received. Did that mean Edith was also affiliated? Could be his place was just a one-off like a safe house. Or the Accountant's Office housed clients in one spot so they could be better safeguarded. So they could help protect each other.

Something else Russ had told him—facts not names.

Not that Isaac wanted to be singled out. Sure, he was liable to protect the people around him that he cared about. There could be a reason he'd been placed here. It could be so that Edith was protected.

He'd only seen two other people on this floor of the downtown apartment building he'd moved into.

Edith reached out with bloody fingers and pointed at a scar on his side. "Make do."

Isaac shook his head. "This isn't a warzone, and I'm not cauterizing this when we're two miles from a hospital."

But he understood needing to keep life under the radar. So what was Edith's story, and would she share it with him? According to Accountant's Office rules, they weren't supposed to speak of the past.

"I've got a sewing kit."

Isaac stared at her. She was serious.

"It's not for repairing buttons, kiddo."

"Does the cop know?"

She tipped her head back and laughed. "Ouch. We need to stop the bleeding, and I don't have two hands. Plus, old lady eyesight isn't going to get the job done."

"You're sure I shouldn't call a doctor?"

"Not unless you know one who will do a house call and take cash with no questions."

Isaac stared at her. Who was this woman?

"You're not supposed to ask."

Isaac lifted the shirt and looked, then replaced it. "Bleeding is slowing." He set her hand over the shirt. "Where's the sewing kit?"

Half an hour later, he had her secured and he'd swept up the kitchen. "Want me to wipe down?"

She was in a recliner in the living room drinking orange juice and finishing the sandwich he'd made her. "You're really not going to ask me?"

Isaac leaned against the open doorway between the kitchen and living room. "I'm not supposed to. And neither are you."

She leaned her head back against the chair, her feet up. The bandaged arm lay on her lap. He should probably get her a sling when he was out today. "Don't need to. I read all about you online." She had an *I'm not an idiot* tone in her voice.

Isaac definitely didn't think she was too dumb to realize, but people believed what they wanted to. "I guess it's not a secret."

"All you did was dye your hair." She made a face. "No one's realized it yet?"

He shrugged. It figured she'd worked it out. He thought she might've believed he was an undercover of some sort, given he'd admitted something was going on with his construction crew. She was the one who'd encouraged him to get information—though she wasn't a big fan of the FBI. Probably more partial to the police.

Given that one of theirs—a local detective—had been revealed as a serial murderer recently, Isaac wasn't about to hand over information that would get lost in the PR nightmare they had on their hands.

Name of the game over at the police department right now was convincing the public there were plenty of honorable officers left.

As for him? "I was exonerated. People who don't care if I might've been working against America don't ask questions, and those who do care don't associate."

"So you're stuck with that caliber of people for the rest of your life?"

He wanted to shrug again but couldn't brush that off. He'd made his life what it was through his own choices. He wasn't going to blame anyone, least of all the two people who could've, should've—whatever. It was done. He didn't need to drag up the past just so he could feel it all over again.

"Are you working today?"

Isaac nodded.

"You get anything last night?"

He pressed his lips together. She hadn't known he was going to try. Edith was only guessing. "How do you know I got anything?"

"Come on, you didn't get home until after one. You think there's anything good on TV? I need excitement."

She was tracking his movements. That should bother him, but for some reason it didn't. "This blows back on you and—"

She chuckled. "Don't worry about me. I go out in a blaze of glory, kiddo. That's the only way this ends."

"Who are you planning on taking with you when that happens?" He'd had a team, a family, and they'd watched each other's backs. Until honor had dictated he do the right thing by leaving them.

Now he had an eighty-something-year-old woman watching his back.

Her chuckle turned to outright laughter. "I'll try to control the damage, but you can't always contain on the fallout."

Isaac shrugged at that. "You've gotta do what you've gotta do."

"Tell me about last night."

"Mitch made a call." Isaac let out a long breath. "I handed over photos of who they met with after. The exchange that happened. Turned it over to the feds in town."

"Russ's niece? Guess that's better than nothing."

"You think your grandson wants me for a confidential informant?"

"Maybe you'd be friends."

Isaac frowned. "Did you tell Eric about me?" If she had, he might have to move. Who knew what the guy would think about Isaac being friends with his grandmother?

"Pshh. That boy wouldn't know what hit him. I'd watch his head spin."

"I take it he doesn't know about you?"

"What's to know? I'm a harmless, but fit and fabulous, older woman. I definitely don't have an illegal shotgun in my closet." She looked away.

"You're not even trying to fool me." If she was, he had no doubt he'd never realize. Something about her reminded him all too much of CIA agents and undercover feds, and special-ops-trained people he'd known over the years. Official and unofficial.

This woman had been someone in her day.

But that wasn't fair. She was certainly someone now. What was that expression? *Retired, extremely dangerous.* Yeah, that was it.

Isaac pushed off the doorway. "I'll keep you posted on what's happening at work, but I want regular texts through the day, so I know you didn't pass out. And you don't wipe down the kitchen. I'll do it when I get back if Eric doesn't get to it."

"I'll call his sergeant. Have him come by when he's off work."

Isaac nodded. "Sounds good."

He headed back to his apartment to change. The front door was open, which gave him pause while he tried to remember if he'd gone out too fast and not closed it behind him.

Isaac pushed the door, but didn't go in. "Anyone in there?"

"Just me." Russ's voice rang out down the hall. "No need to shoot first."

Isaac closed the front door behind him and toed off his sneakers. "I'd need a gun to do that."

"Like you don't have one." Russ had the coffee pot in one hand—the brew Isaac set up before he went to bed.

Isaac got a fresh shirt, then headed back to the kitchen. "Need something?"

Russ handed him a mug. "Everything okay?"

He'd cleaned up the blood, so that wasn't what Russ referred to. "Just helping Edith with something."

Russ nodded. He'd probably head over there as soon as Isaac left for work.

"What's up?" Russ wasn't due to check in until next week. Did he know about Mitch, and the guys' extracurricular activities? Nothing about the phone or the envelope would lead back to him.

Not this fast, at least.

"I struck out once already. I'm hoping that won't happen here."

Isaac frowned over his coffee.

"There's something I need to tell you, but it's more than that because she needs help even if she doesn't want it."

I'm not going to like this. "What's going on?"

"It's not bad, you have to know that. It might actually be really, really good."

"For who?"

Russ gave him a half smile. "I'm sorry you still feel like you need to qualify that. Everything I do is so you can have the best life in this situation. And if it takes time for you to believe it, that's fine."

Isaac figured it might take a lifetime.

Russ unclipped his phone from his belt. He tapped the screen, then showed it to Isaac.

A woman in profile. Blonde. Gorgeous. But that wasn't what caused the mug to slip from his fingers and hit the floor like Edith's glass. Coffee and stone shattered on the tile and ricocheted.

Isaac fought to speak. "She…she's here?"

5

———

Sweat beaded on her hairline. Lyric gripped the wrench with both hands, fingers slick, and tried to move the bolt.

Two seconds later she landed on her backside on the bare wood planks of the floor she'd taken up in the cabin bathroom. Except the pipes under the bathtub that still had to be disconnected from the plumbing. She'd already turned off the water because she wasn't completely dumb. She was, however, not as strong as whoever had tightened this bolt. Or the thing had rusted through the threads, and it would never budge.

A snicker by the door brought her head around.

She hadn't even noticed the guy standing there. Lyric pressed her lips together and got up to sit on the side of the bath. How could she have been unaware there was someone else in the room?

She was losing her touch. This was the natural end of not being that person anymore—the past as far from her as the east from the west. Her history had begun to fade away, and she was starting to forget.

She assessed him. Eyebrows raised, as though he'd dared to disturb her. Anyone that would laugh at someone trying to make a living didn't get the benefit of the doubt as far as she was concerned.

That might not be fair, but it was honest.

Two-thousand-dollar shoes—or thereabouts. A suit that probably cost more than she took in for one month worth of bookings. Fancy haircut, and more product than she used in a week. Clean shaven. No jewelry. She was surprised there wasn't a handkerchief in his breast pocket.

She stared long enough he must've realized she wasn't going to speak first.

Long enough for him to squirm when it became clear he didn't impress her. She dialed that back a notch just so she could flip the script if she needed to. Lyric had been trained to use words first, but not like a diplomat. More like a politician. Guns were a last resort—or anything else that could be wielded to cause physical damage.

She lifted her chin.

He smoothed down his tie. "Ms. Thompson, I'm Brandon Jones with Allerton and Sons."

Ah, the developer that had sent her a dozen or so letters about selling her property. Lyric flicked her wrist and looked at her smart watch. Maybe she should give their information to Russ so he could take care of the situation.

"I won't take up too much of your time." Jones smiled, but she didn't buy it. "But my boss requested that I make contact with you." He chuckled. "You're lucky. You work for yourself, so there's no one ordering you around, telling you where to go."

She nodded. Said nothing. It was an interesting tactic, trying to create a bond between the two of them. He'd alienated her at first and was now attempting to connect.

"Like I said, lucky." He shifted. Was her silence making him uneasy?

She still said nothing.

"I'm sure you've seen the letters from Allerton and Sons."

Of which, Jones wasn't one. How did that make him feel? She could probably use resentment against him.

Maybe she was rusty in her skills, but throwing him off his game would be worth it. This company thought they could throw money at her, and she would give up everything she'd built since she got out of the CIA? That was just nuts.

Clearly they considered this nothing but a business transaction.

"Mr. Allerton is prepared to make you a more than fair offer for your property here," he said, boxing her into the bathroom. "He believes in what this place could be." Sure, she hadn't forced him to have this conversation in the living area, but he blocked the doorway. Which put her at a disadvantage and allowed him to prove he had power over her.

Lyric got up from the bathtub. She strode fast toward Mr. Jones so he had to jump out of the way or she'd have barreled right into him. The refrigerator still stood in the kitchen—she was leaving that area alone for the most part—waters inside.

She twisted the cap off a bottle and downed the whole thing while he waited in the living area. If he boxed her into the kitchen now, she would know it was intentional.

She threw the empty bottle in the can she'd set out for recycling. "What does Mr. Allerton believe this place can be?"

A gleam in his eyes said he thought that was an in. "The town of Benson is expanding. It will reach your front drive before you know it, and there will be residents surrounding you looking for amenities. Places to eat, and shop."

"So you want to turn this into one of those live-work-eat places?"

"Community gyms and pools, a movie theater." To his credit, he seemed excited and not just that this was a sales pitch. Although, maybe that *was* part of the sales pitch. "Clubs and restaurants."

"Schools and churches?"

He blinked. "Of course. An oasis of sorts, both physical and spiritual."

"Right." She owned eight acres.

Hundreds of square miles of trees surrounded her. For them to want her particular property meant they saw something of worth in it. Otherwise, they'd go around her.

Why go through her, mowing her down in the process?

"You need to buy my business to do all that? Must be some undertaking." She leaned her hips back against the kitchen cabinets and whistled. "You've done it before elsewhere?"

Lyric had already done an internet search on them. She knew exactly where they'd done it before, and which residents and businesses they'd ousted in the process. She'd be impressed by their determination if they weren't a giant cliché.

He beamed a smile at her. "With great success."

"For you. Not so much for people like me who have to get out of the way of progress, or they'll get run over."

"We'll make it worth your while. Like we did with the others."

"Will you now."

"In more ways than one." His gaze matched her tone. A spark of life in his eyes. "If you're interested, this could be mutually beneficial."

Lyric wasn't entirely sure what would happen next, but

she knew he likely didn't anticipate the fact she could kill him and dispose of the body in a way no one would ever know what happened. Even if his company was aware he'd visited her. Only Russ would know she had the skills to pull it off.

She could make this guy disappear.

Even if it was a lifetime ago, she'd learned how to do that. She remembered her training. Lyric had tried to hold true to a semblance of morality in the CIA. But going up against honorless monsters, gangsters, and criminals with no code and no feelings? It hadn't lasted forever, no matter that she'd held out longer than her mentor expected.

After her mentor had been killed, the slippery slope began. Ending at rock bottom when the government betrayed her, Lyric's enemies captured her, and she was left for dead. If it wasn't for the men of Chevalier Protection Specialists pulling her out of that Syrian death camp four years ago, she'd be lost forever.

She still didn't know how they'd found her, or who had requested they do the job.

She knew that Chevalier had led to the Accountant's Office, and her life had begun again. New ID. New location. No contact with anyone from her past, and no jobs in any field related to her previous work.

Second Chances had been born. The opportunity to make beauty from ashes.

And now these guys thought they could take it from her?

She pushed off the counter and walked toward him. "I lose everything that's mine, and you walk away the victor. Where's the win in that?"

He tipped his head to the side. "Perhaps this isn't a 'win or lose' thing?"

"Everything is a win or lose." That was how life worked, whether people realized it or not. "That's something winners know. Losers are the ones who think things aren't a battle, because they're too blind to see it."

This was the language of people like him. Companies who thought they could get whatever they wanted and were used to exactly that.

"Fair enough." He took a step toward her, interest in his eyes.

If she gave him even a hint of an "in," he would take it, try his luck.

Lyric planted a hand on the counter beside her and leaned over to him. "Go back to Allerton, or his sons, and tell them too bad. I'm not interested in anything they want to give me." She folded her arms. "My life isn't for sale."

She knew what it felt like when it was. That wasn't going to happen now, no way. No how. It wasn't what she'd signed up for when she allowed the Accountant's Office to provide her a new life and a safe place to be. If the government wanted to find her, they eventually would. Her enemies could —she would never believe she was perfectly safe.

Safety, like freedom sometimes, was only an illusion. Naïveté would get her killed.

If she reached to the back of her belt, she'd be able to subdue him in less than two seconds. If that was necessary.

"Allerton isn't going to back down." Jones stood straight in front of her. He wouldn't push it in a physical sense unless he lost his cool. She'd call the cops and file a police report if he did that. His boss would likely be unhappy with that considering their thing was dealing people out of their property and livelihoods and making money from it.

"He's not taking my property. He can ask until there's no air in his lungs and send as many emissaries as possible. I'm not signing anything." She pointed at the cabin door. "So get out."

"You think this place is going to survive? Death cabins as vacation homes?" He barked a laugh. "Bookings are down the last few weeks, right? That's what happens when you let another person get murdered on your doorstep."

"Ah, so it's to be a smear campaign?" Lyric planted a hand on her hip. "Bring it on. I'm not leaving."

He huffed, spun on his fancy shoes, and strode out the door.

Lyric followed to the porch and watched as he eased his Mercedes down the lane. He had to pull over to let a pickup pass.

He would undoubtedly go back to the office and craft some narrative about her for his boss's benefit.

Two cabins had cars out front. The hunters were off again, doing whatever they did during daylight hours. It was almost lunchtime now. The sun was high in the sky, but the air still had the crisp smell of a Spring that hadn't arrived. At least it wasn't raining. That was forecast for later.

The pickup rounded the landscaped circle in the middle of the cul-de-sac. Came all the way to the porch where she stood and parked.

Lyric wiped her hands off on the sides of her jeans, ready to meet a new customer.

He climbed out and shut his door. Looked around. Nice build, brown hair. But just a guy like all the rest. He worked construction, given the clothes and the tools in the back of his truck.

"Can I help you?"

He came around the front of the truck. Solid stride. He knew how to take care of himself—and any problem he faced. This was a guy you didn't mess with if you had the choice to walk away.

He looked up at the end of the front walk that led to the murder cabin.

Lyric's legs gave out, and she found herself sitting on the top step. *Lord.* She barely knew what to pray. All she could do was stare at him as he moved toward her.

Dark hair to match his dark eyes. She'd always been able to see the shadows deep inside him.

"Lyric."

"Isaac." He was here. "Did you come to kill me?"

He flinched.

Apparently not. "You aren't supposed to be here."

"Russ told me you had a job needed doing." The frown was still there. "A renovation."

That was it? No greeting, just duty. As if she needed help from someone like him. "I'm not supposed to contact anyone from my past life."

Did he know about the Accountant's Office?

"Russ sent me to fix your bathroom. He said you needed help."

Lyric shook her head. This was who Russ had been trying to tell her about. "I don't."

Not from him, anyway. Why did he have to affect her like this? Nothing had changed. Her feelings went haywire every time she saw him, even though it had been years. Decades aside from that one glimpse. Just a figment of her imagination.

"I'm on my lunchbreak right now." His face held a blank expression she didn't like. "But I'll be back later to get to work."

Lyric got up and strode past him. "Don't bother."

The last thing she needed was Isaac back in her life. This was about the past being over, gone. Not about it coming back to haunt her.

6

———

Isaac primed the roller, lifted it, and spread a vertical line on the wall. He could do this particular job in his sleep. Not good, considering that just led to his mind wandering where it would always inevitably go.

She's been here since you got her into the program.

He couldn't believe Lyric was in Benson. Well, she wasn't *in* Benson since she was outside town in that tiny rental cabin village. Second Chances. Seemed fitting. He could use some of that. It was supposed to be what the Accountant's Office had set up here for him.

The opportunity to start over.

She'd been here all along. The pre-teen he'd lived with for a few months at fourteen—when his mom had dated her father. Being a family with them had been one of the happiest memories of his life, except it hadn't even been real. His mom had been pregnant with his half-sister Hannah at that point. That was the beginning of the issues there, most of which he didn't want to get into even if it was only in his mind.

Lyric had been a tiny thing, twelve years old, with all that blonde hair Isaac's mom had secured in two braids.

The woman she was now? Isaac had been practically speechless. Then she tossed him out for all intents and purposes, as though he meant nothing to her.

The four of them had gone to baseball games and eaten out. Spent weeks playing happy family. Then it was over.

His mom packed their bags in the middle of the night and loaded Isaac in the car like he was just another possession. Not that anyone would be surprised to hear it. Everyone familiar with his mother knew she was exactly the kind of woman who played the people around her to get what she wanted. Then she walked away.

No remorse.

According to the official record, she'd died in the hospital months ago. His father had been killed in Africa, witnessed by a friend of his.

Isaac hadn't let himself think too long on either death. Not because he'd hated them or needed to grieve for them. His mother wasn't dead. His dad had been supposedly dead for years.

He didn't want to get swept up in the lies anymore. Mostly he figured all of it was yet another smoke screen. His mom was somewhere he wasn't. In a way, his dad was, too. Something he considered for the best on most days, and a source of hurt on others.

He expected any day now to get a phone call. Or for Russ to approach him about them. The truth was, that's what Isaac had expected Russ to say. Instead, he'd told him that Lyric was here and she needed help.

The whole thing was so messed up he didn't know what to think.

Something with the density of a rubber band ball hit the back of his head.

Isaac glanced over his shoulder.

"Distracted much." Adam lifted a cigarette he wasn't supposed to be smoking in here and took a long drag.

Isaac tossed the roller in the primer tray. It wasn't like anyone else was doing any work either. A couple of the guys were hauling more drywall down the hall. The rest mostly stood around because the boss wasn't back from his own lunch meeting.

"Thought your thing was about another job. One you're doing *solo*." Adam smirked.

Isaac clenched his teeth. "It was."

They were not going to see Lyric, ever. Not if he could help it—which he planned to. This was definitely a job he'd do solo.

"It's just hauling out a bathtub." Even if he planned to do the whole job. "The lady who owns the place can't do it alone."

Hopefully they'd think she was older. Certainly not that she was the most beautiful woman Isaac had ever seen. The fact he knew her better than he knew anyone else here made it even more so.

And she'd kicked him out.

Isaac turned back to his work. He heard Adam approach, but with everything that happened with Lyric at lunch, he hadn't even thought about the guys and what they were up to all morning. Just a cursory assessment. None of them were high or hungover, so that sale hadn't been about getting something for them all to enjoy. It was likely contraband, but what? Isaac needed to know what they planned to do with it.

He'd been unable to follow the boss to his meeting.

"So tell us about her."

Isaac glanced back. Adam and a couple of his buddies were far too close. "I told Mitch about it just so he didn't think I was moonlighting, but that job doesn't have anything to do with you guys."

He didn't turn his back to them. That would have been a mistake.

"That's not what I asked." Adam took another step into Isaac's space and shoved his shoulder.

"Don't touch me." It was telling that none of them had picked up on warning signs. They should *not* mess with Isaac.

Or they believed they were hot stuff and he didn't factor, regardless. According to them.

Adam didn't back up. "Who is she?"

"No one." As if that would ever be true.

"Guess I'll just have to ask Mitch about it. See if she needs more help than just you."

"I'm sure you guys have better things to do after hours than help a lady with a bathroom remodel."

Adam smirked. "Because you called dibs, or what? I don't work that way. I've been here longer than you. Means it goes by me first."

Isaac wanted to call him on that "dibs" comment but didn't. The last thing he needed was to get dragged into a longer conversation. He could wind up getting fired if he wasn't careful.

This was a tight-knit group, and he was an outsider. Unless he could get in with whatever had them meeting that guy and making the exchange.

Now that he had Lyric on his radar, he was tempted to drop the whole thing. Forget that they were breaking the law. Walk away. He'd only been following them and getting evidence for the FBI because it was right. It wasn't like he had anything else to do after work. It was either investigate this or go back to his empty apartment alone. Watch a movie he had no interest in.

He'd rather go hiking, but doing that after dark while exhausted was never a good idea.

If anyone who'd known him in his previous life knew what he was up to now, they'd be proud of him.

The people he'd worked with and considered his friends were the kind of people he wanted respect from. Because it meant something to him.

Even if he couldn't get it, because he wasn't allowed contact with them now, it was enough that *he* knew they'd be proud of his work.

Isaac wasn't sure he could give it up, even with Lyric on the horizon. She didn't want anything to do with him. Still, he planned to show up like he'd said he would. He was always going to show up for Lyric—the way he'd been doing for what seemed like forever.

He just hoped he'd be able to do both, or he'd have to give up one for the sake of the other.

If she knew what he'd done since the last time they saw each other she wouldn't want anything to do with him anyway, so there was no point hoping for what would never happen.

Isaac finished the whole wall before Mitch got back from his meeting with the building inspector.

Everyone stopped work when he showed up. Most had been giving it half effort at best, which frustrated Isaac because he had to go slower than he wanted or it would look strange. They'd snap into action once the boss was working, but not before they waited to see what he had to say.

Mitch held up his clipboard, a paper pinned to the front. "Inspection for the daycare from last week was signed off on. We're good to go."

Isaac lifted his chin while the others gave halfhearted cheers. He tuned out the rest of the conversation since his phone buzzed in his pocket with an incoming email. It was from the FBI. Special Agent Addie Franklin, Russ's niece. She'd responded to the dummy email account Isaac had set up so she could write back to him about the evidence he'd left for her.

He headed for the portable bathroom outside so he could read what she'd written.

Halfway down the hall to the lobby, he felt that familiar tingle of attention on him. Isaac glanced back over his shoulder and saw Adam at the doorway.

"Bathroom." Isaac motioned with a tip of his head to the front door.

The skin around Adam's eyes flexed.

Isaac locked the door and thumbed through to the email. Addie had looked over what he sent and was glad he'd reached out. She wanted to meet him in person so they could talk through everything.

She was probably going to turn him into an informant.

Isaac stowed the phone without replying. He finished out his workday and grabbed a burger from a drive through place. The soda lasted until he reached the lane to turn into Lyric's property.

She'd always been like a homing beacon. Drawing him somewhere he'd have hope for his future, while the rest of the world swirled in chaos around him.

He didn't want to think what it meant that he came to do the job whether she would talk to him or not. Now that he knew she was here, he couldn't stop thinking about her. Which was probably why Russ hadn't told him about Lyric living local until now—when she needed help.

Either Russ had waited for a reason Isaac needed to walk

back into her life, or the only reason he'd mentioned it was because he didn't like Lyric having no help.

Isaac hadn't needed convincing. He was the one who stuck his neck out for this woman. As far as he could tell, that hadn't happened for her much in her life. Not after her dad died, at least. When he discovered the CIA had abandoned her to rot in that Syrian prison, he'd sent an anonymous request to the same team he'd been working with at the time —Chevalier Protection Specialists—and called out sick that week.

They'd saved her.

She'd enrolled in the Accountant's Office program as a client. He'd assumed he would never see her again.

The fact they were now in the same town was something Zander, his former team leader, would call a God-thing. If that was true, Isaac should figure out how he was supposed to show his gratitude.

He eased his pickup past the front office. Upstairs the light was on, which he figured meant she was home. Isaac wanted to get some of the work done before they saw each other again. If things went badly, she would still need help and the last thing he needed was Adam or any of the others getting her information.

One look, and Isaac would have to camp out on her doorstep with a shotgun.

Sure, he felt that older brother protective instinct flare. He'd filled the role for her a lot over the years, whether she knew about it or not. But there had never been anything of a sibling in how he felt for her since they'd both become adults. She'd been a cute kid, but she knocked him flat with one glance as a woman.

Winded.

Who knew what she had to deal with? No wonder she lived a solitary life out here.

Isaac pulled out his toolbox and picked the lock on the cabin. He cracked a couple of windows and took stock of what all she had.

Lyric had printed off a spreadsheet with everything she'd bought for the project, grouped in a way he could easily figure out what related to what.

He smiled to himself, thinking of all the lists she'd made as a kid.

He'd never met anyone as organized as her. Raised by a top-level government official who Isaac had eventually figured out worked for the State Department. He'd run a division of black ops.

After her dad's death, Lyric followed in his footsteps and became a CIA officer. The kind of person who gave it all for her country. Who tried to make the world safer for the people who lived in it.

Isaac had been raised by a woman with dubious loyalties, who often broke the law to achieve her aim. His father had been her soviet handler—a guy who did whatever he thought he had to in order to get a result.

He'd never had anyone to look up to. But so many people could say that, so what was so special about him?

Lyric was probably right to want nothing to do with him. But he was still going to protect her.

He'd do whatever it took to ensure she had the life she wanted.

Whether that included him or not.

7

Lyric let go of the drape. If she didn't, she'd end up looking at Isaac's truck outside the cabin for hours. *Get a grip.*

"So he's there?"

She held the phone with her other hand. "Yes, Russ. He showed up just a few minutes ago."

After a whole afternoon of peace, he'd come back to disturb her life again. As if she needed him doing that for the hundredth time, or however many it was now.

"He's got the skills to help you do the renovation on the cabin." Russ paused. "And I thought…" He sighed. "Maybe this isn't what I thought it was."

"What exactly do you think it is?" Lyric paced her living area, above the office on the ground floor. Essentially it was a one-bedroom apartment, as she'd always figured if she needed more space she could add on. Or move to another cabin with more room.

All that was contingent on her being here long term. Something that was looking less likely while people kept dying here, and developers wanted to con her out what God had given her. Or persuade her to let it go.

Who knew what tactics they'd come back with?

"Tell me what the problem is, Lyric. Maybe I can help."

He probably thought she would talk about Isaac. Instead, she said, "Allerton and Sons want to buy the cabins from me. They want me out so they can build some kind of residential community for when Benson expands out here."

Russ didn't answer right away. "Do you want to sell?"

"I want to live my life, my way. Like all those verses about taking hold of what God has for you. I thought it was this. But doing it means not being pressured and having slick guys in suits show up to proposition me while they're trying to scam me out of my livelihood."

The words came out before she even realized she felt half that much frustration over what was going on. Between Allerton and the guys in cabin three, she had more than enough to handle without Isaac showing up.

Lyric needed to feel like her life wasn't out of control.

"Why not let Isaac know about all this?" Russ asked.

"Because I can take care of myself." Lyric stopped pacing and set a hand on her hip. "I didn't say I couldn't handle it. I'm just saying it's a lot, and the last thing I need is Isaac and whatever agenda he has going on right in the middle of it."

"Were you listening at all at church last Sunday?"

Lyric sighed. Attendance at services was a stipulation Russ had recently added to the terms of being a client of the Accountant's Office in Benson. He'd only signed on a few weeks ago, while she'd been here for years on her own with just a phone number to call in case of emergency.

Now it was like having a handler again.

Church had been about the chance at a fresh start. She'd

never gone growing up, so why not explore that avenue with her new life? She'd discovered a relationship that only required faith, and in return she got more than she could've dreamed she ever would.

Last Sunday? "I was distracted thinking about this company trying to steal my livelihood out from under me."

"Maybe you can sit with Isaac this weekend, since you know him?"

"I'm not supposed to associate with people from my former life." Lyric didn't know why she had to remind everyone else of that when she'd had it drilled into her.

"So you're friends," Russ said. "Or is it more than that?"

"What are you talking about?"

"I just assumed you guys had history, since he's the one who sponsored you for entry into the Accountant's Office program."

"He—" Lyric choked on a gasp. "He *what?*"

The Accountant's Office was about getting a clean slate. For someone like her, betrayed by the government and left to rot with no protection from her enemies. After being burned as a CIA officer, the Accountant's Office had been her lifeline. A second chance she desperately needed.

And she was just now finding out it was all Isaac?

"Says right here on your paperwork. He paid the whole bill while you were recovering, wrote your reference himself, and signed off on everything." Russ paused. "I kind of figured you knew."

At first sight of Isaac, she'd dropped to sit on the stairs, so floored by the fact he'd been in front of her after so many years. *Flabbergasted* was a good word. Russ had tried to tell her, but she hadn't let him.

Lyric refused to allow that reaction to happen again. Isaac wasn't going to make her weak-kneed, no matter how many nights she'd dreamed of him. How she'd kept memories of the two of them close during missions, captivity, and everything in between. She'd fed on those glimpses of the good she'd had to keep her sane. Hold her together.

Even if they were nothing like what reality had turned out to be.

"You didn't know." Russ's voice echoed in her ear.

"It doesn't matter." She couldn't let it.

Isaac was the one thing that threatened everything God had done in her over the last four years. She could move on if Allerton somehow got her property. She'd already suffered the worst humans could do to one another. There was nothing left except him. That ability he had to cut through everything and leave her as that scared kid lying on the floor.

"At this point," Russ said, "I'm thinking I can dig for twenty years, and I'll never figure you out." Isaac had, and it didn't take that long. But he'd always been the exception.

"Maybe that's the point." She had to keep everyone at arm's length, or her peace of mind would be shattered beyond repair.

The doorbell downstairs rang, indicating someone had come in the office. She looked out the window but didn't see Isaac in cabin eight. He might be out of sight, though. Didn't mean he was the one downstairs.

"I have to go." Lyric hung up, knowing that wouldn't be the end of this conversation with Russ. He was the most hands-on person she'd ever found herself under. He didn't have authority over her like a boss or a mentor even. But he wanted to be there for her, as much as she would allow.

After years of fending for herself, she couldn't help thinking there was some design behind all of this happening now. Or it was simply a giant coincidence.

If she believed in that stuff.

Are You doing something, Lord?

Lyric stowed the phone in her back pocket and headed downstairs.

The lobby counter stretched across the mouth of the bottom of the stairs, giving her a few feet of clearance to make her approach. One man occupied the area, wearing jeans and a hooded sweater. Hair mussed. The lingering stench of old beer surrounded him. It was the trained guy of the group of hunting and fishing friends occupying cabin three the past few days.

The ones who'd propositioned Lyric and Addie.

Lord, give me strength.

"Can I help you?" She stepped up to the counter.

"Checkin' out," the man said.

Lyric flicked the mouse, and the computer came to life. "How was everything?"

"Not sure you wanna ask that."

She'd had disgruntled customers before. Truth was, it would never be possible to please everyone. Some people said, *Why try?* But she wasn't willing to be so cavalier with her business.

"I'm always interested in feedback, no matter what it is. After all, my aim is to provide a relaxing atmosphere for my guests to get away from their normal lives."

He lifted his chin. "Maybe I'll just leave a review online later. Then everyone can see what I really think."

That was certainly his prerogative. She couldn't—and wouldn't—stop anyone from leaving a poor review. Especially if it included things she should genuinely work on improving. But this seemed like something else.

He leaned both elbows on the counter. "Unless you think you can change my mind."

"Would there be a point to arguing with you about your

experience?" That usually didn't serve to turn around some-one's opinion.

He reached out and touched her arm. "Not what I'm talking about."

Lyric shifted her arm from under his fingers and checked out the group on her computer. The printer whirred to life and spat out the receipt showing they were paid up in full and she'd charged his credit card for the final balance.

"My friends and I are still packing up. We'll be out of here soon." His voice had a dissonant note to it, hardness mixed with an ooze of something likely supposed to intrigue her.

Maybe.

She could usually read people, but this guy wasn't the target of an operation that could change the fate of the country. So who cared? She wasn't about to waste time on it.

"You could come by. Offer up something that might change our minds." He glanced at the clock, then headed around the counter. "We have some time. Could even be persuaded to leave tomorrow morning instead. Spend one more night." He walked right into her space, leaving them facing each other far closer than she was comfortable with.

Because he thought he could intimidate her?

The guy looked her up and down. She wondered when he'd try his luck at touching her.

Lyric lifted her chin. "No, thank you."

He exhaled out of his nose. "So quick to dismiss us? Play nice, and we could leave a five-star review. Tell everyone we know how great this place is."

"I already gave you my answer."

"Still…" He wrapped his fingers around her arm, just above her elbow, and put pressure on the nerve there.

Was it intentional?

"Swing by the cabin with me. Just to make sure it's all good before we leave." He shifted closer to her.

Lyric wasn't about to back down. She reached with her free hand for the empty spot on the back of her belt. Before she could register the fact she hadn't armed herself, he grabbed her wrist.

"This can go either way." His hot breath wafted over her face, and she felt a shiver of fear move through her for a second. "Could be pleasant for you. Maybe even fun. Or you won't like it."

She wasn't going to like either route because no way would she go willingly.

Lyric knew what it cost to have that taken without consent. She'd lived it. Seen it. Felt it. Known the aftermath of it. No way was she going to live through that again.

"Let go of me and get out of my space."

He had both her arms secured, but that didn't mean she was defenseless. Lyric had worked hard not to be.

She shifted, just to gauge his reaction.

He moved with her and didn't let go of her arms. He'd expect her to lift her knee and try for the bull's-eye. Instead, Lyric was going to surprise him.

She lifted her knee but brought her foot down on his shin.

The guy howled just as the door slammed open and Isaac barreled in, a thunderous expression on his face. "Let her go!"

Hunter guy had already let go of her, so she shoved him away for extra measure. He stumbled. Isaac caught his arm and whipped the guy around the counter, then marched him to the door, pushed him out, and shut it behind him.

In the porch light she saw him stumble off the steps. He

didn't go down, though. Just caught his footing and hobbled away because of her shin strike.

"Lyric."

She twisted around to Isaac.

"Are you okay?"

"I had that handled." She'd been about to take care of her own problem.

"Sure, that's why he had his hands all over you and he was behind your counter, all up in your space." He pulled out his phone. "I'm calling Russ."

"Excuse me?"

It was like she'd said nothing.

"Yeah, it's me." Isaac winced. "Sorry it's late."

Lyric snatched the phone, her hand almost shaking from the adrenaline now coursing through her. She was going to take it out on Isaac. She just knew it.

She put the phone to her ear. "Everything is fine."

Lyric hung up on Russ and tossed the phone on the counter. It clattered.

He started to bluster. "Everything's—"

"Get out. I don't need your help."

"Yeah?" Isaac folded his arms, probably to keep from strangling her. "Like you didn't need my help with General Yemenov?"

Lyric sucked in a breath. "How do you know about that?"

8

"You're unbelievable."

Isaac could only stare at her.

Face flushed, her hair all mussed. She was beautiful, even if it was because she'd just been in an altercation with a guy and Isaac had stepped in to save her. It was also a whole lot more than that.

Circumstances didn't change the facts.

As a pre-teen she'd captivated him with her laughter, the light in her eyes, and those braids he'd tugged on until he got her to punch him back. Then he'd taught her to take care of herself.

Even if he'd demonstrated to her the foundation of the skills she had to take care of herself, he'd still stepped in just now.

Isaac had been out on the porch headed for a tool he'd forgotten from the back of his truck when he'd seen the guy up in her space and everything washed red.

He didn't remember sprinting to her house. Just shoving the guy out.

Isaac walked back to the window and made sure the guy had retreated.

"They're checking out," she said.

"Good." He watched two guys get into one of their vehicles.

"I had that handled."

He turned back just so he could see that fire in her eyes.

It was her. It had always been her.

Isaac had tried to ignore it at first. There was nothing about his life that wouldn't destroy her. Then he'd figured he could help her out. Discovering she'd followed her father's footsteps and gone into the CIA had made sense, as much as it had completely freaked him out.

He'd fought the pull of her, trying to drag it back from obsession, for years. Kept busy. Checked in when he could. Helped out.

Lather. Rinse. Repeat.

"Isaac."

He blinked. "I wanted to help."

She studied him, and he wondered what she saw. Until she sighed and he realized he probably didn't want to know. "You're seriously going to try and tell me that you had something to do with General Yemenov?"

He needed to tread carefully, or he'd be breaching the nondisclosure agreement he'd signed with Chevalier Protection Specialists—and the one the Accountant's Office had him sign when he came on as a client.

The fact she'd already been a client—something he knew since he was the one who got her into the program—made him wish to see her. Even while he knew it was completely impossible.

Their lives had never meshed. Could they now?

Isaac would have to start with a lengthy explanation. "Do you know…"

"You worked for a security company. You were in prison, and you've been exonerated." But she knew more. He could see it in her eyes.

"What about my mom?"

"Lana…" Her voice trailed off. "I don't want to talk about your mom again, or what it did to my dad when you guys just up and disappeared in the middle of the night. No note. No explanation. Nearly a year living together. Being a family, and a baby on the way. I know now it wasn't my dad's. Then one night you're gone?" She shook her head, and he thought he might've caught the sheen of tears in her eyes, but she was a former CIA agent. So how was *that* possible?

Right now he was feeling as human as her. Isaac rubbed a hand over his chest and tried to erase the burn inside. He'd cried in the car as they drove away. Fourteen years old, and he'd cried like a little kid. Cried the way he had as a toddler when his mom left for eleven years. And when she'd come back, pregnant with Hannah. Until his mom told him to shut it, and he'd figured out how to keep his feelings to himself.

"Now you tell me you had something to do with an operation?" She lifted her chin.

"You can say, 'CIA.'" He shifted to lean his hips against her counter, figuring she wanted some distance between them. He wanted zero but wasn't prepared to act like the guy he'd just thrown out the door. "I know you were an officer of the government because I checked in on you regularly. Kept tabs. If you needed help, I pitched in. Whether you knew it or not."

"Because I needed the kind of favor you're supposed to be good at?"

"It's not arrogance. I was helping."

"According to you."

"Don't turn this into something it wasn't." Isaac tried not to get defensive. "It wasn't about throwing my weight around, and neither was it about you not being capable of doing your job. I know what it feels like when a mission kicks off and things go wrong. When that happens, it's all hands on deck."

"So tell me what you did."

Isaac didn't like the guarded tone. And yet, knowing this would be a long road made the fight that much sweeter. He didn't like cheap victory. Isaac wanted the long haul. The drawn-out battle that proved far more satisfying in the end. "Yemenov had you, and your team couldn't find you."

"That's the part I know."

Isaac's stomach roiled. "I called in every favor I had at my disposal." He'd burned a lot of bridges and didn't care one bit. He'd have razed the whole world to find her. "I got a lead on where you were and sent it to the CIA. Anonymously. Took them longer than I wanted to get in and get you out, but I couldn't reveal my presence at the time. I'm sorry about that."

"And yet you 'revealed your presence' in Paris."

So she had seen him. "That was a coincidence."

Lyric rolled her eyes. "I'm really supposed to believe that?"

He shrugged. It was true he hadn't expected to see her. If he was going to become a Christian, the way the Accountant's Office seemed to think was an important part of his new life, he'd be inclined to thank God for that glimpse of her from across the ballroom.

"That was then," he said. "This is now."

"I'm supposed to believe it's a coincidence the Accountant's Office placed us both in Benson, Washington, by accident? Or did you orchestrate this as well?"

"I didn't know." Before she could argue he said, "Maybe they did." His friends in Last Chance County might've sent him here because of Lyric. It certainly seemed like Russ thought something should happen between them. As though the crusty old former deputy marshal saw himself as some kind of matchmaker. "But what's done is done."

"Unless you ask for a transfer." She lifted her chin.

"Because you were here first?"

She said nothing.

"Maybe after I'm done with your bathroom."

Lyric pushed out a long sigh. "I've spent years getting space from the person I was."

"Instinct is still there." After all, she'd acted quickly hitting back at that guy trying it on with her.

"Maybe it's you being here that's dragging all that back up."

"And you want nothing to do with it?" Did she want nothing to do with him as well?

"It's not who I am now." The tone of her voice betrayed grief, but he didn't know what she might be grieving. "The pastor said something at church about being a new creation. It sounded good. Like I could walk away clean. Be somebody else because I don't want to be that person anymore."

"Was she so bad?" The person she had been was the woman he'd lived half his life in love with, even if he didn't want to admit it to anyone else.

Lyric shrugged. "She isn't who I am anymore. At least, not who I want to be."

He wasn't sure it was so easy to rewrite all those patterns and habits. "Can I get to know you now? Can we do that?"

She stared at him with those blue eyes. She was a warrior, and still he wanted to protect her with everything in him.

Maybe he always would, no matter what she could do. Or how strong and capable she was.

"I don't need protection." She stared at the window. "Things might not be perfect, but they're blessed beyond measure."

He wanted to fight everyone causing her problems. Make her life perfect, even if it killed him. And she knew it.

Lyric shook her head. "Do you seriously think we should…date?"

Hope surged in him, but he worked hard to tamp it down. "Maybe that's exactly what the people we are now would do. Have coffee. See a movie and go to dinner…I don't know what else. I'll ask around. Figure out how normal people get to know each other when it doesn't involve running from bad guys in a hail of gunfire."

She smiled, her eyes lighting. "I'm not sure I'll know what to do with that."

"Right?!" He grinned back. "Seems so…calm."

She burst out laughing, and he had to join in, captured by her light. After living with darkness for years, he wanted to be as close to it as possible. The only spark had been his friends, and the family he'd made for himself with Chevalier. Even if he'd known it would never last, he'd tried to believe it was real.

Isaac's phone buzzed in his pocket. He dug it out. "One of the guys from my crew."

She nodded and moved to her computer, the moment broken.

He swiped his thumb across the screen and put the phone to his ear. "Yeah?"

"How is she?" Adam asked. "Any good?"

"What do you want?"

"Oh, so I'm interrupting? Sweet."

"I'm hanging up now—"

"Boss wants you." Adam didn't sound all that happy about it. "We're rolling, and he wants you on board for some reason I do *not* understand."

"Maybe he wants someone he can actually rely on." Was this his in? He'd be able to get back with Special Agent Franklin and give her something more concrete than a couple photos of a duffel bag.

Lyric shifted to glance at him.

What would she think about him getting in with a bunch of guys up to something, and turning informant for the FBI? Maybe she would think better of him. And call him shallow, but that was a good enough reason for him. At this point, putting his life on the line didn't even register on his risk scale. Her life? No way, too much risk. His? Isaac would get the job done, regardless of whether that left him whole, broken, or lying in a pine box.

"Whatever," Adam bit off. "O'Callaghan's, one hour."

Adam hung up.

Isaac shoved his phone back in his pocket and walked to the door. The guy who'd harassed her was taking his sweet time packing up and getting out of here. If they were going to cause trouble, Isaac would deal. But as far as he was concerned, they had ten minutes tops and then they were done here. After that he wouldn't be here, so neither would they.

Lyric sighed. "You're thinking about signing on as my bodyguard, aren't you?"

"I have to go out soon." He didn't turn back from the window. She didn't need to see the truth on his face. She already knew plenty. "Gotta meet up with the guys I work with."

"Oh, okay."

He spun around. "But that doesn't mean this conversation is over."

Could he really spend time with her and keep his word to himself as an informant for the FBI? She didn't need his protection. She would tell him that. But he wanted to get to know her. Find out what the problems were that she was having, and yes, he was probably going to try to solve them for her. That was who he was.

But running with the guys he worked with in order to be a confidential informant meant leaving her unprotected.

And the result? They would likely be in jail, and he would be proud to tell her what he'd achieved. It was the right thing to do. But was it what he wanted?

She captivated him.

If Isaac gave up this whole life the Accountant's Office had given him, rented a cabin here, and spent all day every day helping her and getting as close as she'd let him? That would not suck.

He would be at risk of dying a happy man.

Which was the first time he'd ever considered that a possible end to his life. Or simply one that didn't involve being torn apart in an explosion. Or shot.

In order to be the man he wanted to be, he'd have to let her take care of herself. But that didn't mean he was going to let her go.

She frowned. "Why am I getting a vibe from that look on your face?"

"Because I'm thinking about coffee." She was the one who'd mentioned dating. "And the movies. And dinner. And whatever else people like us do to hang out and get to know each other."

One of her eyebrows rose.

"What do you say? Are you in?"

She looked at her computer, but it wasn't a dismissal. Lyric clicked the mouse. "Sure. That sounds fine."

Isaac grinned. This was going to be fun.

9

———————

F*ine?*

Lyric could hardly believe she'd said that. As if she was prepared to spend time with Isaac for long enough to get to know him better. See more of that smile on his face, and all the hope there touching something in her.

She'd been forced to admit—if only to herself—that he was her weakness. It had served her well in the CIA, keeping her relatively untouchable because no one knew. They couldn't get to him, so she had no vulnerability.

These days she felt so far from that person it was as though it'd been someone else—after all, that was the whole point. She'd never looked or acted like a spy even when she'd been one. It was part of blending in that she'd come across as a nomad, a student. Being unassuming got her into a lot of places unnoticed. Unless she wanted to get noticed— something she'd also managed. Mostly by playing up her looks.

Her outward appearance was a weapon she'd used to manipulate. Something she'd done by playing it coy with whoever the target was. That wasn't what she wanted to do these days. Maybe if she spent enough time with Isaac, he'd see the truth she hid so hard beneath the surface.

Could be a bad idea, though.

Lyric sighed and locked up the front office. She was too antsy to go back upstairs but did it just to grab her phone and call Russ. She probably should've grabbed her Bible and read some psalms.

He didn't answer.

And what would she say anyway? *Thanks for nothing. I don't appreciate your meddling.*

The rest of it wasn't anything she should say. Half of it was classified. The rest just hurt too much to speak aloud. The way Isaac and Lana had shown up in her and her dad's lives, made them feel like a family for a while. Before they took it away.

There had been a hole in her life ever since.

Russ would only tell her to go to God to fill that hole. Lyric had accepted God as the ruler over her life—the One who would shepherd her to good things. Still, Isaac's arrival showed her clearly she hadn't figured everything out.

All that stuff she'd buried and walked away from was back in one swoop. Isaac had simply dropped into her life through no effort of her own, and he planned to stay there whether she did anything or not. The past still had a hold on her.

Lyric grabbed her keys. She needed a milkshake.

She did a walk around of the property. The hunting guys were gone and had left the cabin door open. She gave inside a cursory look and noted it would need the full cleaning service her housekeeper offered. She locked the front door and continued on, strategically ignoring the cabin where Isaac had some kind of tool whirring as he worked on the bathroom renovation.

Like she even wanted him there.

After dropping the bomb on her about General Yemenov, he'd kept going. While Lyric battled the adrenaline of being accosted, he'd basically laid out the fact he wanted to date her. She couldn't even process it, and then she suggested dating.

All she'd been able to think was that she hadn't needed his help. She could run these cabins alone, and that meant taking care of everything and herself. He'd basically insinuated she couldn't do that. Then she'd gone and told him, "Fine?" As if that were remotely true.

Nothing was fine. It never would be.

She wasn't wrong that God had given her this peace for the last four years.

Still, maybe Lyric had too much baggage to ever be truly free. Isaac being here only brought more of it to the forefront when she'd been trying to move past it. She wanted to live a different life—the one she figured the government owed her enough to leave her to since they'd left her to die. She wanted to embrace what God had for her.

Lyric didn't want to be found. And now the biggest part of her past had walked in like seeing her was everything he wanted. She'd thought she wanted to be left alone to live her life. To run her business and have her peace all to herself.

Now it seemed like she had no idea what she wanted.

Lyric shrugged off the day by driving to the diner for a milkshake. She wanted to check in with Clara anyway and see how things were going. It hadn't been more than a couple of days since she and Russ had given the girl a hundred bucks in her tip. Lyric did it when she could and tended to stay away long enough the gratitude would've worn off. She didn't need Clara gushing over the extra money. That wasn't why she gave it.

After spending ten minutes assessing the parking lot to make sure everything was copacetic, she headed inside. The usual customers sat in their spots. Couple of guys from out of town at a booth.

No waitress in sight.

Lyric stood by the door long enough she drew attention. She headed for a spot at the end of the counter with a sigh. Enrique pushed through the swinging doors to the dining area. "Coffee?"

Lyric shook her head. "Clara in tonight?" Maybe it was her night off.

Given the immediate shift in his expression, she didn't think so. Enrique's face pinched. "That girl. No good, like all the rest."

"What happened?" Clara had told her that Sasha never showed up for her shift the last time she was in. Before Russ showed up. Now Clara wasn't here?

He frowned at her. "You police?"

"No."

"Then what business is it of yours?"

"Clara is my friend."

"Then call her. Tell her to show up for work." He walked away without taking her order.

Lyric slid off the stool and headed for the back hall, and the bathroom. She checked for a camera and found none.

The door marked Employees Only was locked. She pulled her debit card out, slid it between the door and the frame and bumped the door open.

The office smelled like cigar smoke, and the tiny window high on the wall was cracked open. Wood wainscoting, unpainted. A metal desk covered with papers. She bypassed a PC so old it was probably purchased last century and pulled open the first drawer of the file cabinet. She found employee files and hunted for Clara's. Took some doing, since it seemed Enrique kept records from everyone who'd ever worked here—since the '60s.

Clara's listed an address on the form that she'd filled out in purple ink. Lyric took a photo of it with her phone, put everything back, and listened to the hall for a second before she shut the door behind her and went to the exit at the end. The alarm bar had been taped over so the sensor couldn't read if it was closed or open.

A gust of wind blew down the hall.

She stepped out and hustled to her car, then drove to the house listed on Clara's employee application. Lyric didn't let her mind drift to thoughts of what might've happened to her. Whatever it was could have something to do with the other waitress who hadn't shown up for work. She was surprised Enrique hadn't called the police to report it, but maybe he simply didn't care. Or employees flaked on him all the time.

After all, Lyric didn't know anything was wrong. All she had was this raw feeling in her gut that instinct and hard-won experience had put there.

She pulled up outside the house, pocketed her phone, and tucked the gun from her glove box in the back waistband of her jeans. Under the jacket.

The feel of it pressed against the skin at the small of her back should be comforting. It wasn't. She'd never believed Benson would be Mayberry, or whatever those quaint crime-free towns were called. Real life existed everywhere, even if it seemed most folks were trying to find some kind of eutopia to live in.

She'd believed the pastor's words on that. *In this world you* will *have trouble.*

That was for sure.

She'd lived it, breathed it. Until it sank into her skin and became part of her. Not even creating an oasis for herself kept the trouble out. After all, it had bothered her tonight.

God, can You help Clara if she needs it? Help her. She might need You right now.

Lyric felt that deep peace settle in her heart. She uttered a quiet, "Thank You."

She didn't want to think about Isaac in the same terms, but the truth was that she wasn't trying to be difficult. His appearance was out of left field, and she felt like she was reeling. The fact was, he had a hard row to hoe with her. If he wanted to stick around, he'd have to do it long enough she grew to trust him enough to let him in again.

Right now she didn't even know if that was possible.

Lyric parked down the street, around a corner. She walked the neighborhood as if out for a stroll. The house was painted tan, with brown trim. The bushes hadn't been trimmed back in the fall, and this wasn't a neighborhood where the HOA held people hostage until they fertilized their lawns.

The front had no doorbell cameras. Lyric couldn't do the debit card trick again, or the plastic wouldn't survive.

She grabbed the handle to check if it was actually locked, since a lot of folks didn't even bother locking their front doors in Benson. Something she'd always thought was crazy.

But it wasn't locked.

In fact, it wasn't even closed.

As she grabbed the handle, the door swung inward. Lyric palmed her weapon before she even realized she'd reached for it by reflex.

Inside was dark. She didn't flip the light on, just stepped inside and listened first. A pedestal table by the front door had been knocked over. There was an indent about head height on the wall, as though someone had punched it. Or they'd shoved a head against the drywall hard enough to leave a dent.

Lyric made her way through the house, cleared each room and didn't find Clara.

The bed had been slept in recently. In the kitchen, the scent of lemon cleaning product hung in the air. Clara was making something of her life. Getting by, doing her job, and keeping things in order. What had happened to her?

The sound of an engine outside cut through her thoughts.

Lyric went to the front window and spotted a black-and-white police car at the curb. She stowed the gun back in her waistband and debated a second before she went to the back door. She slipped outside and down the lawn, jumped the fence into the neighbor's yard, and crept to the street that ran parallel to Clara's. All the way to her car, where she slipped into the driver's seat. That was when she realized she was shaking.

Clara had been taken.

Lyric had the skills to find her. Get her back or figure out what happened to her. All she had to do was become the person she'd left behind years ago when she walked away from her life. It was the price of caring about people that she now felt the driving need to get to the truth. She had to try to save her friend.

Lyric knew she *could.* The issue was what it would cost her to do it.

That woman she had been was the person she'd left behind when she became a believer. Since she already had enough problems with Second Chances Resort, she could walk away and let the police deal with this. Follow the Accountant's Office rules that said she shouldn't be involved in any activity related to her former life. But even as she thought through all that, Lyric knew there was no way she'd let this go. Not when Clara was important to her.

Even if it was just for her peace of mind, Lyric would find her. The way Chevalier had found her in that prison.

Even if it meant walking back some of her convictions, Lyric wanted to help Clara. To be the kind of person who did what was right.

No matter what it cost.

10

———

It was after midnight when Isaac pulled into the warehouse district. Not much happening this time of night, but it seemed like the whole crew hung out at the storefront where they kept supplies, and where Mitch's sister —or aunt, Isaac hadn't figured out which—ran things with an iron fist in which she held a cigarette.

He pulled in beside Adam, who stood by the hood of his car under the yellow streetlight in the parking lot. The last thing Isaac wanted was to get into it with the guy about Lyric but Adam didn't give him a choice. He waved Isaac over.

"I should get inside." Isaac motioned to the rolled-up loading dock, where music and light spilled out.

Adam shook his head. "Job's out here." He shifted and came over, the screen of his phone illuminated.

"What's that?"

Adam assessed him, but didn't say anything about Lyric still.

Isaac got the impression maybe he wanted to but there was no time.

"I've got something I need you to drop off." Adam

walked to his car, pulled the rear door open, then handed Isaac a backpack.

The weight was enough it could be several things. Weapons. A couple of kilos of drugs. Isaac figured it could be a head formerly belonging to a living person for all he knew. "Do I wanna ask?"

"Not your job. Kind of like looking inside. I'd advise against it, especially if you want to stick around this outfit any length of time." Adam sniffed. "I'd hate to have to go tell that girl of yours something bad happened to you."

"Sure." Isaac caught himself before he rolled his eyes. Of course Adam would *hate* going to see her knowing Isaac was out of the way. The guy probably figured there was a high probability Lyric would cry on his shoulder.

She might. She also might stab him. Hit back, like she had with that guy in her front office.

Isaac wanted to get to know her so he could tell those things. He didn't like not being able to make those calls about what she might or might not do. It felt like something was missing—and there would be until he learned all about who she was now.

Adam said, "Now you put that girl out of your mind and you focus. Take the bag to the Sunset bar on Genistein Boulevard. Ask for Petey and give it to him."

"Is he gonna give me anything in return?"

"He'll be giving that to me because I'm going with you."

Great. "Sounds good." Isaac took half a step back and turned. "Your car or mine?"

"I'll ride with you." But instead of heading for the passenger door, Adam motioned with his fingers. "Your phone."

Isaac blinked. He'd figured the guy would ask for the keys, not Isaac's phone. "Why?"

"Security precaution. Hand it over. And let's go, or we're gonna be late."

Isaac handed over the phone. It wasn't like Adam could get in it without the passcode since he'd never loaded his thumbprint. As if he wanted an electronic record of that. Adam didn't try, he just slipped the phone into his jacket pocket.

Isaac figured if Lyric called he'd answer it and try his luck. Better to get this over with and get his phone back. He wanted to know what the crew was up to badly enough to suck it up and drive.

The bouncer waved them in. Isaac held the backpack over one shoulder, willing to cover the risk by praying the contents wouldn't detonate or misfire and injure him just from carrying it.

The decibel level inside caused his ears to ring. Too much damage from gunfire and explosions. He'd probably be deaf at fifty-five. He winced away the discomfort and scanned inside. Women on stage he had no interest in. A crowd of spectators. Busy bar.

Adam tapped the outside of his arm and waved to the left. "Over there. VIP area."

Isaac spotted stairs that led to the floor above, no doubt more expensive with the décor, but the view wouldn't be all that much different from down here. Maybe the staff up there were paid more. The perks were higher quality. Isaac's interest level remained in the basement.

This wasn't the life he wanted, so he had no stir to induce him to partake of anything a place like this offered.

And it was clear from the activities going on in the VIP area that they offered whatever a person was willing to pay a wad of cash for. Places like this, everything was for sale.

He'd just tell them he left his wallet in the truck.

"Guy at the back," Adam yelled in his ear over the music. "Gray suit."

Isaac lifted his chin and weaved through the crowd with Adam right behind him. As they approached the man, two women got up from the booth and exited as though they'd been ordered to do so. He didn't look at either one, just focused on the threat.

He'd already clocked the two guys at the bar. The one on the rope at the top of the stairs and the female security guard in the corner with the buzz cut who was the real threat.

Who he didn't care about?

The guy in the plush seat grinned a million-dollar smile and flashed the Rolex on his wrist while he sipped amber liquid from a squat glass.

Isaac might want to consider the guy nothing more than the punchline to a joke, but he'd be remiss in overlooking the fact he was also lethal.

The guy lifted his chin. "That my stuff?"

"Special delivery," Adam announced.

"I see that." All the guy's attention was on Isaac. This didn't bode well.

Isaac swung the backpack off his shoulder and set it on the table.

"Nothing to say?" the guy asked.

Isaac didn't respond.

Adam cocked his head toward Isaac. "You really wanna pick a fight with this guy?"

"You brought him." Rolex guy sipped from his glass. "This supposed to be a show of good faith?"

Given the way Adam hesitated, it was likely the complete opposite. "Just making sure everything goes as agreed. None of us wants to lose out on this deal."

If Isaac knew what was in the bag, it might help. Too bad

he couldn't simply come out and ask it. Not when the name of the game here was deflection. The last thing that would be said aloud in a situation like this one? Precisely what the person speaking meant. He'd learned from the master—his mother.

Compared to her, these guys were amateurs. Choir boys on their best behavior.

"So you brought this guy on your crew? Mr. Secret Agent Hotshot, who managed to get himself cleared of all charges." The guy leaned forward. "I heard he was killed on the way out of court."

"Seems I'm here after all." Isaac looked at his arm, though he wasn't sure why his sleeve would indicate if he was alive or dead. "In the flesh."

He was going to have to do an internet search on rumors of his death. That wasn't something he'd been aware of.

"So you are, alive and well." The guy grinned around another sip. "Your mother must be proud."

Isaac said nothing. He didn't want his mother in any of this.

"And now you have the product," Adam said. "Which means payment is required."

"Sit a while. Have a drink."

Isaac started to shake his head.

"Let's not drag this out," Adam said. "Mitch won't be pleased when I report back you gave us the runaround. Yeah?"

The club owner pressed his lips into a thin line. Flicked his hair off his forehead. "Whatever." The guy motioned with two fingers at an associate who disappeared into a back hall. Then he turned back to Adam and did the finger flick in Isaac's direction. "Ask Mitch how much for him."

Everything in Isaac stilled. Each muscle turned to stone.

It had to. This was a matter of survival because if he didn't hold it together, he would explode, and this guy would learn quickly what happened to anyone who tried that with him.

He acted the same way if someone he knew was caught up in that dark world of commerce where people were traded as possessions to be used and discarded.

The guy tipped his head back and laughed.

"I'm getting a drink." Adam sauntered to the bar. Likely due to the fact the female security guard spoke to the bartender. He eased up next to her as if he didn't even notice.

As though, if they wound up talking, it would be pure coincidence they'd run into each other.

Adam had an edge. But when he was with women, things occasionally turned darker in a way that left a sour taste in Isaac's mouth.

The guy with the Rolex was no different. "Still got nothing to say?" he asked.

Isaac wanted to tell him he was out of that life, but in order to hand evidence to the FBI, he'd have to cooperate with these guys to an extent. "I don't work for Mitch."

"Yeah, I didn't think so." He sent a sly grin in Adam's direction. "I pay well, you know? Better than Mitch, and you don't have to rip up carpet soaked in cat urine."

Isaac wondered if the FBI wanted this guy rather than Mitch and his cohorts. Could be he was higher up the food chain. More connected. He'd have to send an email. "Tell me your name, I'll think about it."

"Orlando Salvatore." The guy took a sip of his drink. "Don't think on it too long. My offer doesn't last forever."

Isaac glanced at Adam. He wanted to ask what Mitch supplied him but figured that would only serve to make him look clueless. Not a good impression.

"Keep a tight leash on that one." Salvatore nodded the drink in Adam's direction.

"Why's that?"

"People tend to disappear around him…if you know what I mean. So watch your back. At least until you make your decision about whether or not you want to come on board."

Isaac lifted his chin in a nod.

The guy who'd disappeared showed up.

Adam made a beeline back over as well, but not before Isaac could take hold of the envelope. He tucked it in the inside pocket of his jacket and reached out a hand. "Pleasure doing business with you."

Salvatore laughed. He didn't shake Isaac's hand.

Isaac turned to Adam. "Ready to go?"

"It really is a shame you don't want a drink. I'd love to ask you about the suitcase nuke."

Of course he would. "Maybe some other time."

Especially if Special Agent Franklin wanted him to work his way up the food chain and provide information on all these guys.

The fresh eruption of laughter brought attention. He saw a couple of people spot him. If they knew who he was, Isaac didn't care. He'd made his own path in the world. No one had the right to judge him for it.

Regardless of the court's ruling, it only really mattered what he thought of himself and what the people he actually respected thought of him. Which he would know if he was allowed to contact them.

They headed down the stairs, through the club to the street.

"It's done." Adam stowed his phone.

"What is Mitch into with those guys?" He didn't let on Salvatore had told Isaac his name.

"Just keep your mouth shut, okay?" Adam shot him a look over the roof of Isaac's pickup. "You did your job."

"Right. Not the one you told me it would be."

"Got something to say to me, hotshot?"

Isaac didn't like where this was going. "Yeah, I don't appreciate being paraded around like a set piece just because Mitch wants a show of power. He thinks that guy is gonna cross him? He doesn't have what it takes."

"Mitch *always* thinks they're gonna cross him," Adam said. "That's why he's untouchable."

"Then you don't need to worry about me, do you? So give me back my phone." Just so Adam wouldn't think anything of it, Isaac said, "My girl is supposed to call," then climbed in the driver's side, and Adam got in on his.

"She didn't yet." Adam handed it over. Of course he'd checked the screen.

Isaac turned the truck on. The cold steel of a gun pressed against his temple, and Isaac stilled as he always did with a weapon pointed at him.

Adam's low voice filled the cab. "Give me the envelope."

11

Lyric tied off the trash bag. The only thing keeping her from going crazy was the music in her headphones. If it wasn't for her high school playlist of the greatest hits of the early two-thousands she'd have added to the destruction by now rather than cleaning it up.

And there was still a whole other room full of empty beer cans.

The floor was on another level. She'd have to get the carpet cleaner out of the storage shed and hope it all dried before morning.

She set the bag off the front porch, on the gravel beside the planter. Next to the other three trash bags she'd filled. Her housekeeper's child was still at home sick, and the new booking would show up in the morning. She couldn't wait but didn't mind doing dirty work since it gave her time to think through what might've happened to Clara.

She needed a plan to figure out who had caused that destruction in Clara's house and where she was. Lyric had called Russ earlier and asked him to check in with the police department in Benson. Surely they were investigating, and whether they gave it high priority or not didn't matter. She would figure this out.

The young couple across the cul-de-sac were leaving. The woman opened her door on a wave, which Lyric returned, while the guy loaded their suitcases in the car's trunk. All they had to do was leave their key in the lockbox on her porch.

She used the skin of her forearm to brush the hair off her forehead. The gloves she wore made her hands sweat, but they were clean, and she was less liable to cut herself with them on.

Lyric took a moment to feel the sun on her face before she went back into the cabin. She'd cracked all the windows and had the fan on, circulating air that had stagnated over the four days those guys had caroused here.

Her phone rang. She looked at the screen of her watch and didn't bother answering. She had no interest in what anyone from Allerton and Sons had to say. Not right now, when she was looking at the reality of a spring break that had barely broken even. Three open cabins. One being renovated. She needed bookings soon, or she would have to begin to dig into her emergency savings to cover costs.

It rang again. She nearly didn't look, but it wasn't Allerton. Lyric tugged off one glove and grabbed her phone from the breakfast counter. "Second Chances Resort, how can I help you?"

"Yeah, I'm interested in one of your cabins." His voice was too smooth. She instantly pictured him as some too-tanned, manicured middle-aged guy in an expensive suit. Whether the front was real, or not. "The brown one, at the end? Is that open this weekend?"

The brown one was the color of the cabin being renovated—before Lyric repainted it, rebranding it *not* as the place where teens had been tortured. That color was five years out of date.

"Hmm, I'm not sure which one you mean," she said. "The cabins are all pastel colors, purple and blue, a yellow one. But I have some openings this weekend if you're interested in staying."

"I'd like to come in on Friday." He paused, and she pictured a smarmy smile. "Stay two nights. Can I ask…yours is the place where that young man was murdered a few weeks ago, right? Where those kids were captured and held years ago?"

She'd fielded this question so many times. There were several ways she typically responded. "Second Chances Resort is about escaping from the day to day," she began, "and that includes news stories about crime. It's about retreating and recharging. I hope you'll come and stay for that reason."

"Sure, but you can't deny the pull of your resort being the location of crimes that connect over the years," he said. "Who knows how many more terrible things have happened on that very land? Do you know if it used to be an Indian burial ground?"

"I think you mean indigenous peoples. And no, why would I have cause to know that?"

"Maybe the whole place is *haunted?*"

Lyric looked at the ceiling. "I assure you, it is not."

"Could be a draw, you know? Get customers in. Halloween at the murder cabins."

As if that was something she'd entertained for more than five minutes. Even that much time spent thinking on it was a waste. Despite the fact she might make money, Lyric had no intention of selling out like that.

"I'll make the booking online now. We can chat about it

in person." He paused. "Any coupon codes I should know about?"

"Not currently."

"I've been looking for you on social media. Your reach isn't much to speak of."

Lyric felt like a runaway train was about to hit her.

"If I take some pictures while I'm there, tweet and insta about my experience, you'll see some traction. We have thousands of followers. You could get hundreds of bookings in just a few days. Why don't you fix me a coupon code? I'll keep it to myself, of course. I stay for free this weekend, and we'll see what we can make happen for you." After a long silence, he continued, "We all want our businesses to have as much exposure as possible, don't we?"

A shadow darkened her doorway.

Lyric knew it was Isaac before she even turned. "I look forward to seeing your booking come in for this weekend." She hung up on the guy and blew out a long breath.

"Everything okay?"

"Fine."

He looked around, strategically ignoring the complete lie that was her answer to his question. "They really did a number on this place, didn't they?"

She shrugged. "It happens. They won't get their cleaning deposit back."

"I've never really thought about what running a place like this would be like. It's a lot to do all by yourself."

"I have help, but my housekeeper's kid is home sick from school today." She couldn't quit thinking about her booking spreadsheet.

"Tell me." He stood close now.

But he was still a stranger. "I wanted to do it by myself.

So I could prove I was capable of being a success without anyone's help."

"You have." He glanced around. "I'm proud of you."

"I don't know that I've done it." She glanced at the window over the sink. She needed to see the trees. "When will I know that I have achieved what I wanted to? I'll probably be too busy working to realize I've 'made it' and keep chasing it until then."

"And you're doing it." He touched her hand, giving it a small squeeze. But he didn't hang on—though, she'd have admitted she wanted to if he asked. "What's going on?"

"This place always had a reputation," she said. "People who want to stay where those kids were held. Addie and Jacob, and their friends." One of whom turned into a seriously bad guy. "But then that kid, Austin, was killed here a few weeks ago. I'm never going to get the stain out. Doesn't matter that you're renovating, it'll still be the cabin where a young man was killed." She bit her lip.

"Is it affecting business?"

If she said yes, was he going to suggest she take the payout from Allerton and Sons? "I'm okay, but if I'm going to feel like this is a success, I have to do something. And I don't want my only option to be turning this place into one long Halloween party between Labor Day and Thanksgiving."

"That's not the vibe the rest of the year, though."

She shook her head. "It really isn't. I've been ignoring the idea, but maybe I need to lean into it even if it feels like selling out. That might be my only option outside of selling this whole place to Allerton and Sons."

The only way that would happen was if they were to irritate her into agreeing to sell so that she'd be left alone. And then where would she go? The Accountant's Office had placed her in Benson, and she'd decided to try to run this place. Make a life for herself.

It seemed like God had given her this.

Could she walk away?

"It wouldn't be a failure." He eased in another inch, not too close but near enough that it felt like a comfort. "It would be taking a new path. Which isn't necessarily a bad thing."

"I wanted this to work." She didn't want her whole future riding on being so bullheaded she refused to fail and wound up making the situation worse. "But I'm also not going to dig my heels in."

"We were both trained to pivot quickly when things change. To improvise."

She nodded.

"What do you want?"

There was a loaded question.

She avoided his gaze, not wanting to see what might be there.

He was asking about the cabins. Not them. There wasn't even a *them*. Maybe there never would be. How could they tell the future? A quick pivot and improvising meant things were never set in stone. Expectations had to shift.

She couldn't set her heart on one outcome only to watch it slip through her fingers.

Not again.

"I want to feel good about who I am, and the kind of life I live."

Isaac nodded. "I know exactly what that feels like. And I agree." It seemed like there was more he might want to say, but he didn't get into it. "Whatever decision you make, it needs to be the one that allows you to maintain that hold you have on integrity and honor."

"I feel like I'm figuring out what that means." She

shrugged. "I have the skills to do whatever I want. Not that I'd just go ahead and dismantle the company Allerton has built for years from the inside in one night so that he realizes the error of his ways in being a crooked developer and walks away to live clean."

"He could always die in a suspicious accident." Isaac showed her a hint of a smile. "Happens all the time."

"Maybe, but I know I don't want to be that person. It's taking the easy way out to do whatever I want and make everyone else live with the consequences." She knew too many spies, or former ones, who would've done exactly that to get Allerton off their back. "I'd rather do what's right."

"Me too, which means not kissing you now even if I want to."

She stilled.

"Is it really so strange? We were best friends."

"I was twelve."

"Cutest kid I ever saw."

"You left. In the middle of the night."

By all rights, she should hate him. There were so many reasons why she should want nothing to do with him.

Lyric folded her arms. "Don't you have a bathroom to remodel?"

He nearly smiled. "That was all my mom. You know that, right?"

"She was on a job?"

He said, "Hiding out."

"Because of the baby's father?"

He nodded.

It was confirmation enough to support what she'd managed to dig up on Lana over the years. Lyric just didn't know what Isaac's mother had wanted from her father.

Though, she could guess considering he'd been CIA. Something even she didn't know until later.

Before either of them could say more on it, a black-and-white police car eased down the lane.

Lyric went to the open front door. "They're probably here to talk to me. Someone I know went missing last night." She'd figured sooner or later the cops would show up to ask her questions.

She turned because he hadn't responded.

The cabin was empty.

12

───────

Isaac lowered himself to the grass below the bathroom window. He could've snuck out if she hadn't been airing out the cabin, but it was certainly easier since she had left all the windows open.

One peek around the corner of the house told him Lyric had wandered down the steps to speak with the officer who approached. She smiled and reached out a hand to shake his. Probably so that any of her residents aware of the police presence wouldn't be alarmed. They'd believe this was a friendly visit.

Isaac crouched so no one would see him spying and strained to hear.

Lyric's soprano tone drifted over, but he couldn't make out the words. He'd have to read lips if he wanted to know what they were saying.

The police officer began his questioning. The subtle shift in his body language indicated it wasn't a pleasant visit. He showed her the screen of his phone, and she nodded. A woman's picture—the missing person she'd mentioned as he ducked into the bathroom. He couldn't see the person clearly from this distance, but enough to piece things together.

The last thing Isaac needed was to land on the radar of the local police. Not only would that blow his cover if he managed to continue feeding the FBI information. It would also serve to draw unnecessary attention he didn't want. The Accountant's Office was all about laying low and not being noticed.

He grabbed his own phone and swiped for the camera. If the FBI wanted his help, he was going to make sure the favor was reciprocated—at least in part.

He emailed a photo of the cop to the email he'd set up to communicate with Addie Franklin, using the new untrace-able phone he'd bought that morning. Along with one word.

LEGIT?

The cop wrote notes in a pad while Lyric talked. She seemed as antsy as she had in the cabin, though that had been about making this whole place a success. Something he might be able to help her with. As long as she didn't figure out it was him behind it, and that he was "helping."

Before he could figure out how he was going to do it, the FBI agent replied.

CALL. I'LL TELL YOU.

Isaac gritted his teeth. He pushed out a breath and looked at Lyric and the cop. They were wrapping things up. He'd be able to get the lowdown from her as soon as this guy took off. Find out what was going on.

In the meantime?

He used the burner to make the call, since he didn't want the FBI to have access to the phone he used to communicate with his boss and coworkers.

"This is Special Agent Franklin. Who is this?"

"An interested third party," Isaac said. As if she didn't know. "And the cop?"

"Eric Hummet is as solid as they come."

That settled things at least. The cope who'd come to visit was Edith's grandson.

Mitch, Adam, and all those guys didn't hold the cops in this town in high esteem. Not just because the men he worked with were likely involved in criminal activity. It was also because lately the police in Benson hadn't scored high on the public relations front. One of their own had framed an innocent citizen when it turned out he'd been killing for years. A Benson police detective of all people.

The guy was dead, but the problem hadn't gone away with that.

Addie continued, "You seem like you know what you're doing, so I'm guessing you'll know that being anonymous won't fly."

"I'm a friend of Russ," Isaac said.

She fell quiet for a second. "From the marshals?"

"A more recent acquaintance."

"Ah."

He figured given her tone, she knew about the Accountant's Office.

"You got a name?" she asked.

Isaac worked his mouth back and forth. "You're not just gonna call me 'confidential informant'?"

"You're prepared for that paperwork? I can do legit if that's what you want." She sighed. "But we can also keep this off the books if that works better for your…situation."

"You see me in person, you'll know why I hesitate."

"What about your cover with Mitch and the boys? Do they know who you are?"

Isaac wandered to look at the creek behind the cabins. It

figured she'd concluded he was connected to the men he'd informed on. This wasn't a coincidence.

He stared out at the landscape. Lyric had a great spread. Something out here relaxed him, and it didn't happen downtown in his cramped apartment. It was like being able to breathe. "They know who I am. So do you."

"Yes, I do. Isaac."

He squeezed his eyes shut. "You followed them?"

"Saw you working earlier today. Put it together."

"You surveil all your potential confidential informants?"

"Honestly?" she asked. "Yeah, I do. It's not worth the risk of being strung along."

Isaac explained about the club the night before, why he had no evidence since Adam took his phone while they were inside, and what his presence there meant.

She caught on quick. "They wanna use you. Throw around the weight of what having you on board gives them." She fell quiet for a second. "How do you feel about sticking with it, even knowing that's what they want?"

He pushed out a long breath. "I can do it."

"That wasn't in question, Isaac."

"Then you're just trying to do damage control, or what?" Isaac didn't like that she might be assuming he would do something to mess this up. Or that he'd snap and kill someone.

"I'm thinking that the damage won't matter with this guy you just told me about, Orlando Salvatore. Even if no innocent civilians should be caught in the crossfire."

The threat wouldn't come from him. Isaac knew that much. "I was better trained than that."

"I know. Problem is, so were they."

Isaac frowned. "You think my sense of honor will make it so this fails?"

"They could mean for this to go somewhere you don't want to go," she pointed out.

"At least they don't think I up and found a moral compass." Isaac thought over his interactions with Adam. "And I can continue to give them the impression I'm just like they are."

"What if they push you to do something you wouldn't normally? Cross a line you don't want to cross?"

"I've talked myself out of worse situations." And he didn't just mean escaping from prison. He'd lived a lot of years going on missions, getting the job done with no boundaries. He knew where his limits were.

Zander had taught him by example how to live honorably. Isaac intended to do right by his former team leader. Whether Zander ever found out, or not.

Because it was what his friend would've done.

Addie said, "I've got some background if you're interested."

"Yeah?"

"Francisco Salvatore owns the club. He's sixty. The son is Orlando."

"What do you have on them?"

"Orlando is listed as the person of interest in several assault cases. Either the witness recanted, or the charges were officially dropped. Or both. He's never been charged with anything."

"Dad covered for him."

"The father has been under investigation for years by the FBI. DEA. ATF." She paused. "You name it, no one has been able to make it stick."

"So it'd be a boon if I get you something that goes up the chain." Taking down a whole criminal organization just by working with Mitch and his guys would make this new life worth it.

"What do you get if I co-opt you into helping me take them down?" she asked.

"A sense of satisfaction?" He didn't even know if he could explain it to her. Everyone knew him as an operative, a guy tangled up with a rogue operation. The one who'd been in possession of a nuke. Who'd escaped from federal prison.

He'd been fully exonerated, but that didn't mean he believed in his heart he wasn't still guilty. Of one thing, or all of it, didn't much matter.

Someone behind him cleared their throat.

"I should go." He knew it was Lyric. Whether the cop was still with her didn't matter, so he didn't turn. "Send me some ideas. We'll make a plan."

"Why do I have a sneaking suspicion whatever it is, you'll ignore the plan and do this your way?"

Isaac felt a smile tug his lips. "It's good you get it." He hung up to the sound of Addie's laughter.

Instead of turning, Lyric came to stand beside him. Close.

"What is it?" he asked.

She bit her lip and stared out at the trees.

In the creek between them and the woods, the trickle of the water was little more than a burble of water over rocks. A soothing, rhythmic sound. He wanted to take her hand.

"Someone I know went missing," she finally said. "The police think she was abducted from her house."

He twisted to her. "A friend of yours?"

"Waitress at the diner I go to. And another one of them went missing days ago." She shrugged, pain lining her face. "Something is going on."

He moved close and dipped his chin. "Don't get involved."

"Did telling me what to do ever work?"

"Shoot." He wanted to run his hand down his face. Instead, he moved this forward rather than going around about the same thing. "Please be careful."

"There's no reason to believe I'm in danger."

"You're always in danger. It's the nature of who we are."

"Then tell me what that phone call was. Because you certainly weren't talking with a librarian about the book you have on hold." She folded her arms, putting that barrier between them.

"I'm working on something."

"So you don't want *me* working on something of my own, because you'll need to micromanage it in order to make sure I don't get even one hair on my head mussed."

Isaac closed his mouth.

"That's what I thought."

"So I should apologize for caring about you?"

She laughed, but there was no humor there. "I'm surprised you haven't moved in yet." Her cheeks pinked, and she shook her head. "To a *different* cabin than the one where I live."

He nodded, pure gentleman. "Of course."

"So we both have missions to carry out here, I guess." She lifted her chin.

Great. There was going to be no changing her mind now. He sighed. "You're going to find your friend?"

"Would you leave that to chance…or the police?"

"No," Isaac said. "I don't suppose I would."

"Did you eat before you came over?"

He twisted to look at her.

"I have some chicken in the fridge."

"Are you asking me to eat with you?"

She shoved his shoulder. "No, I'm asking if you want to watch me eat."

Isaac chuckled. He remembered how she'd brought him sandwiches at lunch when he had to do summer school in her town. They'd split them so they each had one grape half and one strawberry. "Dinner sounds good."

"You can help me brainstorm ways to convince people they can vacation here without being murdered." She wandered away.

Isaac nearly tripped over himself catching up with her. He felt a whole lot like that fourteen-year-old who couldn't get through a whole day without needing to see her smile or hear her laughter. They'd been each other's reason for hope. For believing in the power of family.

Now all they had was each other.

"It's Sunday tomorrow." She held the door open for him.

"Yeah?"

Lyric didn't move inside. "Do you want to meet at church? Go together."

He'd take any time he could to spend with her. And likely Adam and Mitch and the rest of them wouldn't be up to much on a Sunday morning other than sleeping off the night before. They'd told him they were headed to a sports bar across town tonight to watch some game. After the club, he needed a night off. They knew where he was, anyway.

"It's okay, if you don't—"

Isaac cut her off. "I want to. I was just thinking whether I have a clean shirt."

Lyric smiled. "Okay." She pulled back on whatever she might've said and led him upstairs to a small apartment she'd filled with a riot of colors. Artwork, decorative bowls. A million toss pillows. She lit a lamp beside the couch and set the kitchen to dim. "Salad?"

"Sure."

"Wanna watch a movie?"

"Depends. Have your tastes changed?"

She grinned. "Since the seventh grade? I'd like to think so."

He moved to her kitchen, drawn like she was a beacon in the night. She always had been. "What can I do to help?"

Lyric stilled. She stared at the inside of the fridge. "You're already doing it."

13

"Feel free to pick up the phone and let me know if you need anything. Instructions are beside it." Lyric smiled at the woman.

Her hair had been trimmed to a pixie cut. She was in her early thirties. Something strong about her manner said she kept herself in top shape.

The woman turned in a circle in the cabin's living room and nodded. "Thanks. I will."

"I'll leave you to it." Not just because Lyric had somewhere to be.

She was getting vibes from the woman who'd checked in with ID that said her name was Sheila Janning. Not that Lyric had any reason to believe that wasn't her real name. People checked in for more reasons than just wanting a vacation. This woman could need help or be on the run from something.

Or here for another reason altogether.

Lyric checked on everyone else. Two other cabins had residents. Isaac left after dinner the night before and was probably at work by now. They'd spent most of Sunday together. It was nearly eleven on Monday morning, and she was still thinking about that dinner. It was kind of like how she'd spent half the night the past two nights thinking about it before she gave up and decided to read a book instead because she wasn't sleeping anyway.

Back in her cabin, she wondered if she should ignore the drive to go to her computer. Then she did it anyway, pushing away the niggle in the back of her mind. Sometimes it was better to do without thinking and face the consequences as they came.

She pulled up a database that searched online and typed in Sheila's driver's license number without looking it up. Sometimes she wished she didn't remember things so easily, but it did come in handy. Isaac could also…

She cut off that thought before she was sucked back into the vortex. The lingering glances. The way they'd spoken about nothing, and everything. Enjoying each other's company. Pretending, at least for one meal, that they were normal people. Watching an action movie about an alien invasion, because it was the only thing they'd been able to agree on.

Lyric found her lips curling up. Her body's betrayal of her mind's determination not to be affected by him. There were still too many unanswered questions about his involvement in her life. She wanted those answers before she just handed over her heart.

Which she knew she would do, sooner or later.

Lyric had to get out of her house, or she'd spend all day thinking about Isaac. Since she needed a few things from town anyway, and everyone was settled, she entered the waitress's name into the same database. Not Clara, who as far as she knew was still missing. She entered the name of the first missing waitress, Sasha Welkins, whose last name she'd seen in the office files the same time she got Clara's address.

The database gave her Sasha's, which made her wonder why it returned nothing of note on her new renter yet.

Lyric forwarded the landline to her cell and grabbed her keys.

The drive to town gave her time to listen to some music. When a popular country song ended. The DJ started talking and Lyric punched a different preset button. The music that came on was an upbeat song about the love of God.

Her finger hovered over the button to change it, but she lowered her hand back to the bottom of the steering wheel. Tapped her finger to the beat. She let the words resonate in her rather than push them away, determined to figure it out on her own.

The song brought with it a sense of peace she needed the time to ponder, except that she was at Sasha's house already. She parked out front. The door didn't have police tape over it, so she likely hadn't been taken from the house. If she'd been abducted like Clara at all.

Lyric had no idea what the police thought. But she planned to find out what happened to Clara, so she needed to know if the same had happened to Sasha.

Even though it was broad daylight, Lyric parked down the street and picked the lock on the front door. She'd simply tell them she was worried about her friend if anyone caught her here. Her phone chimed from her pocket. Given the beep it was probably a text. She ignored it and trailed through the house. She did it in a way that didn't disturb anything, but the look still told her Sasha had some issues. The woman seemed to have leaned into her vices rather than trying to move past them.

Given what she'd seen at the diner, that wasn't surprising.

Sasha frequently disappeared into the back hall with customers, returning with mussed hair and a flushed face. The whole thing was immensely sad. It also had nothing to do with Lyric, or how she felt about the woman's choices.

Not only was it not Lyric's jurisdiction to judge someone else, but she also had enough problems of her own to deal with. People got to make their own choices.

Whatever ones Sasha had made didn't mean Lyric shouldn't try and save her. Unless something happened to her that she in no way invited into her life.

Lyric found a matchbook for a club on Genistein in the pocket of a jacket hung on the back of a chair. For some reason the owners had chosen an upside-down number eight as the logo for the Sunset club.

Somewhere Sasha had been recently? She figured it was worth a drive by at least.

Lyric noted down a few things from Sasha's most recent bills, including a new car insurance paper that Lyric always forgot to put in her car. She noted down the make and model and license plate in case she needed that later and locked up the house.

As she walked to her car, Lyric felt a sensation on her back. She was being watched.

Rather than look around and make it obvious she knew someone observed her, she headed for her car with her head ducked. Projecting the air that she grieved her friend, and was worried about what happened to her.

It was true enough.

She'd been gone an hour, but still had some time before she needed to pick up her grocery order. Lyric drove by the club. The place was shut down and didn't open until two in the afternoon. She wasn't sure what kind of people would visit a place like that so early in the day. It probably lit up at night, bustling with people. The parking lot was cracked in daylight, and the exterior needed to be repainted.

The number eight sign rotated above the building like a church spire, beckoning worshipers to come and give their lives believing enjoyment was everything. That life was about satisfying their feelings and wants, no matter the consequences or who was hurt in the process.

Lyric circled the parking lot out front a couple of times before choosing a space. There were a couple of vehicles already here. Two expensive German cars, top-of-the-line models. More were older and told her the difference between those who ran the place and the employees.

She had no idea how the club even played into what'd happened.

It was unlikely there wasn't a connection at all. She had time and her body wanted to move instead of sitting in the car all restless, so she got out. Lyric strode around the club for the sake of burning some energy.

A delivery truck pulled out, and she saw a loading dock back there.

The side door clicked shut before she walked into view. She would be on camera walking back here, no doubt. Places like this might sanction nearly any activity a person could get up to, but they protected their investments.

The dumpster at the end overflowed, ready to be picked up.

Beyond it someone had parked a blue compact. Lyric checked the license plate and realized it was Sasha's car.

She peered in the windows but saw nothing inside. The hood was cold, so it had been parked here long enough the engine lost its heat. Without breaking into the car she couldn't check the trunk. She also had no reason to—especially not if she'd be recorded doing it.

The club's back door swung wide and hit the brick wall beside it. A middle-aged woman with headphones in both ears carried a trash bag to the dumpster. Lyric wondered if she called out to her to ask about the car, if the woman would hear her—or did she have noise canceling on? Ambient noise meant she could hear someone trying to sneak up on her, so Lyric always used it. Didn't mean others followed suit.

The woman swung the bag.

Her arm dropped. The trash bounced off the edge of the dumpster and fell on the ground beside her foot.

The woman screamed.

Lyric raced over as the woman backed up, still screaming. Lyric took her arm. "Hey, it's okay." She looked in the dumpster.

A woman's bare foot poked out from between two trash bags, dirty and scratched.

Before her mind could assimilate what that indicated the woman had been through, Lyric turned to the bystander. "I'm calling the cops."

She'd let the woman decide what to do with that. Lyric wasn't afraid of the cops and hadn't asked Isaac why he'd avoided the one who came to her cabins.

Was it Clara? It might not be Sasha. But the odds of it not being one of them weren't great.

Lyric realized the dispatcher had answered and explained the situation. After she hung up, a suited man came out the side door. She clocked him as the owner almost immediately.

He touched the woman's shoulder, right by her neck. "Go inside."

She scurried away, tears on her face.

"The cops are on their way," Lyric said.

He glanced at the foot, a disinterested look on his face. "And my employee's involvement?"

"I think you'll be busy explaining why a missing woman's car is parked behind your club." She motioned to the compact.

Lyric didn't plan on doing this guy any favors. After all, it seemed clear he didn't care at all about there being a dead woman in his trash.

Discarded. Probably used. Thrown away, kind of like the way the CIA threw her away when they left her for dead.

The man studied her. "Anything I can do for you?"

Because she wanted to owe him? Or did he think that keeping his employee's name out of it meant he owed her? "You gonna hang here until a black and white pulls in?"

"I have a lot of work to do." He pulled a business card from his wallet. "But if you think of anything you might need, let me know." He looked down to her feet, then back up. "Or if you'd like to go to dinner."

Lyric pocketed the card without looking at it.

The guy turned and went back inside. Expensive suit. He walked like he was born to that life, so he'd had money a while. Or played the part like a pro.

When he was out of sight, she pulled the card and read it. *Orlando Salvatore.* Underneath was a phone number. Nothing else.

He might be small time, owning a club in a city like Benson, Washington, but she'd met his type the world over. He lived for the power he had, and nothing else.

A cop car pulled around the end of the building.

That feeling of being watched was still there. And she had no idea who would have her under surveillance. Some killers returned to the crime scene, but that might not be what this was.

The cop saw the body and paled. He grabbed his radio and asked for the crime lab and additional personnel. The second he let the button go, he asked, "Do you know who it is?"

"From a foot?" She hoped it wasn't Clara. But did that mean she hoped it *was* Sasha? Or some other innocent whose life was snuffed out?

"Don't go anywhere," he said. "I'll need a statement."

Lyric sighed. It was going to be a long trip into town.

14

———

"Eric is on his way home from his shift." Edith settled into the armchair. "So tell me quickly."

Isaac handed over her mug. He'd opted not to have a cup of her tea, since that would leave evidence she'd had a visitor and her grandson would ask questions. Isaac had pieced together that Eric Hummet was the same cop who'd shown up at the cabins to talk to Lyric about her missing friend. The one Addie told him was a good guy. Good cop.

That meant Isaac had to be even *more* cautious about landing on the guy's radar.

"Spill. You said you had dinner with her on Saturday." Edith took a sip of her tea. Her hand shook slightly as she lowered it to the side table. The kind of strength she had didn't have a thing to do with physicality.

Isaac let out a long breath and looked at his fingers, linked in front of him. Elbows on his knees. "You want me to sum up?"

"I don't have time for you to beat around the bush, Son."

Isaac grinned.

"You've got it bad for her." Edith eyed him. "She's the one?"

"Always has been," Isaac admitted. "That was never in question."

"So what's the problem?"

He figured he had some time, since visitors were announced by phone notification from the security guard downstairs and use of a guest key card to get up the elevator. No one else could enter the building. He'd even tested it. It turned out sneaking through proved difficult. Isaac had emailed his conclusions to Russ, who apparently passed them on to the building owner who lived in the penthouse so he could shore up the holes Isaac had found.

"Isaac."

He shook his head. "Sorry. The problem is life. It always gets in the way."

"So you've tried to make it work before, and failed?"

"No." He couldn't shake his head again. That would be redundant. "We've never had the chance."

"Until now."

"A friend of hers is missing. I've got this whole business going on with Mitch and being a confidential informant for the FBI." Isaac ran a hand over his hair. "How do I know life won't move us apart like all the other times?"

"You don't want it to, then don't let it." Edith shrugged. "Why should it be more complicated than that?"

He wished it was so simple.

"Mitch doesn't have anything going on tonight?"

"He called," Isaac said. "Told everyone to lay low. He's worried about heat for some reason."

Isaac hadn't put the pieces together about that yet. He also didn't know where Adam was. Mitch had told him the guy was AWOL, something no one was especially worried about since it happened every couple of weeks. The guy had serious problems, and sometimes they had him out of commission for a few days.

"I'll bet." Edith winked. "If you're gonna play with fire, sooner or later you'll get burned."

"You should write greeting cards."

She tipped her head back and laughed.

"Do you need anything doing?"

She shook her head. "Eric can help me with dinner."

"And your arm?" She'd worn a long-sleeved sweater today. He doubted Eric even knew about it. "How's it feel?"

"Fine, dear. Thank you."

Isaac leaned down and kissed her cheek. "Only woman scarier than you is my mother."

Her eyes flashed. "Is that supposed to be a complement?"

She was playing it off, but he didn't buy it. Before he could ask her about that, his phone beeped with a notification. Someone was coming up—a guest for him. The photo came a second later. Lyric in the lobby where she'd checked in.

"That your girl?"

Isaac nodded. "I told her where I live." He hadn't thought she'd visit so soon, though. He showed Edith the picture.

"She's beautiful." The older woman frowned. "But she looks upset. Go find out what she needs."

He'd been about to leave anyway, but still said, "You're the best."

"Yes, I know, dear."

Isaac let himself out of her apartment, smiling. He wished he had half that much enjoyment over life as she did when he reached her age. It was the goal, at least. But the question remained whether it would come with people in his life he cared about. Not just the way he'd cared about his brothers—his teammates. He wanted relationships as well. Love. A family of his own.

People who would stick around.

She's the one?

He'd told her straight. Lyric had always been the one for him. As much as anyone could be a soul mate, he supposed. He didn't know if he believed it, but he'd also seen it happen for his friends. So how could it not be true?

The idea he could have that for himself wasn't something he could quite grasp. It would mean he'd earned it, or it would mean that kind of thing didn't have squat to do with merit. And how would that be remotely fair?

The elevator doors opened. Isaac stopped by his front door and frowned. "What's going on?"

She shook her hands and strode toward him like she struggled to hold herself together.

He opened the door. "Come on. You can tell me what happened."

She strode into his apartment. "I was close by. You said I could come over whenever." She laid her phone on the breakfast bar and clutched the edge of the counter with both hands.

"Water? Coffee?" Isaac said. "Or something stronger?"

She straightened. "It's always coffee. Everyone knows that."

He headed for the pot and set it up. "What happened?"

"I found Sasha." She paused. "Well, the janitor at the club did." Then she proceeded to tell him about a body in a dumpster at the same club where he'd gone with Adam to make the delivery.

"I've met Salvatore." Isaac frowned. "He knows who I am."

She said nothing, but she didn't need to. As much as it didn't sit right with him that they'd used his presence to make a statement, she was fully aware if she wanted to drop his name he had no problem with it. Because it was her.

It's always been her.

"Come here." He waved her around the breakfast bar. When she got into his space, he tugged her against him.

Lyric inhaled, wrapped her arms around his waist, and let the breath out slowly.

Isaac held on as long as she let him. Then he went back to making coffee while she unashamedly checked out his living space. "I haven't been here long."

She said, "It's a nice place."

"They furnished it for me." He barely had personal belongings, so it wasn't like any of the stuff around here meant anything to him. "Tell me what the cops said."

"To me? Not much." Lyric leaned against the counter. "But I got a decent look at her when they asked me to officially ID her. I don't know what they're going to tell her parents." She blew out a breath.

"It was bad?"

"Stabbed multiple times. Beaten." She winced. "It looked like rage, and he tossed her in a dumpster when he was done. Something happened that didn't go to plan."

"And he threw her out."

Lyric swallowed.

"Do the police think it's related to your missing friend?"

"They can deny the connection."

Kind of like Isaac, and the fact this woman had been dumped behind the same club he was at just two nights ago. It could be a coincidence, but it would be crazy if it was. And he'd never understood why some people assumed everything was random. There had to be a connection. Even if it wasn't closely related to Mitch's business, there was a link. "Did they tell you if they have any leads on your friend's disappearance?"

"They're going to investigate this murder." She worked her mouth back and forth. "Follow the evidence. But no one knew who took Sasha. How are they going to find Clara?"

"Evidence means leads." He didn't want to say aloud that the dead body might be a good thing, because whoever left her could've also left DNA. Or another clue that pointed the police to him. "That means more ways to find her."

"But will it be quick enough?"

"What about the club owner?" he asked. "You think he knows anything?"

She shrugged. "Seemed more like he didn't want to be inconvenienced. He played off his surprise, but it was there."

Isaac got down two mugs and started to pour hot coffee into the first.

"Unlike you," she added.

Isaac frowned at the dark brew.

"You ran as soon as the cops showed up."

"I don't need the attention." He replaced the carafe and turned. "Not from a department in shambles. That's why I'm working with the FBI. Want me to see what they can tell you about the two women? See if they can find your friend?"

She moved to the fridge and pulled out his creamer. "You avoid the police and make friends with the FBI."

"She's Russ's niece."

"Ah, Addie Franklin. The victim turned cop."

Isaac frowned. "It's not like she and I are best friends."

"Sure." She took a drink, not meeting his gaze.

Isaac didn't pick up his mug. He moved to stand in front of her, took her mug, and set it on the counter beside her.

"That would start a war in some countries."

Isaac slid his arms around her. "Addie Franklin is in my life because I need to do the right thing. Being a confidential informant for the FBI is a way to live with the kind of integrity and honor I want to believe is in me."

She flinched. Laid her hands on his shoulders. "You don't think it's there?" Before he could answer her, she said, "You forget I know you better than anyone."

"Do you?" He wanted to believe that was true. He was supposed to be reassuring her. "Addie is a means to an end. That might sound callous, but it's true because I'm more of my mother's son than I'm usually willing to admit."

"She tried to make you like her. I knew it wouldn't work." There was a sadness in her eyes he didn't like. But life didn't often produce laughter for people like them. Not even after the good days they'd had recently. They were overdue for the other shoe to drop.

Was that what'd happened today with the discovery of a woman's murdered body?

He leaned in. "If you need any help at all, I'm there."

"You can't do it all."

"When it comes to you, I'm going to try." He leaned in, until their noses were almost touching. "If that's okay with you." He smelled coffee. Felt the warmth of her in his arms. Lyric was the only woman he'd never been able to get out of his head. That had to mean something.

"It's okay with me," she whispered.

Isaac touched his lips to hers. He kept it light, so they could both take a second and feel out the possibility between them. Instead, he got swept up in a tornado.

Lyric shifted, closing the scant gap between them. She angled her head, so he did the same. Letting her lead as their lips danced together for a moment.

It was easy to let the doubts creep in. To allow the hurdles between them to loom larger than they were.

Harder still to push all that out of his head and let this be what it was.

She broke off but didn't go far.

"I knew it."

Lyric tipped her head back and laughed. "Such a know-it-all. You always were."

"You're telling me that was a surprise?"

"Maybe it was." She shrugged one shoulder. "Would that be a bad thing?"

Isaac pressed his lips together to keep the smile from taking over.

"I should get back to the cabins. I've been gone a long time." She nudged him back, shaking her head.

"I'll go with you," he said. "I've got work to do."

"I'm thinking that's not a good idea." She grinned. "A cooling off period is a good idea."

"You're sidelining me?"

"I'll see you tomorrow." She stopped at the door, all the heat still in her eyes. "Right?"

Isaac snapped a salute. "Yes, ma'am."

15

———————

The doorbell above her front door rang just after seven in the evening, and Sheila stepped in. She wore workout clothes and had a decent sweat going, as though she'd been exercising in her cabin.

Lyric waved. "Hey, how's it going?"

Sheila smiled. "Good, actually. It's really nice here."

Lyric smiled back. It was great when customers enjoyed themselves. They were the reason she did this. It was kind of a double-edged sword when so much of her success relied on catering to people's needs—and some people had crazy ideas about what they had a right to. The payoff was worth it, though.

"My boss appreciates the Wi-Fi." A wry look crossed Sheila's face.

"Oh no! It's nice to get away, but sometimes the tradeoff is twice as much work when you get home." Lyric smiled. "Do you need anything?"

Sheila shrugged one shoulder. "Just to stretch my legs. I feel like I've been at the computer all day." She grinned. "At least the whole time you were gone."

"Right. Sorry about that, if you needed anything." Even though she'd forwarded the phone specifically so any of her guests could contact her. She didn't want to hire someone to cover the front desk all the time, but it had crossed her mind that at some point she might need to.

"I didn't. I just saw you leave, and then I saw you come back." She leaned over the counter a fraction to tell Lyric a secret. "Too much staring out the window."

Lyric shared another smile. She didn't sit at a computer all day, but she could imagine well enough.

"Did everything go okay with whatever you were doing?" Sheila asked.

The woman was astute, that was clear. Lyric didn't want to share the murder with a guest, even if this woman seemed like someone she might get along with. "I had something to take care of, and it took longer than I thought. Then I went to see a friend of mine."

She felt her cheeks heat just thinking about Isaac.

"Whoa." Sheila grinned. "Seemed like you might've had a bad day, up until then."

"More like a bad life," Lyric said. "And he managed to always be there, apparently even when I didn't realize."

Sheila blinked. "Like a stalker?"

Lyric laughed. "Not in a bad way. He's pulled me out of more than one jam in my life, even when I didn't know it was him. Just because he cares about me."

"Wow. That's some kind of friend."

"He really is. Actually, his mom and my dad were in a relationship for a while, so we were brother and sister, I guess, for a little over a year." The best year of her life. Even if her dad thought that his mom's baby was her little sister or brother. Turned out Isaac's mother had been a liar. She blew out a breath, pushing away the bitterness as she'd had to for years. "Now he's here and it's like new and familiar at the same time. Kind of weird." She lifted both hands, palms out. "In a good way."

Sheila chuckled. "I'm glad. What did you do before you moved here and took over this place?"

"Travel agent." The lie slipped off her tongue like the seasoned pro she was. Except this time it left a sour taste in her mouth. "I got to see the world." Toppled a few regimes. Stopped crime by dismantling entire organizations. Saved lives. Retrieved stolen weapons. Drugs. Art.

"I spent a semester in London in college."

Lyric made a face. "Eww, permanently gray skies? No thanks. Only British people know the truth of what the word *drizzle* means. And I'm not talking about a caramel sundae."

Sheila grinned. "I don't mind the rain."

Lyric shuddered. "I prefer South America. Even with the risk of being abducted and ransomed back to my family."

"Did that ever happen to you?"

Once or twice. "Not really. Mostly sun and drinks with umbrellas. Schmoozing clients, you know? Now I get to be my own boss."

Sheila nodded. "That does sound better. Maybe I should think on that."

"Sometimes you pivot in your career because you can, sometimes because you have to. Either way you hopefully land somewhere better in the process."

"I like to be where the action is," Sheila said. "This place is great, but for more than a couple of days? Pretty sure I'd go crazy."

Lyric shrugged. "I get that. But it's nice to be surrounded by so much peace."

Sheila studied her for a second, and Lyric wondered if she would ask about the teens who were abducted and brought here years ago. Or Austin, who'd been killed recently. Instead, she simply said, "Second Chances."

Lyric nodded. "Sometimes they land in our laps. Sometimes we make our destiny."

She didn't want to think she'd forced it. The Accountant's Office had given her several options of where to go, and what to do with her life. She hadn't liked the sound of any of them until this one landed. A place to be out of the rat race. Away from danger.

"I should head out." Sheila patted the counter between them. "Have a good one."

The bell rang again as she left. Lyric shut down the computer and flicked off the lights, turned the sign over the door to Closed, and locked up.

Sure, she'd been gone hours today talking to the police and then seeing Isaac. Nothing seemed to have suffered in her absence. It wasn't like she could go on vacation without shutting the whole place down. She typically took a week off in early November, before the holidays. She'd gone to McCall, Idaho, because people didn't bother each other there. They didn't stare. They just let others live their lives in peace.

Maybe she should go again.

No.

Bad idea when this place had barely gotten off the ground. Now wasn't the time to bail, especially not because things got hard. What a dumb reason to quit.

At least, that was what she told herself.

Freedom didn't mean she could go anywhere she wanted whenever the urge struck her. It meant doing something important that she believed in. And she spoke those words over and over to herself as she ate dinner and eventually climbed into bed with her e-reader.

The fact Isaac was someone important to her, who she believed in, wasn't lost on her. She'd have to think about that some more.

Eventually she'd read so long her eyes started to close of their own volition. She shut the front cover and reached to set it on her bedside table.

A creak in the floor sounded. Far enough away it might've been downstairs.

Lyric slid out of bed, moving silently to the closet where she entered the keypad for her gun safe. The thunk of the mechanism was loud. Maybe too loud. But she'd get a new one later. If she was alive.

Her weapon was loaded, and the safety lever in the trigger would be depressed along with the trigger itself as she squeezed off a round. Ready to take a life any moment.

If it was necessary.

Lyric eased the bedroom door open and didn't step out. She just listened.

She held the weapon with both hands, elbows bent, and took one step into the hall. Another floorboard creaked, this time around the stairs to the left.

She could either turn the light on and take a stand at the top of the stairs to warn off whoever it was—or wait and see what their plan was.

Lyric lowered one hand. Her gun barrel dipped with the other. If the person ran off before she got a look at their face, she might never know who had taken Clara.

But if she let this play out, she'd see what they wanted. Why they'd broken into her house in the middle of the night.

She should've grabbed a stun gun instead. Or a knife. Either was better than a gun if she wanted to get up close and personal. She also didn't want to have to tell the police what'd happened, and wind up with more of them crawling all over her property. Running her ID, seeing how new it was. The Accountant's Office had the best tech people, but no one was perfect. Her identity was a lie.

The intruder started to climb the stairs.

Lyric eased in a retreat to the bedroom and put her back to the wall beside the stairs. She might be about to come face-to-face with the man who'd abducted Clara. Which could mean the waitress was about to die, if he was here to take Lyric. Or she was already dead.

Clara had put up a fight. Given the state of her place, she'd made it clear to the police that something serious had happened in her house.

Had this guy left DNA on Sasha?

Lyric slowed her breathing so her heart rate did the same. Long inhale and exhale. Mouth open to make no sound.

She felt more than heard him step into her room. Then a shuffle of clothing. An inhale, breathy. Sharp. Adrenaline pumping through him, nervousness. The understanding of what he was about to do.

He took a step toward her bed.

Lyric lifted the gun a fraction. She closed her eyes against the dark, reached for the switch, and flipped the light on. Half a second of orange glow behind her eyelids to take the edge off the sudden brightness, and she opened her eyes.

He spun to her. Jeans and a sweater. Ski mask over his face.

"Don't even think about it." She pointed the gun at his chest.

He roared. Whether to scare her, or out of frustration, she didn't much care.

"What do you want?"

"You'll pay." He lunged for her.

She hit back at him with the gun in a two-handed grip. The noise of his nose breaking was an audible crack, and he howled. Instead of reflexively reaching for his face, he pulled back his fist and punched her faster than she could move out of the way.

His strength hammered into her temple.

Lyric gasped.

He grabbed her hands. Squeezed her fingers around the gun. Pinching her skin. She cried out because what was the point of expending energy pretending? He knew he was hurting her.

That was why he was here.

She brought her knee up. He let go of her hands, and she lost her hold on the gun. Lyric grabbed his ski mask and pulled his hair as well.

He wriggled out of her grip and shoved her against the wall. "You'll pay for that." His forearm pressed against her neck.

She shoved at him, her fingers cramping so that she couldn't get purchase.

His free hand roamed. Squeezed. "They said to scare you, but this is gonna be better."

"Let. Me. Go." She bit the words out.

"Why would I, when I get to enjoy the fight?"

Lyric worked her fingers into fists and then straight. Enough times she could grip again. All the while he felt her up in ways she wasn't going to think about. It would only send her back to that night years ago.

Fear shuddered through her like a cold wind that chilled her bones.

She had one shot.

Lyric swung her arms up and slammed the sides of his head. Given the ski mask, it wasn't as effective as it could've been, but it disoriented him for a second. The pressure on her neck eased, and she grabbed two fistfuls of his jacket. She swung him to the right, using the door frame for leverage and sent him sailing out of her bedroom.

Down the stairs.

He hit the bottom with a thump and a groan.

It took her a second to realize she'd done it. He was away from her.

Lyric raced to the bed and reached for her phone. No, the guy was still there. She flicked on the hall switch and bathed the stairs in light.

He was gone.

Lyric stumbled back to her bedside, and the phone. She stared at the screen and realized she was on the floor. She nearly dropped it twice but managed to dial the most recent number.

She woke him up.

"Isaac?"

16

Isaac headed downstairs to meet the person at the front door. Rage boiled hot in his gut. When he saw it was Russ inside, the tight anger on his face matched what he also felt, which made Isaac let go of some of it. He blew out a breath and managed to rein in the urge to put his fist through her wall and make a hole.

He would only have to fix it later.

"How is she?"

Isaac unclenched his jaw. "She decided to take a shower." He had to pause, then fought to get out the rest of the words. "Some bruising on her throat from where he tried to choke her. She's shaken up. Probably will have a black eye tomorrow because he punched her."

Russ nodded. "If she tries to ignore that and pretend it's not there, she'll only wind up having to face it later."

Isaac figured that was why she was in the shower. But thinking about her crying alone under the spray of water so he couldn't hear her didn't sit right. He wanted to help her out. He also knew some things were better dealt with alone.

Russ glanced back at the front door. "Shouldn't the cops be here by now?"

"She didn't call them, and asked me not to," Isaac said. "But we agreed on calling you."

Russ's jaw flexed, but he didn't say anything about that. "Did she get a look at him?"

"Ski mask."

"I'll need a full statement when she gets out of the shower."

Isaac nodded. "I'll make some coffee, and we can sit. She can talk us through what happened." The words came out, hollow sounding, but Isaac wasn't even sure what he was saying made sense. All he could think of was the sound of her voice on the phone. The way he'd found her, sat in a tight ball on the floor gripping her phone hard enough she could've cracked it.

"Want a distraction while we wait?"

Not really. "Sure." Isaac wandered to the living area she had set up as a lobby and stared at the shelf of used paperbacks people could borrow while they stayed at the resort.

He was surprised none of the occupants of cabins currently being rented had come over to see about a disturbance, to ask why he'd sprayed gravel in the parking lot and raced in the house like his shoes were on fire.

"I got an email. A follow-up request, from your mom."

Isaac stared at the books so hard his vision blurred.

"She wants to come here. Stay a while. See you." Russ kept his tone easy. He had no personal stake in this, so he wasn't trying to convince Isaac to see his mom. But the guy surely had the lowdown on what his mom was like.

He ran his finger down the spine of a book. "The Accountant's Office took her on?"

"That doesn't mean you need to see her."

Isaac lowered his hand. "When I was eleven, my father sold me to a guy. Turned out the man ran a whole operation trafficking children. He'd put a GPS tracker on me so he could find me later, but the guy had me change clothes." He swallowed against the lump in his throat.

"My mom hit the roof when she found out, but she'd given me this digital watch, and it had GPS." He blew out a breath. "Do you know what she did when she rescued me? Gave me back to my father and disappeared again. For two more years."

Russ muttered something under his breath. But it was past time when pity would've helped ease the knot inside him. "How long?"

"Hours." He shrugged. "Days."

"She's dead."

Isaac spun to see Lyric at the bottom of the stairs, hair wet. Pajamas on. Red marks on her throat.

"He's dead right? Cause I'm gonna kill her for giving you back to a guy like that." She turned to Russ, face tight. She was not joking. "Where is she?"

"Girl, I'm not gonna tell you."

"Fine." Lyric sniffed. "It'll take me slightly longer to locate her."

Russ shook his head. "You're not taking her out."

Isaac ignored them both. He'd made his own peace with his mom, mostly because his father had been killed, and had even worked for her for a long time. She did what she'd had to do so the mission wasn't compromised.

Still, he'd needed Russ to understand the depth of what'd happened.

"Is she really trying to make amends?" Isaac asked.

"I won't push you." Russ shrugged. "That won't ever be what this is."

Isaac pointed. "Can you grab frozen peas or an ice pack from Lyric's freezer?"

Russ turned to her. When she nodded, he headed upstairs to the tiny kitchen in her apartment.

Isaac walked to her. "What do you need?"

Lyric lifted her chin. Holding it together because she didn't want to break down…again. "You aren't going to let me kill her, are you?"

"Will that actually make you feel better? Because people have tried, and she seems to manage to live through it every time."

"They weren't me."

He knew the bravado was only about being strong after she'd been attacked. "I don't want you to kill her."

"Because you want to protect me. Not because of her."

He figured either way it was the right thing. He would fully admit the point here was to keep her from harm, but considering she'd just been attacked, this might not be a good time to mention it. Aside from moving into the cabin he was renovating, or sleeping on her couch, he couldn't keep her safe. She would never accept him as a bodyguard, and besides, he had a job to do for the FBI with Mitch.

His loyalties were divided right now. And he certainly didn't like the toll it was taking.

Russ returned with a baggie of ice.

Lyric touched it to her face and hissed out a breath, teeth clenched.

"Any idea who it was?" Russ had turned on "cop" mode. Which was oddly reassuring.

Isaac was far too close to Lyric to see straight. He wanted to drag someone from their bed and start punching. Probably not the best response if they didn't even know who it was that had done this. He needed to calm down. Get some perspective and not go off half-cocked in a way that made her mad he was trying to fix her problems himself.

Which was what she'd wanted to do with regards to his mom.

Isaac fell a little more in love with her realizing that. They connected on a fundamental level, and the idea she would fight on his behalf was as satisfying to know as it would be for him to do the same for her.

Isaac led her to a chair and had her sit. He parked it on the coffee table in front of her.

"I thought it might be the guy who took Sasha—and killed her—but he has…Clara." Her voice cracked. "Did he try to take me as well because he's done with her?"

Isaac touched her knee.

"Anyone else you can think of?" Russ asked.

"The developer?" She paused. "I mean, he didn't say anything about me selling. I don't think this guy came here for that. Because of Allerton and Sons. Or if he did he changed it up pretty quickly. I made him mad."

Russ nodded. "Go on."

"I broke his nose."

Russ shifted to look toward the stairs. "Did he leave blood? I can have it tested at a private lab."

"Won't that take time?" Isaac said.

"A few weeks, but even if this is all over by then—"

"It'd better be."

Russ frowned at him. "We still have evidence in hand. Not just our word. It'll mean something to the police when we get this guy off the streets, which is how we deal with things now." His voice had a tone. "We don't go vigilante. I know who you both were, and what you're capable of. Sometimes we have to let go and do things in a way that gets justice. That means living clean."

He shot Isaac a pointed look.

Isaac didn't think too closely about what that meant. Russ knew about the informant thing, and how Isaac worked with Addie, Russ's niece. The FBI agent knew who he was, and their connection. Things would turn out the way they were meant to.

Russ turned back to Lyric. "What about cameras? You got any surveillance on this place?"

"Only to look at the wildlife."

Russ flinched. "Say what?"

"A couple of local conservationists, they work with the university. They have cameras set up facing the trees so they can see what comes and goes."

"But no security?"

"I don't live that life anymore." Lyric crossed her arms.

"It's basic safety."

"I don't want to be recorded. No one gets to watch me, not even a camera I set up. That's why I live out here."

Isaac squeezed her knee. "It's okay."

"I'm not being naïve."

"We know that, honey. That's not what Russ is saying." At least, Isaac didn't think so. "We just want to find this guy and take him to the cops." That last part was for Russ's sake. Addie could write up the case, even if they dropped a suspect in her lap with all the evidence. He figured she wouldn't mind an easy win.

"Can you write down everything you remember about him?" Russ handed her the scratch pad he'd grabbed from her front counter.

Lyric took it, then raised the back of her hand to her mouth to cover a yawn. She was fading fast.

"Make your notes," Isaac said. "Then you should head to bed. Try and get some sleep." She glanced to the side, and he caught the sheen of tears in her eyes. "Do you want to pack a bag and stay with me?"

Russ shifted. "I can get my stuff. Come here. Watch this place for a couple of days. If you want?"

"I don't want to put you out."

"I'll bring Mona." Russ turned to Isaac. "That's my niece." To Lyric he said, "She might enjoy helping me out, pitching in. Who knows? She might want to keep doing it. If you need another pair of hands, or someone to cover if you want to take a day off."

A tear ran from the corner of Lyric's eye.

Isaac wondered how long it had been since someone offered her help. He didn't begrudge her not asking. He was the last person who'd admit he needed assistance with anything.

"You guys get squared away here, lock up, and get over to Isaac's place. I'll be here first thing in the morning, and Mona can come over after school."

Lyric lifted her chin. "Thank you."

Russ nodded. Encapsulated in that one move was the fact he'd do it regardless. She'd earned it. He considered it his pleasure to help her out like that.

Isaac stood. He offered Russ his hand, and they shook.

"Call me in the morning?"

Isaac said, "Will do," and waved as Russ left. He then turned to Lyric and saw she'd stood.

She shifted from one foot to the other, and he spread his hands. She walked into a hug, and he held her gently.

"You did good." She'd broken the guy's nose after all. "You did really good."

She sucked in a choppy breath and let it out slowly. "We need to find Clara."

Isaac frowned, his chin against the top of her head.

"Okay. Let's get packed up and head to my place. First thing in the morning we'll make a plan."

She leaned back and he let her go. "He's not going to get away with this."

Isaac nodded.

"I don't want to see your mother. She's not a nice person."

Isaac burst out laughing. "I love you." Then he realized what he'd just said. "I mean, I…that's not what I mean."

"I'm too tired to figure this out." She moved to the stairs. "I'm gonna get my stuff."

Isaac shut his eyes. Found the wall. Laid his forehead on the cold drywall and tamped down the need to bang his head.

Stupid.

He shouldn't have said that. It wasn't a lie, but now definitely wasn't the time to tell her how he felt. She'd just been attacked.

The last thing he wanted to do was pressure her when she was already vulnerable. She was probably going to find somewhere else to stay, and he didn't want that either.

Now he'd gone and messed everything up.

He heard her footsteps on the stairs and met her at the bottom. Her face was pale, her expression blank. "I can carry your bag."

She slipped the tote off her shoulder, grabbed her purse, and locked up.

As they crossed the porch, he realized what a terrible job he'd done of parking. His door was open, the interior light on. He'd parked halfway on the grass and might've run over a bush. He winced. Then he felt her fingers slide against his, and she held on.

Isaac said, "Let's go."

17

____

The car rolled down the highway toward the cabins, but that wasn't where they were going. Lyric stared out the passenger window at the clouds.

Isaac's fingers touched the back of her hand. She turned it over and held on. Nearly a day since she'd been slammed around. Freaked out. In the light of day the fear was like a fire that had banked, now just smoldering embers. When night fell things would likely be different, but she planned on being back at his apartment by then.

"Doing okay?"

"I'm good." She shifted in the seat. "You know Edith doesn't like me, right?"

"What? No way."

He was in denial. "Trust me. She doesn't like me."

He'd walked her over to Edith's when he came home on his lunch break, hung for a few minutes, then left. She'd tried to talk to the older woman for an hour, but Edith didn't want to engage. She'd actually seemed kind of mad. Or just stand-offish. Lyric couldn't get a read on the woman at all. Except for one thing.

"Maybe she doesn't approve of me for you."

"And you're worried that might be a deal breaker?" He squeezed her hand, but only gently. "Because it's not."

Lyric shook her head. "I don't like causing dissent."

"You have nothing to worry about."

Sure, that was why she'd been awake half the night. Instead of thinking about what happened she'd been thinking about what Isaac said. How he felt.

I love you.

She wanted to wrap those words around her like a blanket. Hold them close.

"I need to focus on finding Clara." Since Isaac had driven her to his place, she also needed her car. Hers was on the drive at her cabin. She'd have to get him to drive her back, and something told her Isaac would rather she stuck around with him for as long as he could convince her to do it. "I don't like being taken care of."

"How about partners?" He let go of her hand and held the wheel with both.

She didn't like the hurt in his voice. "When I know Clara is safe, and whoever took her is caught, then I can think about other things. I have to keep focused."

After all, leaving it to the police only got her an intruder in her house.

"Do you think your assailant is connected to Clara and Sasha?"

"It's a serious escalation from harassing me if it's that developer," Lyric said. "But I'm not ruling them out."

"You think this Enrique guy they both worked for will tell us anything?"

"I know he's going to tell us something." She wasn't prepared to leave until then. There had to be a correlation, and work was the place their lives intersected. Aside from at the diner, Sasha and Clara didn't hang out. They weren't friends.

What else could it be?

"Sure you feel up to this?"

Lyric twisted around in her seat. "How was your day at work?"

"You forgot to add 'dear' on the end."

"You want me to call you that?"

Isaac shrugged. "Might be nice."

"We were supposed to date first. Did you forget that? Because it was your idea as far as I recall."

"Are you mad at me?"

Lyric blew out a breath. She'd been thinking about what he said the night before about his mother. She couldn't believe what both of his parents had done.

Everyone knew Lana had questionable methods. Morals. Tactics. She'd been a Russian double agent and then ran a special operations group that worked privately with no allegiance to speak of. Except to herself and what she thought needed to be done.

"I am mad," she said. "But not at you."

"Sorry your quiet life got disrupted."

Lyric tried to think if that was what it was. She hadn't allowed herself to consider it much. "I like my cabins. I want to do that."

"But it's hard to switch off what you used to be."

"It all came back. His arm against my neck, all of it just kicked in." She shook her head even though her face hurt where she'd been punched. "I could've killed him. But why deal with the police?"

"You'd have been within your rights to do it. He intended to harm you in your own home."

"I had a gun."

Isaac glanced quickly at her. "Why didn't you shoot him?"

"I…I knew I could figure out why he was there. Then I just wanted him gone." She ran her hands to her knees, trying to loosen the tension. "I don't want that life back. It didn't want me, so why try to keep it?"

"Because the government left you for dead."

"They burned me." And he was the one who'd sent his friends to rescue her. The one who'd cared whether she lived or died.

Lyric figured she probably did love him. But unless it was to get that spur-of-the-moment gorgeous laugh of his, it didn't work to just blurt the sentiment out. She needed to find the right time to tell him.

"If you didn't want that life, you'd leave Clara's abduction to the police to figure out. But you know you can do this, and you know exactly what it'll cost you."

"Yes." What else was there to say?

He pulled into the diner parking lot and found a parking space, then squeezed her hand.

She squeezed back. "Thanks for driving me."

"Let's find your friend."

They headed for the diner, walking like partners rather than a couple. In the CIA showing affection for someone meant you had a weakness. A vulnerability.

Maybe he was right. As much as she wanted a life that was nothing like the one she'd had, the training stuck. She'd done that job for years. Given them everything.

Now what did she have?

Isaac held the door open for her. Lyric jolted out of her thoughts and stared up at him. He grinned and cocked his head for her to go in.

Maybe she had a lot still, whether the CIA took what she

had or not. They might have left her to die, but they'd never factored in Isaac. *She* hadn't factored him in either.

And yet, she'd always had him as part of her life.

In a way, she always would.

Lyric headed for the counter where Enrique wiped the surface with a ragged washcloth. He spotted her approach, clocked Isaac with her, and his face hardened. "Whatever you want, I'm not interested."

"And if I'm here to ask for an application to waitress for you?"

He stilled. "Are you?" Didn't seem like he thought that was a great idea.

"No. But if I get one of them back for you?" She didn't give him much time to think about that. "Sasha's dead, but maybe I can find Clara."

He made a face. Then he motioned to the end of the bar with a skinny arm and that long-fingered hand. The hall she'd snuck down to raid his office. "Over here."

She followed him to the end. "You have no idea who I am, and it will stay that way." She wasn't going to ask him to trust her. "What did you tell the police when they asked about your missing waitresses?"

He shrugged the shoulder of his ragged T-shirt. "They worked for me. I don't get involved in their personal lives. I don't know who they saw or if they were into something. They work, I pay them. That's it."

"What do you know that you didn't tell the police?" She gave him a second to think. "Someone who paid them a little too much attention. Hung around, maybe when they were leaving. Anyone like that?"

His thick brows furrowed. "You think I'm gonna narc on paying customers?"

"You want blood money?" Surely he held a little concern

for his employees? He was now forced to do their jobs. That had to inconvenience him enough. "Because someone has Sasha's blood on them. She didn't get that way and they remained unscathed. You get what I'm saying to you?"

"Have I noticed anyone with wounds she might've inflicted? Or cracked knuckles from beating her?" He shot Lyric a pointed look. "Like you?"

"I was attacked. Likely by the same person who took them."

Enrique sniffed. "So you know who it was."

She'd certainly landed on the guy's radar. If it was the same man who had Clara. Was she dead, or still alive by some miracle? Lyric intended to find out. And until then she couldn't think too much about what might be happening to Clara. It wasn't going to help her find the woman who was the closest thing Lyric had to a friend right now.

"I wouldn't be here if I knew who it was," she said. "I'd be kicking his door in."

The skin around his eyes contracted.

"I'm not a cop." She motioned to Isaac. "Neither is he. That's why I'm going to find her. So tell me what you didn't tell the cops."

Enrique sniffed again and rubbed his nose. "They hang out here every few weeks. Moving through town. Too chatty, trying to get my waitresses to go with them. Like they don't know what being groomed looks like. They're too smart for that."

"So you think they followed them home? Took them?"

"One was here about a week ago. Not part of them, but hung around when they showed up. Like he wanted to be in on the action. Seemed like he was down on his luck, looking for something. Sasha went with him. Didn't come back the next day."

"Can you give me his picture from your security cameras?"

"They're just for looks. Not even plugged in." Enrique looked guilty. To his credit.

She wasn't going to give him much, though. "Did he come back at all?"

Enrique shook his head. "Haven't seen him."

"Local guy?"

He nodded.

"Vehicle?"

He frowned. "A truck. New by the look of it."

"And the guy?"

"Dark hair. Thirties. Goatee." He paused. "Tries too hard. There's something off about him when it comes to women."

"When was he here last?"

Enrique gave her a day and a rough time.

"Give me some paper," she said. He pulled the order notebook from his apron, and she wrote down her name and number. "Call me if you see him. I wanna know."

He stuffed it in his apron and went back behind the counter.

Isaac wandered over. "Ideas?"

"We need to hit the gas station." She patted her pockets but realized she had her debit card but no real money. "Got any cash?"

"What do you need?"

"Forecourt footage." She went first, heading outside to the gas station next door. "They've got cameras. Let's just hope they're plugged in." She pulled her coat tighter around her as they crossed the pitted parking lot. The air held a slight chill, and her body struggled to retain heat.

"After that, we're getting a hot drink and some food," Isaac told her.

"Good." She picked up her pace.

Isaac shifted beside her, and his phone rang. "Yeah?" He stalled her with a hand on her arm. "Serious? Okay, but I'm with a friend of mine." He paused. "Will do." He hung up.

"What is it?"

"Mitch needs a favor. I've gotta go." And he was taking his car.

"I'll rideshare back to your place," she said.

He winced. "That'll cost a fortune. We can come back here tomorrow."

Lyric moved out of reach, headed for the gas station. She wasn't dropping this when she had a real lead. "I'll catch up with you later."

She was going to find Clara.

18

I saac watched her walk away.

His phone started to ring, but it was Addie—not Mitch.

"Yeah?"

"I've got her. You go."

Isaac frowned.

"I'm serious. Go."

She could see him. Isaac turned to his car. "Wanna tell me how you've got eyes and ears on me?"

"I know Mitch called you, but I'm not listening to your conversations, so you don't have to worry about that. Me being parked across the lot watching out for Lyric has nothing to do with my job as an FBI agent."

"So you're moonlighting?"

"Russ asked for an extra set of eyes on Lyric. Just to make sure she's safe."

Isaac opened his driver's door and climbed in. "Does the Accountant's Office pay you to bodyguard?"

"It's how I get room and board at Russ's house. For now, at least." Her voice lightened with humor. "Go figure." She paused a second. "Now tell me what that was about with Mitch."

Isaac stared at the gas station for a second. Lyric was out of sight now, but where she was didn't matter. All he knew from the ache in his chest was that he wanted to be there. Not chasing errands for a boss he didn't like.

"Isaac."

He shook himself from that thought train and headed out of the parking lot. When the call connected through his truck speakers, he said, "Mitch was contacted. Apparently, Adam is making a scene at the club, and I have to go pick him up."

"Good. They're relying on you, trusting you," Addie said. "Keep on with that and see where it gets you."

Even if the last thing he wanted was to be "in" with the crew. Doing this would serve as a means to an end. A way to feel clean because he'd done the right thing as soon as he realized the guys were dirty. He was contributing to justice. And he'd be doing it the complete opposite way to how his mom would work the process.

Which was the point here.

He couldn't believe he'd actually admitted to Russ what the deal was with his mom. And Lyric had heard it.

Sure, she jumped to his aid. But did he need her to do that?

He liked it that she got riled up to defend him. It was just that he wanted nothing to do with Lana. Not now, and not for the rest of his life.

If he couldn't have the good parts of his old life, the friendships he'd built, then why should he have to deal with the rest of it? That was the stuff he'd much rather forget.

"You think any of them is Lyric's assailant?" Addie asked.

"Maybe." Isaac followed his phone navigation back to the club, just so he didn't waste time getting there. He wanted to be done with this as soon as possible. Get Adam back home and get back to Lyric.

"Worth a look to see if anyone's got a broken nose."

Isaac gripped the wheel and pushed the gas pedal farther than he probably should. "I'm thinking that club owner."

"Only because it wasn't the guy from the diner," Addie said. "From through the window I didn't see any damage."

"He mentioned some suspects, but it's hard to know if he's just blowing smoke instead of giving us solid leads."

"Want me to look into it?" she said. "I can shake some trees, see what falls."

"Because you need more stuff to do?"

Addie sighed. "Fine. Jake is in Florida telling his parents that we're planning on getting married. Not because he especially wants them to come to the wedding. It's more about damage control."

"Huh."

"So I'm trying to distract myself. It's part of my investigative process."

Isaac felt the curl of his lips. He hadn't been on the receiving end of work banter in months. Betraying his teammates and winding up in federal prison kind of killed the camaraderie. "Thanks, Addie."

"For me diving in with the weight of the federal government?"

"Sure. Let's go with that."

"You know you could just take a couple of photos and walk away," she said. "You don't have to play this out to the end."

"Yeah, I do."

"Okay." She paused. "Also, you're welcome."

He wanted to offer her a long-term thing. Permanent CI. The guy she called on to go into situations none of her badged coworkers could. Places his identity would carry weight, since he couldn't live under a clean one without getting plastic surgery.

That'd been a hard no.

He wanted to be who he was, even if his life had been screwed up by circumstances, doing the right thing, and being his mother's son.

Isaac held his tongue, though. This wasn't about trying to get back what he'd lost. As soon as it was done, he would start a construction company of his own. Or become permanent groundskeeper for a resort of cabins.

If Lyric was interested in a partner.

She already knew how he felt. He needed a way to tell her he was all in with life here, with her. The two of them. Making a family the way Addie and her fiancé were going to do.

Assuming she felt the same way.

Addie was right about one thing. Distraction was a solid plan for now, and what would be should take care of itself. He was supposed to leave it to God to let Him take care of the future.

"I'm at the club," he said.

"Call me as soon as you can. I'll keep Lyric safe." Addie hung up.

That was the only reason he was doing this tonight. She was watching over Lyric while he couldn't. Lyric had proven she could take care of herself. Isaac still planned to be signed up for the job permanently until…hopefully forever.

He climbed out of the pickup sighing. Tempted to pray she felt the same way.

The bouncer lifted his wrist to his mouth. "He's here." He motioned for Isaac to enter.

Isaac walked by the line of people and pulled the door open. The music remained at a muted volume in the lobby until the interior door opened and a security guard stepped through. No broken nose. Isaac remembered him from beside the bar.

"This way." He led Isaac through an employee door to the side, down a hall, and upstairs to the offices. He pulled open a door and stood there.

Isaac stepped into the owner's office. He was behind his desk. No broken nose.

Two men secured with zip ties sat on the couch. One was Adam, the second guy someone Isaac didn't know. Both had been beaten so badly it was impossible to tell, but it looked like probably both had broken noses. Among a ton of other injuries. Both were glassy-eyed, keyed up on something. Disoriented or concussed.

The second man took shallow breaths. In a way that didn't look good.

"This guy yours?" Isaac motioned to him.

"Why?" Orlando Salvatore frowned.

"His lung is punctured."

"Don't worry about that."

Isaac figured that meant Orlando's payback would leave the guy without the means to worry either. "What happened?"

"He started it." The guy gasped and twisted to Adam.

"Just get your guy out of here." Orlando lit a cigarette.

Isaac needed to know if either of them were Lyric's assailant, so he said, "I'm sure Mitch will reimburse you any damages."

Orlando spoke around a mouthful of smoke. "Then you don't know Mitch that well."

"Adam can fill me in," Isaac said. "How long has he been here? We lost track of him."

"Keep this one on a tight leash." Orlando waved the cigarette at the two men. "All this took less than half an hour."

Isaac shook his head. "How many drinks did he have?"

"Sauced when he came in. Hides it well." Orlando paused. "Hides a lot of things is my guess."

Adam swayed on the couch. If Isaac dragged this out any more, he'd have to carry the guy down the stairs.

"Get him out of here." Orlando flicked two fingers.

Isaac hauled Adam up by his elbow. "Let's go."

Adam groaned.

Isaac got him out and loaded into the pickup, which included cutting the plastic ties so he was no longer bound.

Adam winced.

Mitch had texted Adam's address, so he headed there. A rundown apartment complex built in the '70s. Window air-conditioning units, and rickety stairs to the second floor. Mitch's truck was in the parking lot.

Adam motioned to a door under the stairs. He didn't get out a key, just turned the handle and stumbled in.

Mitch waited by the kitchen, drinking from a brown bottle.

Isaac shut the front door.

Adam headed for his couch and flopped down. "I'll take one of those."

Mitch didn't move. "Salvatore reports you attempted to make a sale. More of my product, and you're handing it to buyers for half price under the table. Under my nose." He set the bottle on the counter without making a sound.

Isaac put his hand in his jacket pocket and leaned against the wall like he didn't care what happened next. He couldn't stop it without intervening, which would cause Mitch to think twice about his involvement in their business. Mitch wanted underlings who followed orders—and showed zero initiative.

It didn't bode well for Adam.

"We all gotta do what we do." Adam shifted under the focus of attention.

"Is that right?" Mitch came around the recliner and stood in front of the couch where he towered over Adam. "So I should allow you to continue self-serving? I've let it go long enough."

Isaac slid out the phone and took a couple of pictures. He only got the back of Mitch's head, and Adam didn't notice. He was too focused on his boss to see what Isaac was doing.

Isaac opened his voice recorder app and turned it on.

"Along with other things," Mitch added.

"That doesn't factor." Adam spoke the words like a plea. "It's my business."

Isaac frowned.

"Until you make a mess." Mitch moved closer. "And now there's heat on us. Attention. You think I need that when I'm gearing up for something big. You've become a hinderance, Adam. We're done."

"Mitch—"

The boss pulled a gun from under his jacket, put it to Adam's chin, and pulled the trigger.

Isaac's whole body flinched. His ears rang. He winced around the sensation and slid the phone into his pocket. Some latent sense of self-protection kept Mitch from discovering his true intentions.

"What was that?!" The guy he was here had to be surprised in the moment, but not afraid of what Mitch might do to him. He had to anticipate what was about to happen.

Mitch wiped the gun with his shirttail, cleaning the entire thing. He took Adam's lifeless hand and curled his fingers around the weapon. "The neighbors won't say a thing."

Isaac gritted his teeth. "Did you have to kill him?"

"Before he destroyed everything I've worked for? Yeah, I did." Mitch sounded aggravated. "You of all people know how it goes."

Because he thought Isaac got rid of inconveniences by staging a suicide?

"He was getting sloppy."

"What did you mean when you—"

Mitch held up a hand. "We don't have time for questions." He got the beer bottle and slid it into his coat pocket so the neck stuck out past the zipper and bumped his elbow. The other pocket of Mitch's coat was stuffed full of...something. "Wipe down everything you touched."

"And then?"

Mitch shook his head. "I seriously don't have to explain how this works, do I?"

"It's been a while."

"Going straight." Mitch huffed. "Makes you soft." He clapped a heavy hand on Isaac's shoulder. "Don't worry, we'll get you back to your prime."

Mitch walked out the door.

"Clean this up." The guy paused a beat at the front door. "It'll be good practice."

19

Lyric didn't bother hiding the fact she took a photo of the surveillance printout. Addie stepped up beside her as soon as she'd sidled up to the gas station register. She'd managed to contain her shock and got the attendant to point them to the office so they could look at the security tapes—complements of a hundred bucks after Addie didn't mention she was a cop.

The guy had asked if either of them were. As if Lyric would chain herself down to one department of one agency in one town. That wasn't freedom.

Addie took the photo and stuffed it in the driver's door pocket. "I'm the one who is gonna get an ID on that guy."

"Tonight?" The clock on the dash indicated it was after eleven now.

"I'll call as soon as I figure out who that is. I know you want to find Clara."

Lyric said, "Thanks."

"No problem. I'm going to follow up with an officer I know at the police department also. See what they've got."

Addie took the freeway exit that would get them to Isaac's apartment building.

She didn't want to repeat the same word, saying, "Appreciate it."

"No one wants Clara to be wherever she is a minute longer than necessary. I know how it feels to be trapped and at the whim of some guy determined to make your life a nightmare."

Lyric knew that was true. "So you get it."

"And you do as well?"

The FBI agent was fishing. She wanted to get to know Lyric, which was fine. See why Lyric was so determined to pursue this.

Addie said, "I know she's your friend, and that you helped her out with extra tips."

Training dictated she keep the past to herself. But did she really want to be that closed off spy she'd always been for the rest of her life?

Isaac had brought out so much in the last couple of weeks. Addie wanted to do the same in her own way. They were both determined to connect with her, which meant they saw something worth connecting to.

She could either shut them out or continue to let them in. But would opening herself up to friendship—and more, with Isaac—mean freedom? Or would she feel trapped by the relationship? She'd been living behind a wall for years, refusing to let anyone in because she didn't want to lose another person she worried over.

"Yes, I care about her." Lyric bit her lip and decided to say it. "And yes, I know something about what it's like to be in a situation where you're held against your will."

"What happened?"

Lyric was tempted to talk about the assault, but that was

classified to the highest level the US government used to label covert operations. This? No one cared, no one remembered but her, and no one needed it to stay a secret.

Lyric stared out the front windshield. "After my dad…" She swallowed. "After he died, I was put in foster care. The first home was fine. They just ignored me. It lasted a few months and I was bounced around. Landed in a group home. The guy who ran it…"

Addie was silent.

"He took pictures of me. He was going to sell me."

"How old were you?"

"Old enough to know exactly what was about to happen."

"Did it?"

Lyric bit down on her molars. "I climbed out the bedroom window." He'd locked the door so she couldn't get out that way. "Cut my arm on the glass, but I climbed down the tree and got out of the yard. He chased me about a block, then gave up. Yelling, cussing, and screaming until he realized the neighbors would call the cops. I got away. Lived on the streets for about a year before I landed in a shelter."

Ten years later she'd had the time and the means to find that guy. Along with enough information to hand to the FBI, who arrested him days later. Him and the social worker who placed vulnerable kids in his care.

He was still in prison, and he was never going to get out.

Addie blew out a long breath.

"Yeah. But no one has to worry about him now, outside of the federal penitentiary he lives in." Lyric could have just put a bullet in his head. She doubted anyone would argue about that being necessary. Still, lots of people talked a good game—especially online. But when it came down to doing something about a threat they logged off. Did nothing.

She'd brought justice to all the victims, past and present, as well as saved any future victims. She grieved every day for the ones who had suffered instead of escaping.

Addie pulled up to the curb outside Isaac's building, where her fiancé apparently lived in the penthouse. The guy she'd been through her own trauma with. Now they were getting married this summer, and Addie seemed happy. Open.

Lyric wasn't sure she'd ever be able to say the same about herself. It seemed like too much of a stretch that she would ever get to that place.

She was a different kind of person from Addie. Isaac and his mom had been the cause of her family being destroyed. Her dad's life ended because they'd left, and he hadn't seen a need to go on. Everything Lyric held dear in the world had been taken away. Her sense of security. All the family she'd had. Her innocence.

"Let the FBI take this one. We'll find Clara, and I'll keep you posted," Addie said. "Can you do that for me?"

Lyric cracked the door. "Let me know what you find out."

She got out before Addie could object or try to question her further. It would've been worse with Russ. The guy didn't miss a beat, and he never backed down. He was a great fit for running the Accountant's Office here locally, keeping clients safe. For Lyric to keep her own secrets? The two of them would either know everything, or she would have to keep them at a distance.

Too big a part of her wanted to let them in.

After she found Clara.

Lyric stepped into the lobby and glanced back to see Addie drive away. She checked in with the front desk guy, then threaded her way down the hall to the elevators. Kept going. Found the exit door at the end of the hall and used the back way to get to the street behind.

Two blocks down, she did a quick internet search from her phone and found the address for Brandon Jones, Allerton and Sons' latest envoy. It was a gamble. The image they got from the gas station surveillance wasn't good, but it was clear enough she knew who it was. At least as much as she could be sure.

Because she'd seen him before. In the cabin, and possibly when she'd been attacked last night.

Lyric wanted to know if he had a broken nose.

Half an hour later, she crossed the street and turned the corner onto the row where he lived. For a guy who'd driven a luxury car and worn an expensive suit, he lived in a smaller, older house. But according to the county assessor's website, the place was owned by him. The Mercedes was parked under the carport alongside the house.

Side door by the car.

No cameras visible. No security light.

Lyric let herself in the side door, slid the hairpin back into her pocket, and closed the door behind her. She waited a full minute in case of pets, security, or any other reason her presence might be known.

She made her way through the dark house, moving by instinct more than being able to see anything. She traced a hand along the hallway wall.

A dull distant thud pulled her up short.

When nothing else happened, she continued down the hall. The noise had come from the farthest part of the house, but the next door to her left was slightly ajar.

She eased it open, jaw clenched. No noise. Not even the barest squeak.

Inside the room the TV flashed on the opposite wall, still

on. The volume down. Double bed with a single occupant. A man with dark hair, fast asleep with a nightstand covered in empty bottles. His phone.

His face was unmarred, so he wasn't the person who'd attacked her in her home. But that didn't mean he wasn't the man who'd taken Clara from her house. Was he involved in a trafficking ring the way Enrique had inferred?

She was going to find out.

Lyric grabbed the tie from the dresser. She pulled the bedspread from his lower body, noticing scratches on his chest. But she didn't look long before she pulled one leg across his body and flipped him all the way over. She climbed on the small of his back while he began to thrash, grabbed both his wrists, and secured his hands.

He grunted and strained. "What are you doing? Who are you?"

She tightened the tie. "Stop and I'll get off."

He thrashed some more. "Get off."

"Quit it, Brandon."

He stilled.

"Yeah, I know who you are." She shifted and let him roll over, hands tied under the small of his back. Which would be incredibly uncomfortable. She shifted back to sit on his knees so he couldn't kick her off, then pulled out her phone. "This you? Or you've got a twin, or lookalike cousin I don't know about?"

He stared her down and squirmed.

"Talk."

"About what?"

"You're chatting up the waitresses at the diner. You're hanging around enough you got noticed, which means you screwed up," she said. "How long do you think it'll be before the police question you about Clara? About Sasha?"

His eyes flared.

"She scratch you? Hard to hide that when the police are looking you over." Lyric asked. "And when they scrape under her fingernails. Is that DNA gonna match?"

"So you're here to warn me?"

He thought this was a favor to him? "Where's Clara?"

His eyes shifted.

"You have her. Where is she?"

He bared his teeth at her. She was surprised he didn't try to spit in her face.

She needed to search the house. "Is she here?"

He'd want to keep her close, right?

Lyric scrambled off him. She slammed the bedroom door and reached the hall before he managed to scramble up and come after her. It delayed him a second. Long enough for her to flip on the hall light. One other bedroom and the bathroom. Closet in the hall, which was too skinny for anything but towels. The second bedroom door stood open.

She flipped the light on and found it piled high like a storage unit. Furniture. Boxes. Clothes. A bike. She spotted a computer tower. A pathway.

He roared down the hall, hands still secure behind his back and wearing only boxers.

She slammed the bedroom door. *Please be here.*

Across the room was an old door. For the closet? A padlock. The end of the path. "Clara? Can you hear—"

"Police! Freeze!"

She looked at the closed bedroom door. Then the window. She couldn't scale the mountain of belongings fast enough to get out of that window. Bars hung on the outside of the glass.

No way out.

Brandon yelled, "She tried to kill me!"

"Get down! On your knees!" It was a woman, this cop. Out of sight, but something about her voice gave Lyric pause.

Then a man wearing an FBI vest shoved the door open. "Hands in the air!"

Lyric lifted both. In the second of quiet while he breathed and assessed the room, she called out, "Clara?"

A muffled voice responded.

Lyric moved closer to the closet door.

"Freeze!" the guy yelled. "Don't move!"

"There's a kidnapped woman trapped in there!" She motioned with her head, hands raised. The FBI? This was bad. "She needs help."

"We'll get to her." The guy moved toward her as a woman agent led Brandon down the hall.

Hold up a second…

"After you turn around," he added. "Face the door. Keep your hands raised."

Lyric turned, wincing when he couldn't see her face.

She was being arrested?

Not good.

20

"I guess it's the kind of night for house calls." Addie strode into the apartment, pulled up short, and blinked. "Okay."

Isaac stood in almost the exact spot where he'd been when Mitch pulled a gun and shot Adam. It felt like his heart had stopped he had stood there for so long. When he tried to move, his legs would likely give out and he'd land on his face on the carpet.

"Did you touch anything?"

He glanced over at her, unable to believe she'd think he would compromise evidence—or his standing with the Accountant's Office.

She lifted both hands, palms out. "Okay, forget I asked."

"I should've just called 911 as an anonymous bystander and told them I heard a gunshot."

"In this neighborhood?" She shook her head. "Too suspicious. You were right calling me."

Isaac let out a breath and shifted his feet so the blood started flowing in his legs again. "What happened at the gas station with Lyric?"

Addie shrugged. "Got a picture of the guy. I already entered the image in our database, so it's running facial recognition."

Isaac nodded.

"I dropped her back at your place."

He frowned. Pulled out his phone and looked at the screen. "No one entered my apartment." He'd have a notification if they did. This meant Lyric had never opened the front door and wasn't inside. He sent her a text asking where she was. He would call her as soon as he could, but first they had to deal with this.

Isaac motioned to the dead man on the couch. "What are we going to do with him?"

Addie moved closer to the guy but remained several feet back. "He's pretty beaten underneath the obvious gunshot wound."

The bullet had entered under his chin and exited the top of his head, leaving plenty of evidence on the wall behind him.

"You think he's the guy that attacked Lyric?"

"Impossible to tell unless there's DNA evidence on him," Isaac said.

"Then I guess we'll find out." Addie headed for the door. "I'll get my stuff."

He figured that meant she would be back in seconds, because he didn't need to be unattended with a dead body for any longer than he had been already. Not that he was a child, or would do anything. Isaac had enough history—blood and death didn't bother him. He'd have lost his mind a long time ago if it did. There was just no one he could call to talk through it with.

Maybe Lyric, if she'd respond to his text.

What was she doing?

Addie had dropped her off at his building. She hadn't waited around to see Lyric go upstairs or walked her to the apartment door herself. He didn't want to think badly of the FBI agent since she'd been doing him a favor, but there was a reason he didn't have a lot of cop friends.

These days he barely had friends at all.

He lifted his phone and checked the screen. Still nothing. He tapped the cell against his leg.

Addie breezed back in, an evidence collection duffel over her shoulder. "She didn't call you yet?"

"You get I'm not a cop and I can't help you collect evidence, right?"

"You're not in the chain of custody, I assume you can man a camera, and neither of my associates are answering their cell phones right now." She frowned.

"I'd heard you had a small office in the police department."

She held up one finger. "Next to."

"You have colleagues?"

"From the Seattle office. They keep threatening to leave, but neither has done it yet. I think they secretly like it here, and they just don't want to admit it."

"I had the best kind of teammates."

Addie stared at him, a neutral look on her face.

"I guess you did your homework." He tried to shrug it off, but considering the first shot he'd had at male friends in this town had wound up leading him to witness a murder, he wasn't sure that would look convincing.

"I did." She spoke softly. "I can understand why you'd miss friends like that. And why it might take a while before you felt like you carved a place for yourself here." As she spoke, Addie removed items from her bag. She wandered over with a camera and gave it to him.

"You have some experience with it?"

She shook her head. "I never had friends in Virginia or anywhere else after I left Benson. Coming back was like being face-to-face with every nightmare I've ever had. Things got worse before they got better, and now things aren't perfect, but I can tell you they're the best they've ever been."

He stared at her, the unfamiliar weight of a camera in his hands. "This your idea of a pep talk? 'Things will get worse before they get better.'"

She grinned. "They already did for this guy."

Addie grabbed a clipboard from the bag and said, "Name?"

"Mine?" He didn't want his name on official record.

"No, the deceased." She held her pen poised.

"Adam," he said. "I'll find mail, or something with his last name on it."

"Copy that. But take the photos first." She told him what to get images of, which amounted to a million photos of Adam's whole body and close ups on everything, from basically every angle until his finger ached from clicking.

Isaac straightened and stretched out his back. Lyric still hadn't called yet or replied. He dialed her number because even if she somehow managed to enter his apartment without his knowledge—which she certainly had the skills to do—she should still answer the phone.

But she didn't.

"Here." Addie handed him gloves.

Isaac wandered through the house. He picked through Adam's things, finding mail. The contents of his sock drawer with random items that meant nothing to Isaac but were probably important to Adam. He found narcotics under the sink in an expired prescription bottle still full. A refill he never used—or a bottle he'd filled with what he purchased on the streets?

Addie stepped into view in the bedroom.

He called out, "How are we going to get the body out of here without Mitch seeing?"

"You think he'll come back and check on you, or send someone to look?"

Isaac shrugged and straightened out of his crouch. "Possibly. I could always call it in and say I found Adam after the fact. Or tell Mitch I did, and that's why the coroner showed up."

"You think he figures you'll clean it all up and dispose of him?"

"I can just tell him that's not how I do things. I keep myself clean, talk my way out." Isaac figured there was a shot Mitch would buy it. "Won't last forever, but it can get me through this."

"I'll need a full statement."

He nodded. "We could make that part of me 'calling in the body.'" He used air quotes even though it always looked borderline ridiculous no matter who was doing it. "I have to give you guys a full account of everything—except Mitch doesn't know I told you all about how he did it."

He strode to the bed and hauled up the mattress. The only place he hadn't looked, and the thing big enough he could get out some of this frustration screaming in his shoulder muscles.

Underneath the bed was a shoebox.

"Don't touch it. Let me." She crouched and pulled it out, flipped the lid off. Inside were a collection of photos.

"Those are girls." As if that wasn't completely obvious to both of them.

Addie nodded slowly. Before either of them could say more her phone rang. "Special Agent Franklin."

Isaac was surprised she hadn't already pulled out her badge and slid it on her belt.

"Wait…*what?*" She lowered the phone and tapped the screen, her gaze on the photos.

"What I just said." A woman's voice came through the tinny speaker. "We found Clara in a closet in this guy's house." She paused. "Brandon Jones?"

Addie frowned. "Doesn't ring a bell." She lifted her gaze to Isaac.

He shook his head and figured it was best to stay quiet right now. He used gloved fingers to spread the photos on the bed.

They needed to take care of Adam. And figure out if there was anything here they should know, so while he listened to Addie's conversation, he moved to the closet and looked around. The FBI could process the photos, and he didn't need to worry about what was contained in there.

He knew it would be a trigger. After what his dad had done it would always be a trigger for him.

The woman said, "Apparently, Jones is some midlevel guy at Allerton and Sons."

Now that rang a bell. He'd have to tell Addie those were the developers coming after Lyric's property and land.

Addie said, "How did you put it together that he's the one who took Clara?"

"That's the thing. We didn't." The female, presumably, Addie's colleague, sounded excited. "I had a person of interest I've been trying to get close to. To see if she knows anything. The woman walked up to his house, broke in, and tied the guy up. We got there right as she was about to get Clara out of the closet. She made it sound like she found

Clara herself, but if she did it's probably only so she can cut out Jones and take the woman for herself. Give her to someone else."

Isaac pushed aside a couple of jackets with nothing in the pockets and pulled a cardboard box out from behind. He flipped the lid. Just old shoes. And they smelled like it.

"How is Clara?" Addie asked.

"Headed to the hospital now. We have Brandon Jones and Lyric Thompson in custody."

Isaac rushed back to the closet door, feeling his eyebrows lift. He mouthed, *What?*

"Stella, did you say Lyric Thompson?"

The woman let out a hiss. "I know, I didn't tell you it was the woman you know."

"Because you believe my judgment is compromised."

Stella said, "I also know it involves your family, since your uncle and your sister are at her house right now covering for her."

"Why don't you fill me in on what I don't know?"

Isaac took in the tension in Addie's body. She wanted to get mad, but she held it back and chose to act the professional regardless of her personal feelings. On the other hand, he wanted to grab the phone and demand answers. The FBI had arrested Lyric?

He needed to tell Russ.

Find her a lawyer.

He'd have to pull some cash together and bail her out.

Stella said, "I've been staying at the cabins the last few days."

Addie let out a hiss.

"Lyric Thompson is a person of interest whether you like it or not. She knew both victims, and she found Sasha. That was before I started following her. She knows more than what she's told anyone about the disappearance of these women. That, or she's the next victim and she has no idea."

If they thought Brandon Jones was their suspect, he'd visited Lyric. That could be why their theory was that she could be the next victim. That meant there was a niggle of doubt that she might not be involved.

He moved back to the bed and dumped out the shoe box. A few of the photos had writing on the back, a pound sign and a number.

"You're taking her in?" Addie asked.

"Her and Jones. Kyle and I are on it."

"I'll be there in a couple of hours. No one questions either of them until I get there."

"Understood," Stella grumbled.

Addie hung up.

Isaac was about to speak when she redialed. "Yes, this is Special Agent Addie Franklin. I need the ME and the coroner." She gave the address. After a moment of conversation, she said, "Thank you," and hung up.

"Lyric got arrested?"

"This is getting complicated."

"You think?" He had to convince Mitch the problem was taken care of, or he wouldn't be able to continue being Addie's confidential informant in this situation.

He flipped over half the photos in one swipe. Numbered women. The photos were from up close, distant: surveillance pictures and candids. A few of women were tied up, their faces overcome by fear.

"Oh, no."

It was like she echoed the words in his head.

"That's Lyric."

21

———————

Lyric strode out of the police station two days later. Forty-eight hours she'd been held and questioned. Since they had no evidence she had committed a crime beyond breaking and entering—which led to the recovery of a kidnapping victim—she'd been released.

As if that made it better.

Addie had been suspiciously absent for most of it. The other female agent and her male colleague tried to wear down Lyric and get her to confess.

Addie hadn't done her any favors, but Lyric knew how the real world worked.

Isaac stood on the curb in front of the police station as Lyric stomped down to him, irritation fueling her movements. She tried to walk off the frustration of having been cooped up inside for two days. It didn't work. She rolled her shoulders and shook out her arms, hopped the stairs two at a time. Didn't work either.

"So you're not okay." He looked down, then back up at her.

After the two days she'd just had, that was the last thing she needed.

"Whether I am or not isn't the point." After that assessment she wanted to tell him it wasn't his business either. Her getting arrested had nothing to do with him.

He jerked his head in a flinch, like she'd slapped him. "So what is the point?"

Lyric didn't know if he was here to offer her a ride. She didn't know what to do and had no way to get anywhere without him.

"How is Clara?" She sighed. "At least tell me that. Because those feds wouldn't say a word. They were too busy accusing me of taking her in the first place."

Isaac's expression hardened. "I'm sorry—"

"Don't waste pity on me. I don't need it." She couldn't shake the tension of being cooped up. She needed to move. "I have to go."

"I'll give you a ride." He waved her in the direction of the parking lot across the street. "And we can find out about Clara if you want, but the last I heard was that she's stable. Doing okay now, thanks to you, but understandably traumatized."

Lyric nodded. "That's what Addie said."

She could go see Clara later after making sure everything was okay at her cabins. She was just glad the woman was safe. Because of her, and the actions she'd taken to save Clara. Because she'd risked her freedom, the waitress was alive. Out of that terrible situation.

Brandon Jones was in custody. Eventually, he would talk, or he would go down for the whole thing.

"Did you see…" Isaac's words trailed off. "Do you know…"

It wasn't like he ever had trouble speaking his mind. "You

think they withheld the fact one of my guests is an FBI agent lying to me, and Addie for that matter, about why she's at my cabins?"

"I got the impression Addie wasn't happy with what Stella did."

"As if that makes it okay she lied? That *anyone* would think I had something to do with those women being abducted?" They'd pulled out the fact she had found Sasha. As if it was some kind of misdirection for the police to believe she was only a concerned acquaintance when the truth was that she was the killer.

As if.

They didn't know who she had been before she moved here. So Addie hadn't broken Accountant's Office confidentiality and told them. They had no idea she had the skills to break into Clara's house and find the matchbook that led her to the club, or that she'd follow up on it in her time.

Like she'd known she would find Sasha's car, and her body.

Isaac shifted closer and bumped her shoulder as they walked. "I'm glad you're okay."

"Thanks." She managed to get the word out. He was trying to help her out here. "I should get back to the cabins as soon as possible."

He glanced over. "I thought you were staying with me?"

Lyric lifted her hands and let them fall back to her sides. She didn't meet his gaze. Isaac was the kind of guy who could change her mind. Maybe the only guy who could. "I need to get back or my business is going to fall apart. I can't rely on Russ to run it forever. That's not taking care of my own life."

He had to see reality. She couldn't live with him forever. Lyric had a life here, and he'd only recently come along.

With him had come more disruption than she'd experienced since she moved here four years ago. She might even think her entire life had turned upside down. But that was the Isaac effect.

Truth was, she was dealing with a lot between the missing women and Allerton wanting her land. Now she didn't know where one started and the other ended. She was wrapped up in the abductions, and Allerton was as well—at least through Brandon Jones's involvement. The whole thing was crazy confusing, and her head pounded from lack of sleep and the injuries that guy gave her when she broke in.

Lyric tried to push it off, but the whole thing was overwhelming. She wanted to curl up in her bed and cry herself to sleep.

"I don't want you to get hurt."

She didn't like the edgy thread in his voice. Especially since she figured it meant he thought she wasn't doing what she was supposed to. What *he* thought she should do.

Isaac wasn't a threat to her. Or, he hadn't been so far. But she got the feeling that they were rapidly barreling toward a situation where he thought he had a say over her comings and goings.

"If you're at my place, I can keep you safe." His stride took on a stiffness. "We can stop whoever thought they could hurt you and make sure it doesn't happen again."

"I'll be the one who makes sure it doesn't happen again." It wasn't like she was ignorant about security, or how to keep herself safe. Lyric had weapons, and next time she wasn't going to hesitate. She wasn't going to get hurt just to see what they wanted—what her assailant's plan might be. She was past information gathering, and she'd moved to the place where she intended to hit back.

It was the only way to resolve this.

They reached the car, but Isaac didn't beep the locks. "I don't want to get another call where you sound out of your mind. Where I have to rush all the way to you and find you broken."

She moved to him, slid her hands up his chest, and linked them behind his neck. "You gonna protect me, baby?"

"Don't do that." His expression hardened.

"Isn't it what you want?"

"Not when you're only doing this to push me away."

Lyric let go of him. "I don't need you to save me."

He was the reason her life had fallen apart. Him and his mom. She was just supposed to get over her father's death because of them? They'd tricked her into believing in something that wasn't real, and then they'd taken it—and everything else she'd had—away.

"You know, I did a lot of thinking while I was in a jail cell for two nights. I get that you're here." She folded her arms, suddenly cold. The sun drifted behind a copse of clouds. "We both have to deal with that. But we have our own lives, and our own things to do. It's probably for the best if we go our separate ways."

Lyric had to let go of her arms and roll out her shoulders. She was going to strain her shoulder muscles they were so tense right now. But what did she expect, sleeping on a holding cell cot? Or when they'd brought all those ladies in and she leaned back against the wall instead.

She didn't even want to think about it. She was flat-out exhausted, twitchy enough someone would probably conclude there was something wrong with her—or she was having symptoms of withdrawal. Truth was, she had so much to deal with between the developer and the abductions there was no time for anything else.

Or anyone else.

"Like I said. Pushing me away."

She didn't need to stick around to hear this. "I'll find my own ride to the resort."

Lyric had so much pent-up frustration she should probably just walk there. It would take a couple of hours—or longer—but she likely needed to burn off the energy. Move. Then again, the fatigue made her feel far heavier than she was comfortable with. Maybe she wouldn't make it that far.

"Why do you keep everyone at arm's length?"

She squeezed her eyes shut, but why let him off the hook? "I think you'd be the one person who understood why." With entirely too much time on her hands to think, she'd faced a few things about herself in that jail cell. "I don't need you to fix me, because I'm not broken."

"No? You think I don't see the same thing in you that I see in me?"

"I think you could've walked away from your mom at any time. But you stayed. You worked with her. You allied yourself with her. And for what?"

Pain flashed across his face.

"Meanwhile because of her, I had nothing left. I've made everything I've got with my own hands, and I don't need you to help me keep hold of it. If I lose it, it's because I chose to give it up or let it be taken from me."

"Excuse me for caring about you so much I want to stick around." He lifted his chin.

"Isaac." She squeezed her eyes shut again. He didn't want to stick around—he wanted her to move her life so it fit in his.

He touched her shoulder, but it felt a little too much like trying to get her to move where he wanted her instead of comfort.

Her eyes flashed open and she stepped back, shaking her

head so she couldn't see. She didn't want to see the determination on his face. "Don't."

She was free after hours of being locked up. Was this how Clara felt? Lyric didn't even want to be touched. She certainly didn't want to be managed or controlled. And they thought she was responsible for doing this to others?

She wanted to run.

Past her cabins. Keep going. Forever, free.

"You have your operation. I have my own stuff." She shook her head until it ached. "Those don't mix. We don't mix."

He had to see that. She couldn't be tied down. Held down.

"Lyric…take a breath."

His voice was so soft. It hurt to listen to how soft it was.

But she couldn't let it penetrate. He would take over, and she would lose everything she was.

Her freedom.

22

Isaac swung the mallet and smashed the cabinet on the concrete loading dock. Sure, he could get a screwdriver and take the hinges off. Remove all the pieces.

But why do that when obliterating the thing was so much more satisfying?

He swung again. Glass shattered, and the sun glinted off shards beside the shadow of his sweat-covered body. It might be early spring, but today was warm and the sky clear. Temps would soar to the sixties, and folks would be out walking the paths and parks around Benson.

Meanwhile he was trying to keep the love of his life from being targeted.

No big deal.

He'd stewed over what she said all night. Stared at the ceiling in his bedroom after Russ called to tell him she was back at the resort and tried to figure out how to play this in a way he wouldn't get slapped.

Russ had picked her up on the side of the highway trying to hitchhike her way back to the resort. The fact Isaac had been tracking her cell phone wasn't relevant, but if pushed, he'd admit that he kept tabs on her. Just not to anyone else. He'd sent Russ a general idea of where she was.

After seeing her photo in that shoebox under Adam's bed, what else was he supposed to do? She was in danger. The woman could be a kidnapper's next victim—unless she'd thwarted that whole plan herself by getting Jones arrested. Which was possible.

But the whole thing seemed like a bigger deal than one guy. Unless it was only Enrique spinning lines. Like he had nothing better to do working at the diner than that. Maybe he was part of it and decided to point the finger at someone else.

And yet, his intel had led Lyric to Jones, and Clara.

If she hadn't followed through with it, Clara could very well be dead. Lyric might've saved her life. Probably had. He didn't want to commend her though, because he'd ditched her so he could be an informant and watch Adam get killed. He'd left her but discovered she was on the radar of these people in the process.

The whole situation was so messed up.

Isaac swung the biggest piece up and over the edge. It splintered in the dumpster. Something ricocheted off the side of the metal and hit his jeans. He ignored it.

The woman was infuriating.

I don't need you to fix me.

He was about to lose his mind dealing with her, so it was probably for the best she'd walked off and left him to handle his outburst alone. In front of the police station, he'd barely managed to contain himself. Like when she'd slid up against him and given him the offer of a lifetime.

Yes, he'd very much like to be the one who protected her. Permanently.

But after two days in an interrogation room, he'd been

able to see how stir-crazy she was. She found it difficult to simply hold herself together and not lose it in front of whoever was watching—and him.

Isaac dropped the mallet and winced. Then he realized his phone was ringing.

Two of Mitch's guys stared at him from their smoke break spot by the front door. Like he was their morning entertainment. They should get back to work before Mitch caught them burning his money standing there doing nothing.

Isaac pulled out his phone and saw it was Russ calling. "Did you find out?"

There was a clear pause, where he could imagine the older man's mouth twitching with disapproval. "First you can tell me why I woke up to that voice mail after I picked her up last night?"

Isaac said nothing. Yeah, he'd just yelled at Russ, but he also wanted Russ to keep going.

The guy did. "Acting all mad, hot as you-know-what. Will she answer questions? No, I'm guessing that won't happen."

"But she's home."

"She crashed. Hard. Fell asleep in the truck within two miles and woke up when I got to the resort. Ran upstairs without another word and heard the shower turn on. You think she said anything when she got out, aside from wanting a full rundown on the resort as though nothing happened? Same thing this morning."

Isaac winced. He knew she'd been exhausted but hearing that hurt.

He knew what happened when he bottled everything up and it compounded. When fatigue piled on emotional turmoil. The fallout was never good. Something his former friends could attest to. And his cell block associates in federal prison.

Isaac had the scars to prove it. A lifelong record of what happened when he let his feelings get the better of him and refused to let them out in healthy ways.

"What did you do?" Russ asked.

Isaac shifted to sit on the edge of the dumpster, like it was a park bench. He needed to hit the gym and lift some serious weights, or he was going to light somebody up just to release the tension. "Maybe you should ask Addie what her people did? Because I doubt forty-eight hours in holding is supposed to make a person react like that."

"You and I both know clients of the Accountant's Office don't react like everyone else." Russ took a breath. "Which leads me to you, and your question. So tell me this. Your girl throws down, tells you to take a hike or whatever, and your response is to ask me what happened to her father?"

"I need to know what you found out." There had to be a reason Lyric had pulled up the past like that, mentioning his family living with hers. His mother, and the opinion he'd always known she had of Lana. It wasn't a secret.

Blaming him wasn't a surprise. He knew what she thought of the choices he'd made.

"Okay," Russ said. "But that doesn't give you the clearance to have me tell it. That's privileged information everyone is required to fill out when they sign on. No secrets. You know that's the rule. So tell me why I didn't know about what you told me at Lyric's."

"You needed to know why I am the way I am about my parents."

I think you could've walked away from your mom at any time. But you stayed.

Isaac winced, thinking on Lyric's accusation.

"So now you need information about Lyric." Russ paused. "You okay if I ask her if I can share?"

Isaac ducked his chin. "Please just tell me what happened."

"The death is listed as a suicide." Russ pulled no punches. "Given the dates, looks like about a month after you and your mom left their house. Tore the family apart like nothin' doing."

Isaac winced. "It wasn't my decision."

Lana had dragged him off in the middle of the night. Lyric's father had killed himself a few weeks later? Because his mom had lied about whose baby she'd been pregnant with, taking advantage of a good man.

Tears blurred his vision.

Isaac figured she'd at least found her father afterward, if she hadn't been in the house when it happened.

And Lyric had lived with that all these years.

"Think I don't know that? Lana isn't someone you get to argue against at the best of times. And I don't even know the woman. But at twelve years old? No, I don't think you got a say."

"So what does she think I'm supposed to do? Apologize?" The burn of tears stung his eyes.

"Maybe you ask her that. After she's had time to calm down."

Isaac pushed out a breath. "Thanks."

He hung up before Russ could say anything else. What was the point of chewing over it? He'd done that all night and conclude that Lyric had been having an awful day—understatement. She might think differently in the cold light of day, and she might not. He'd have to try his luck and find out.

Take the risk. Because she was the kind of woman who was worth it.

Until then they were at odds.

"Done taking out your anger on the furniture?"

Isaac twisted around and saw Mitch behind him. He put a hand on the edge of the dumpster and hopped out. He kept the mallet in one hand, just in case things went south. He'd been caught unawares too many times and suffered the consequences. Including in prison. "What's up?"

Mitch stared. "You tell me."

"It's taken care of." The guy wasn't going to like this, but Isaac could deal. "I cleaned up, waited an hour, and then called the cops."

Mitch's eyebrows rose. "You did *what*?"

"Told them I came over, found him like that. They do the cleanup and I walk away." Isaac shrugged. "Besides, I've got a buddy in the PD, and he'll make sure it's all written up as a suicide. That won't be a problem with what I fixed at the house."

Addie was going to keep the accurate report under wraps. No one would find out that Adam's murder and Isaac's statement of what happened were part of an ongoing investigation.

"So it's all good?" Mitch didn't look convinced.

Isaac nodded. "No one needed to see me walking out of the house with Adam in a rolled-up carpet."

Mitch snorted.

"What else is going on?" Isaac needed Mitch to share now. He had no intention of telling his boss about the photos and the possible connection to the abductions. However, he was going to dig if it got him information on what could be a trafficking ring.

Isaac's theory was that something had happened with

Sasha and she was killed intentionally or by accident. To fulfill an "order" for a woman, Clara had been taken in her place.

And now Lyric was being offered up as well. Her photos had been surveillance, taken by someone watching her without her knowledge.

He wanted to smash some more furniture. Or Mitch. Or the guy who'd been arrested, Brandon Jones. He wanted to rush into the FBI office, completely blow his status as a confidential informant, and demand to know what Jones had said. Maybe take a crack at the guy himself.

As if Addie would actually let him do that.

In years past he'd never have let that stop him. These days, the man he wanted to be, Isaac was going to play by the rules. Well, the ones he respected at least. Some rules were just dumb.

Mitch lit up a cigarette and leaned against the dumpster. "Got a meet later. Doing some business, and you know what? Adam would've wrecked that, too. Guy was a liability."

Isaac figured even someone like Mitch didn't murder a man without a reason. Likely it was business and rarely personal.

"Need a second? I could use something to do later." Isaac let out a breath chock full of all the exasperation he felt over being at odds with Lyric. Something that felt fundamentally wrong. "My girl...we're on the outs."

Mitch's head whipped around. "You didn't tell her—"

Isaac cut him off with a head shake. "She knows nothing. Doesn't even live in town."

None of them knew about the remodeling job, so he figured there was nothing to worry about there. Just the tiny issue of her *picture in that shoebox.*

Mitch clapped him on the shoulder. "Geez, man. She's got you all up in knots."

Isaac ran a hand down his face. "You have no idea. Please give me a distraction." He grinned. "I need something else to do or I'll be weak and go grovel."

"Yeah, don't do that." Mitch barked a laugh. "Not a good look on anyone."

"Don't I know it."

Isaac had established himself over again as lower in the pecking order. Mitch thought he was in charge. That Isaac would do anything and everything he asked, which was how both of them needed it to be—and for different reasons.

Isaac needed to find out Adam's connection to the shoe box photos sooner rather than later. Because if anyone took Lyric from him, that person would find out precisely how many laws he was willing to break to get her back.

Whether she hated him or thought he was trash, he would protect her.

"Eleven tonight," Mitch said. "I'll send you the address."

"Sounds good."

Mitch clapped him on the shoulder. "It's good to know who you can trust."

23

———

Lyric used her key to unlock the cabin. The second one she'd cleaned today. The guests for this place had cleared out earlier than their reservation had them staying. She wasn't going to think on that, though. People had all kinds of reasons for changing their plans.

Didn't mean anything.

The cabin seemed surprisingly clean on the inside. Lots of trash in and next to the can, and the dishwasher ran over in the kitchen. She checked the bathroom and found towels, where the instructions hung on the wall beside the door indicated they put them—all piled in the tub. Sheets had been pulled from the bed.

Lyric let out a sigh. Maybe a horrifying display of the mess people could make would've been more satisfying to clean. But she didn't want to deal with a biohazard. This was enough, but nothing interestingly sufficient to distract her from the awfulness of that conversation with Isaac.

She still couldn't believe she'd yelled at him like that.

Told the truth.

Bared her soul.

Lyric winced at the memory of the conversation they'd had. Even if she could barely remember the nuances. She'd been so tired the whole thing felt like a bad dream, and considering she'd slept most of the day away—including when these guests checked out—that was exactly how it seemed.

But it was real.

Lyric wanted to pack a bag, get in her car, and leave. Go somewhere far from here where no one knew her. She could start over. Have a new life.

Or she would fly to another country, backpack for a while. See parts of the world she'd never been to before.

Forget all about Isaac and the fact he'd been part of her life for what seemed like forever. Since he and his mom moved in with her and her dad, spent a few months with them, and gave her the happiest time.

Then ripped it all away.

Since he showed up here, she found out he'd been manipulating her ever since. He'd affected her job under the guise of "helping," saved her life, and landed her here.

Because he knew he would also eventually be here?

It was highly suspicious to her.

Lyric dumped the trash into the outside can and replaced the strap that would keep animals out. She wandered to stand beside the porch and looked at the other cabins. All of them were empty and would be until the new guests arrived tomorrow.

Her business was going under.

She should go to Allerton and Sons, take the offer, and go. But that meant the people behind Clara's situation and Sasha's death would go on preying on women.

Stella had shown her the photos of women. She hadn't explained where they came from. She'd done it after the whole shock of Lyric realizing she was an FBI agent and Lyric hadn't noticed a thing off about the woman's stay here at Second Chances wore off. Which of course, she definitely was over.

The part about Stella being FBI, anyway.

How had Lyric not noticed? She hadn't been a spy for years, and some of her training hung around even now. But she should have realized the woman wasn't really on vacation. That she wasn't working on her getaway couple of days out of town.

Lyric sighed and wound back to the rear door. She stared out at the creek that ran behind the cabins.

Was she really going to give all this up?

Turning it into a viable vacation business proved harder than she'd imagined. Now it was all falling apart and she couldn't even leave because there was a murderer out there.

Brandon Jones hadn't killed Sasha.

Lyric had yelled at him at his house, both of them in cuffs. She'd demanded to know if he killed Sasha. He'd denied it, but she believed him.

Now she was doubting, given Stella had fooled her. How did she know her instincts were right after that?

The only person in his life she knew was his boss, Allerton Sr.

An hour later, Lyric was dressed for a nightclub in a tiny dress she'd never worn and only bought because latent training indicated she be prepared for anything. The heels were ridiculous and seriously uncomfortable, and she would suck it up because the lights were on in Allerton's office.

She parked her car in the nearly empty lot and pushed her way into the building. The interior lighting reflected across the lobby to shine on the bald head of the security guard. She heard the low drone of an action movie coming from under the counter.

Her shoes clipped the floor. The security guard looked up and gaped. Lyric flashed him a wide smile, probably flashing the shimmer of her lip gloss. She fluffed her hair with one hand and held her tiny purse with the other.

She gave him a show like she was a catwalk model and it was Fashion Week. All the way to his desk, where she leaned her assets on the counter.

His gaze didn't lift to her face.

"Hey, handsome."

His eyes flicked up.

She lifted her brows. "The boss has an…appointment."

Those bland blue eyes flashed with disappointment.

"And when I'm done, I'll have to come back down here. Have you *validate my parking*." Whatever that meant, she had no idea. Maybe she could knock him out and he wouldn't remember. She could leave him a thank-you note with a lip gloss kiss on the paper. Make him think he passed out and missed something good.

That held the smile long enough it was believable.

He nodded his head to the left. "Elevator. Eighteenth floor."

"Thanks, darlin'." She figured he watched her walk away, so she sashayed to the elevators and applied more lip gloss, using the shiny metal panel for the buttons as a mirror.

The doors opened.

She heard a distant, "Thank you, Steven," said by someone with a low voice, probably Allerton. She figured the security guard had warned him she was coming up. And yet, Allerton hadn't indicated he had no clue about any "appointment."

Lyric sidled up to the open doorway and rapped her knuckles on the frame. "Knock, knock."

Allerton turned from the window, a short glass with clear liquid and ice that clinked as he took a drink. "I wasn't aware I had a booking."

"Maybe someone thought you deserved a present." She strode to the desk and set her purse on the wingback chair in front, where her phone would record the entire conversation. She turned and sat on the desk, hands clutching the edge by her hips.

Bit the inside of her lip.

He took a sip of his drink. "You think I don't know who you are, Lyric Thompson?"

"My land isn't why I'm here."

"No?"

"Unless you care to make me an offer." He'd think he held all the cards. A man like this wanted to think he held all the cards. The power in every room he entered had to be with him, and this was his throne room. Where he surveyed the world and lauded it over everyone within. Content that he controlled everything.

She lifted her chin.

He meandered to her, a couple of steps that put him within touching distance. "I'm sure we could come to an arrangement." He reached out and ran the back of his index finger down her cheek.

"Far as I can see, I have the land and anything else you might want." She lifted her chin.

"And what do you expect in return?"

She glanced around, assessing his office. She dismissed it and looked back at him. "A little…bird told me my photo is circulating. If I was the kind of woman who didn't know that beforehand, perhaps I would be vulnerable. But I'm not. So I'm here to make my own deal."

"And you think I have something to do with it?" He took another sip.

"Brandon Jones worked for you. A man like yourself can't help but be aware of what his people are up to, even in their free time. But if you don't know…" She lifted off the desk.

His fingers curled around her elbow.

She looked at them, then up at his face. "I make my own deals. My terms. Whether that's about land, or any service I choose to provide."

His fingers drifted up, threaded into her hair, and ran through the strands down to the end, then landed on the small of her back. Low. "Your terms are acceptable."

"Before we negotiate, there are a couple of things." She eased slightly closer to him, so he'd smell her perfume. She'd put mentholated petroleum jelly at the entrances to her nostrils so the odor wouldn't cause her own head to swim. If he kissed her neck, he would be unconscious in fifteen seconds.

"And what are those things?" His voice rumbled with the edge of a slur.

"Where I come from, people who cross you pay the price." She kept her voice soft, rumbling over him. Through him. Like the perfume. "Who is behind the sales? I'd like to know who wanted my cut, so I can pay them a visit."

He winced.

She eased her body close so there was barely an inch between them. It was hard not to think of Isaac and when she'd done practically the same thing to him. Trying to make a point. Get something in return.

The idea made her nauseous, but she pushed that away along with the thoughts.

"Tell me who is behind the sales." She eased her face alongside his, their cheeks almost touching. "Then we can get down to business."

Actually he'd be passed out, but that wasn't something he needed to know.

"We don't give names."

"How do you make an order?" She whispered the question close to his ear.

"Text."

She'd have to get his cell phone. "Who connected you to them?"

"It's referral only."

Lyric opened her mouth to ask another question, but someone approached before she could speak.

"What is this?" The voice sounded like gravel spilled.

Lyric eased back like she had every right to be here. She'd have to talk her way out of this situation if…

Isaac stood slightly behind another man, presumably the one who'd spoken. But the words written on his expression? Loud and clear.

She set one hand on her hip. "Can we help you boys?"

Allerton chuckled and took another sip of his drink. Her perfume was working, but it wouldn't work on Isaac and the man he'd entered with. Presumably the boss he was working with the feds to bring down.

Was his boss the head of this? The one who got Sasha killed and had Lyric's photo in a shoebox.

"Are you kidding me right now?" Isaac strode over, fury on his face.

Allerton moved away. While no one could see Isaac's face but her, he mouthed, *Play along.*

Of course he was going to take over this situation. She reached back and grabbed her purse. The operation was over.

"This is what you blow me off for?" He reached out, grabbed her arm above her elbow, and tugged her two feet so she stumbled on her heels. "So you can make a date of your own? What did I tell you about doing this?"

"It's my life. How I earn a living is up to me." She shrugged, just in case Mitch knew who she was. "You know those cabins don't get many bookings."

"We're out of here." He bit off the words, then turned to his boss. "You mind if I take off?"

Mitch sneered. "Do what you gotta do."

"Let's go." He hauled Lyric to the door while she scurried to keep up.

Great.

24

"I'm gonna fall," Lyric whispered as they reached the hall.

Isaac didn't slow. "I cannot *believe* you."

"You don't need to act all irate. We're out of earshot."

"You think I'm acting?" He jabbed his finger on the elevator button.

"You're just mad because you didn't expect to see me there. Because of what you're doing." Thankfully, she didn't mention the FBI. "Now you can drop the act. Unless they can still see us."

"Don't assume they can't." He managed to get the words out.

"You know I know how to do this, right?"

Isaac knew all about what she could do. Did that keep him from being scared to death she was going to wind up dead—or broken? No. It also didn't apparently keep him from being furious.

The second he'd walked in that office. Her. Wearing that dress, and those heels. Her hair.

He shook his head just to dissipate the effect of the whole

package. He couldn't even see straight right now. All he knew was his instincts screamed. She had dangled herself like bait to see if Allerton would take a bite.

The elevator doors opened.

"So you either have no clue what I've been trained to do, you think I've lost all my skills in the last four years, or you think you're better at it." She strode onto the elevator clutching her purse. "That's great."

Isaac entered after her. "Why did you go to him?"

Instinct had him crowd her. But she didn't back up—she stood her ground.

"Why were you here?"

She moved to reach in her purse.

"Just answer the question."

"The question is in my purse." She tugged out her phone, showed him the screen, and paused the recording.

"What did he tell you?" If she'd learned something, maybe that would make all this worth it.

"My operation is none of your business," she said. "Besides, it seems like you've got your own thing going."

He stared her down. Forced himself not to look at her dress again. His brain would only short-circuit more than it already was, and where would that leave him? "Yeah, and you killed any chance I had of finding out what dealings Mitch has with Allerton."

"Well, *excuse me* for taking charge of my own life."

"You infuriate me."

"Doesn't mean you don't want to kiss me."

Isaac blinked.

Two seconds later, his hands were in her hair and she was clinging to his waist. He moved until her back touched the elevator wall and he took her up on her offer. All the frustration and fear rolled through him, into the hold he had on her and the movement of his lips on hers.

He pulled back. "Is this because of the perfume?"

"I don't know," she said, her voice breathy. "Is it?"

He kissed her.

Isaac might have worried it was too much, but she met him beat for beat. Touch for touch. Clinging just as desperately as he did.

The elevator doors opened, as if from a mile away.

He ignored the whole world and realized this was the only place he wanted to be. Even if it edged fast into dangerous territory. He wasn't going to fault her for wearing the dress. His reaction to it was down to him to control, which was why he kept his hands in her hair. There would be no drifting. Though she got the message on how he felt loud and clear.

He knew it when he leaned back and she started to chuckle.

Isaac wasn't amused. "You're going to say, 'I told you so,' aren't you?"

She leaned so close their noses almost touched. "Forever."

He nearly passed out.

"Oops. Don't get too close to my neck." She tugged on his hand, and they exited the elevator. "You'll get fuzzy."

Isaac shot her a glance. She'd drugged Allerton, asked him questions, and recorded their conversation. He was about to speak when she shook her head.

Right. The security guard.

They strode past the guy, Isaac pulling Lyric by her hand. She twisted around to the security guard. "Bye, sugar. Maybe next time."

"Uh, yeah. Bye." The guy practically stammered the words.

The lobby doors slid shut behind them. Out in the dark of late evening the air held a chill.

"Want my jacket?"

She started to object but caught herself. "Fine." For someone trained to give away nothing, she let him see everything. On purpose, or because she felt free enough to do it. There had to be some trust with him, or she'd have kept her guard up.

Instead, she let him see the core of her. The pain over her father's death. The need to solve these abductions. The refusal to be a target, or a victim.

She'd been attacked days ago.

Held by the police for questioning.

Now she was back on the job, working the problem in her own way. Taking back the power so she could control her own destiny—as much as that was possible.

He settled it on her shoulders. "I got a ride here with Mitch, so I guess we're taking your car."

She pressed her lips together.

"Do we need to talk about that kiss?"

"Nope."

He frowned. Maybe they should, but if she didn't want to, he wasn't going to press her. Frustration still boiled in his gut, too much of it. Like she'd taken hers out on him outside the police department he could easily do the same right now. And he wouldn't have the excuse she'd had. What they had wasn't something he wanted to ruin, if he could help it.

Especially not if that meant he said the wrong thing and she was hurt.

She stopped by her car.

"What is it?"

"I know you're mad, but…" She tugged out her keys. "Here."

Before he could say anything, she rounded the car. He unlocked it and they climbed in—him in the driver's side and her in the passenger seat. She tugged off her heels, tossed them in the back, and sighed. "Better."

"I liked them."

She glanced out the corner of her eye. "Noted. But if I dress like this for a date or something, it'll be a little classier."

He smiled. "Has its charms."

"Mmhmm." Her cheeks pinked.

At least, he thought they did. Visibility wasn't great in the dark interior of the car. "What?"

"We're not talking about the outfit, okay? Tell me what Mitch was there to see Allerton for."

"I don't know." Isaac didn't turn the car on. He wanted to wait until his boss came out. Maybe follow him. See what happened next. "That's what I wanted to find. Then I walk in, and you're rubbing up against Allerton. I nearly lost my mind, but it was more about surprise." He didn't need her to get mad. "Because I know you're a potential target. I thought they'd captured you for a second and you were under duress. All kinds of horrifying things went through my mind."

She winced. "Sorry. I used it to my advantage, told him I heard through the grapevine I was on the menu and that I was there to make my own deal."

"It was a gamble that Allerton was even aware of what Brandon Jones got into, let alone that he was involved."

"Worth the risk," she said. "He admitted someone is running it."

Adam had to be part of the business, maybe a customer. The same was Brandon Jones. But what about Mitch? "Allerton isn't the top of the food chain?"

She shook her head. "You like Mitch for it?"

"Maybe." He worked his mouth around, thinking it over. "I intend to find out."

Isaac pulled out his phone and called Addie. He ended up leaving a message to update her of everything. When he hung up, he said, "I'm guessing she did a deep dive into Mitch when I came to her with my evidence and the offer to be a CI."

"Things like this don't always show up on paper. Maybe he's been clean for years, operating under the radar," she said. "I'm hoping Clara can give the police information when she wakes up. Or Brandon Jones rolls over on the whole operation."

"But you're not waiting around to find out?"

She shrugged. "Neither are you."

"It's time to get aggressive with Mitch. Find out what he's into." Isaac figured he had an angle. "I can bemoan how out of control you are."

"Offer me up for sale yourself." She shifted in her seat, moving like she'd had some great epiphany. "Bring me to the table, but as if you're the only one who gets the commission. No one else."

He wanted to be sick. "Like I'm your pimp?"

She waved a hand. "However you want to play it. We could do it together, figure this out."

Meanwhile his focus would be divided working the men in charge of this operation and making sure she remained safe. It might work with a team to provide backup, but that wasn't something he had access to now.

"You think it's a terrible idea." She shifted in her seat. "Great. I guess I'll just go home and wait for you to fix all my problems. I'll take up knitting."

"Your home isn't safe." And it was too far for him to

reach fast. If anything happened to her at the cabins and he wasn't there, she would be long gone—or gone from this world—before he reached her.

"So I move in with you and my business dies. Or you move in with me and give up this operation to keep me safe full-time."

"Yes, I want you safe." He swallowed down the lump in his throat. Still thinking about being too far away to help her. "I also want to help keep this from happening to anyone else. People like Clara, and the other women in that box, didn't have us to help them."

"They do now."

He nodded. "I just… Can you tell me when you're gonna go on an operation? No more flying solo."

Except that was precisely what he intended to do. Isaac needed to make a plan, but he wasn't going to dangle Lyric in front of these guys like bait. No way. She didn't get their attention any more than she already had it.

He would make sure of that.

The lobby doors slid open, and Mitch strode out.

Lyric let out a breath. "I'd love to know what they talked about."

He didn't mention that he would know. If she hadn't been there. Isaac just waited until Mitch pulled out, then turned Lyric's car on and followed him out of the parking lot.

His phone rang, and the screen displayed Addie's name.

Isaac handed it to Lyric. "Put it on speaker." When she held it up between them, he said, "Hey."

"Where are you?" Addie asked.

"Following Mitch. Things didn't go exactly to plan, but I'll fill you in. Hopefully he doesn't just go home, and we can see what he's up to. Get a feel for how big this thing is."

She remained quiet.

"What is it, Special Agent Franklin?" He used her title since he didn't need Lyric wondering about his relationship with Addie. It was business as far as both were concerned, and Addie was engaged. But Lyric didn't even need one single niggle of doubt.

"Brandon Jones was transferred to county lockup for the night. He was killed two hours later."

Lyric nodded. "Someone got to him." Isaac glanced over, and she continued, "They're closing ranks. Cleaning up loose ends."

"Stella is headed over to make sure Clara is safe," Addie said. "And that she stays that way."

"Good." Lyric's voice hardened. "That's good."

"We'll figure this out." Isaac was willing to promise them both that.

But he was going to do it all himself.

Without help.

25

M itch drove half an hour across town.

"You think he killed Allerton?" Lyric glanced over at Isaac, absorbing his presence with her. After so long alone it was strange to be so close to someone. And for so much time lately.

She'd shared his apartment—sleeping in his room while he took the couch out in the living room and acted like a total gentleman. Shared meals with him. Called him when she needed someone. She hadn't thought about that last one so much, just dialed the number and didn't think too much on why he was her first call when she could barely breathe and nearly died.

"I guess we'll find out tomorrow."

"I thought we were off on a cruise or something." She needed to find another conversation starter. Things had been fine since they got in the car, but now the chatter waned, and they were back to quiet. She had to face the lull and fight the memory of that kiss in the elevator.

Her entire body still felt flush. She could still feel his lips against hers, every sensation. Every inhale.

Even if it was Isaac, going down that rabbit trail wouldn't lead her anywhere good. She'd end up crazy distracted when they needed to focus. She thought about things she shouldn't when she was single and knew what the Bible said about it. Not that she had to act all holier-than-thou about the choices a lot of people made.

Lyric knew the pain life could cause. The way things got twisted. Distorted.

What Clara had suffered.

Sasha.

The others.

Men like Allerton, Brandon Jones, Mitch, and the rest of them didn't care about a woman's choices. They didn't care about freedom. They only cared about what they wanted and making money giving others the same thing. Like women were a commodity to be traded. Unlike a lot of products, sex could be sold over and over again.

Until there was no more of the person left inside the body.

Isaac's hand covered hers. "Hey."

"I wasn't going to let any of them touch me."

"Could you guarantee you'd be safe?"

"Can any of us?" She had to ask him. After all, even he couldn't guarantee autonomy. Things happened to all kinds of people every day in all kinds of places. Just because she was female didn't mean she was more vulnerable.

"I guess not." He squeezed, then moved to let go. Lyric didn't release his hand.

Likely it was a product of her former occupation that so much was twisted around and messed up in her head.

"Are you really okay?"

She winced. "I know I suggested being bait, but now I think I don't want to do it."

He nodded. "Your call."

Yes, it was. "But I'm not going to let this rest. I want to help take down the whole ring, not go home and hide until it was over."

All she'd do was think about her dad's death, how much she hated his mother, and that kiss.

The kiss.

Lyric brushed back hair from the side of her face. She was never going to forget that kiss for the rest of her life.

"What if working on this costs you success with your cabins?"

Lyric let out a long breath.

"Let me ask you this," he said softly. "What do you see yourself doing in five years?"

Ah, the five-year plan question. She hadn't ever thought much about goal setting, whether at the new year or any other time. She might have put together a business plan to get the loan for her start-up costs. That didn't mean she'd stuck to it.

Lyric said, "I'd need to think on that."

Because she couldn't say she wanted to be running the cabins still. And maybe she wasn't ready to admit it yet.

"What about staying on the land? You see yourself there?"

"Of course. With the freedom to go when I want, come back when I want." To be free.

"Sounds like you need an RV." He squeezed her hand.

"Maybe I do. But being on the road gets your face on cameras. You can be tracked, and the last thing I need is to get noticed by someone." It was better if she stayed in one area, as much as she didn't like being tied down to a place.

"Putting down roots isn't bad. Neither is a relationship."

"And when your mother comes for Thanksgiving, and I stab her with the cheese knife?"

Isaac barked a laugh that went off like a gunshot in the interior of the car.

"Maybe I wasn't joking."

He squeezed her hand again and turned the corner, following Mitch at a distance, using one hand. "I'd preach to you about what the pastor said Sunday. Forgiving others because Christ forgave us. But that would mean I'd have to forgive her first, and I have no interest in being a hypocrite."

"I've never understood forgiving people." Though, things were square between her and the Lord. "It's not like they care that they did you wrong and you've absolved them of it. If they cared, they wouldn't have wronged you in the first place."

"Maybe that's the point."

Lyric frowned. "What do you mean?"

He shrugged. "Maybe it isn't for them. Maybe it's for you…us. It's true, my mom probably doesn't care she did either of us wrong. She thinks everything is a means to an end."

"She still wants you in her life."

After a moment of stillness, he nodded, conceding the point. "She does. Why, I have no idea. I mean, it's obvious I don't want to see her."

"Maybe she wants to apologize. Start over." Lyric figured if more people did that, the world would be a better place.

Up ahead of them, Mitch pulled into an industrial complex. A tile store, warehouse, and office building above— recently built—beside a contractor building supply store. The whole street was like that.

"You guys get your stuff here?"

Isaac nodded. "The guy who runs the building supply store is Mitch's brother-in-law."

"Is he married?"

"I think he is," Isaac said. "He just doesn't wear a ring. He keeps it tight though. You'd never know he's sampling any merchandise if that's what he's doing. If the guy has proclivities or vices, he's keeping them hidden like a pro."

"Eventually they all slip up."

"Yeah, we do."

Lyric frowned. "He's parking."

Mitch pulled in through the open gate for the fenced area where wood had been stacked high.

Isaac headed around the back of the neighboring building. "Let's see if we can get close enough to hear him."

Lyric pulled the duffel from the floor behind her seat. She tossed the running shoes inside on the floor by her feet and tugged out the leggings. "Give me a sec."

He nodded and climbed out, affording her privacy. She shimmied the leggings up and smoothed her skirt back down over them. Between the shoes and dress she was going to look ridiculous, but if anyone saw them the bizarreness of her outfit was going to be the least of her problems.

She wasted no time with the shoes or the gun from her glove box. Another firearm registered to the corporation behind the Accountant's Office. Done that way so if it showed up in commission of a crime, they would know, but the police might not necessarily be able to find the culprit. Plus it wasn't good to use the same gun all the time—or even the same type of weapon. But Russ hadn't agreed to her having a sword yet. Or throwing stars. Some rubbish about them being illegal, as if that was the point.

So what if she was unlikely to need one. Was that the point?

"Ready?" Isaac's lips curled up. He held out his hand for her duffel.

She put it on her shoulder instead and raised her brows. "Honey, I was born ready."

He shook his head, chuckling. "Okay, I walked into that one."

They quickly settled into a jog and rounded the back of the building. Overhead was barbed, but the fence itself could be cut easily. She used more items from the duffel and opened a big enough hole in the wire they could squeeze through.

A quick glance indicated he had his game face on.

She prayed there were no dogs patrolling this area at night, but she didn't hear any barks indicating a visitor had arrived at the front, so maybe they were safe. At the far end of the rows of stacked supplies, headlights were visible. She took a circuitous route and got them close by the offices.

Lyric saw Mitch sitting on the hood of his car. A man emerged from the office.

She pulled a camera from the duffel and got it ready for collecting surveillance pictures.

Isaac squeezed her shoulder.

He hadn't brought his things? Probably just planned on taking photos with his phone camera. As if that would ever replace the feel of a real camera in a person's hands. Cell phones weren't necessary for living, despite what a lot of people thought. Before Isaac she barely looked at hers.

Now...

She pushed away thoughts of him since he was right beside her anyway, and that was distracting enough. She didn't need to get on another trail of thoughts that would make anyone who knew her now believe she'd been a terrible CIA agent. She'd been top-notch—likely because she'd been completely unaware of Isaac in her life. She'd gone to work, trained until she scored higher than anyone, completed every mission possible—some would never end with success, that was just how life was—and generally strived to impress everyone above her in the agency.

And why not?

That was her dad's legacy. Being the best at what he was —a CIA legend.

Until he ended his own life.

Lyric aimed the camera and took every picture she could. Wide angle, both men. Individuals. License plates. The business name. More close ups while they chatted. An envelope exchanged hands, from the man to Mitch. A payment of some kind. It looked like money stacked in a manila envelope. A lot of money, if they were big bills.

"I want to get closer, but it's not worth the risk," Isaac whispered by her ear.

Lyric nodded, motioning with two fingers to indicate they should head out.

He held up one.

Probably wanted to wait until the conversation was over. They could sneak out in the quiet.

Lyric lifted the camera to her eye and looked through. She zoomed. Mitch shifted. She snapped the shutter as he drew out a gun and fired it at the man. Muzzle flash exploded across the screen. She kept taking photos, even with her eyes closed against the brightness.

Isaac's arm came around her back, and she realized she listed over in her crouch. She heard him hiss out a breath through clenched teeth.

Mitch's car door slammed shut, and he gunned the engine.

Isaac said, "That's two people in two days."

"Brandon Jones."

"Mitch is cleaning house."

Lyric whispered in the dark, his hand on her shoulder. "So we give everything to Addie. Let her do her FBI thing. She can bring him in. Take him down."

They'd brought her in, and if someone was actually guilty, then that was a good thing. Stella had made far too many assumptions, and then jumped the gun for the whole breaking-and-entering thing.

This was murder.

A man cried out, a roar of anger and pain.

Lyric's head whipped around. "He's alive?"

Isaac shot out of his crouch, and she raced after him to where a man was sitting up on the ground. The guy pulled apart the snap buttons of his shirt.

Isaac flipped on his phone camera flashlight. It glinted off the slug in the center of the man's chest. Embedded in the vest. "You knew he'd try to kill you."

The guy flinched. Grimaced. "Now you're going to finish me off?"

"Not unless you try to kill us." Lyric showed him her gun.

The guy was probably in his sixties. Jeans and boots. Gray stubble on his face. He frowned up at them. "Who are you guys?"

Isaac looked at her and grinned.

Lyric grinned back. "Mitch is gonna go down."

26

Isaac strode into the diner as if they had plans. Mitch sat alone at a booth, halfway down the room. Drinking coffee, presumably waiting on his order.

Isaac and Lyric had breakfast with Addie, after the fed spent time with the man from the night before. The one who knew he was going to get shot. The FBI had his full statement. They were working on a deal for immunity in exchange for his testimony as to his brother-in-law's activities.

Addie had found more photos at Brandon Jones's house. The FBI had catalogued them all, found most were the same as the ones in Adam's shoe box, and had the police department correlating—running the photos through facial recognition to see who they were. After that they would track each one down.

Mitch spotted him.

A man who had murdered multiple people this week, as well as ordered one to be killed. Two of those, Isaac had witnessed. Which meant to an extent Mitch needed to keep Isaac quiet. Something that could play in Isaac's favor.

If Mitch didn't opt to kill him, too.

Now he sat sipping coffee as if he hadn't done all that. Like he was some regular guy with a regular job. Maybe a wife and family at home, trying to figure out how to scrape together money to give them a good summer vacation.

He slid into the booth. "Hey. Glad I found you."

Mitch glanced at his phone screen, the device on the table. All that was visible was the time. "How did you find me?"

Isaac shrugged. "Word is you have lunch here every once in a while. I tried two other places first." *Right.*

He didn't need to let on this was the kind of lunch where the FBI had an agent in a van outside. Sure, it was the male agent and not Addie, but Kyle seemed like a decent-enough guy. He hadn't been the one to accuse Lyric of being involved with traffickers.

"So what's up?" Mitch asked, tension in his voice. His tight face displayed impatience. Despite looking for all the world as if he had the afternoon to sit here doing nothing.

"Just wanted to chat." Isaac couldn't push hard, or Mitch would close off and he'd get nowhere.

The waitress came over and took his order: a roast beef sandwich and fries.

"Thanks, darlin'," Isaac said. When she was out of earshot, he poured cream in the coffee. "Just checking in. Seeing how things went with Allerton."

Kyle was the one who'd checked this morning. Allerton was alive as of eight. He'd also been in the process of packing up so he could head out of town in a couple of days on a last-minute cruise with his wife.

Isaac couldn't help being frustrated he'd had to adapt when Lyric had been there. He wanted her nowhere near Mitch, and anything the man was into. But getting her out cleanly and the fastest way he knew how meant he hadn't heard anything of their conversation. Or had a chance to ingratiate himself further with Mitch and whoever he was in business with.

The number of questions with no answers wasn't helping.

"Allerton's fine." Mitch's burger and fries arrived.

The waitress said, "Your food will be out shortly."

Isaac nodded. To sell the part, he stared at her backside as she walked away. That was when he noticed Edith across the room eating lunch with a dark-haired young man who had her nose.

Eric Hummet. Local cop. Edith's grandson.

The older woman said something to her grandson, along with a slight chuckle he couldn't hear but saw light her face. She caught Isaac's gaze, a question there about her lunch companion.

Isaac gave her a tiny shake of his head.

Edith lifted her iced tea.

"What about the rest of business? How's things going?" Isaac felt the need to make up for whatever ground he'd lost last night. Even if, along with saving Lyric from what might've been, they had witnessed another murder and had the photos to prove it was Mitch that corroborated their story.

Mitch swallowed a bite of his burger. "Shifting some things. Too much heat, you know? But that doesn't mean things are done here. Just…refocusing."

"And my girl's role in that?"

Mitch shrugged one shoulder.

Isaac's sandwich was delivered.

"She can have whatever role she wants. Or what you decide. If you'd like to make an offer." Mitch took another bite and spoke around it. "Some women are like that. They need an extra…helping hand. To understand how the world works."

"Sure." Isaac was sure if he took a bite of sandwich, he would throw up on the floor. "If I was the kind of man who needed help with that."

Mitch nodded. "Of course. If that's the deal you want. But you could make some money, too. Woman like that? You could charge extra. Make a deal of your own."

He wanted to tell Mitch to shove that idea. That Lyric wasn't for sale and never would be. Which, of course, was the absolute truth. Instead, he said, "And if I wanted a different kind of deal? Something extra for me."

Mitch's lips twitched. He dug out his wallet and slid a card across the table. Cream. Gold embossed digits of a phone number. No name. "Text, give your order."

"And my girl, Lyric?" He figured Mitch might as well know. "I found the shoe box under Adam's bed." He was making an assumption Mitch was aware of the photos and that he knew who she was.

"Ah," Mitch said. "Saw something you like."

"Just curious how all this goes. Seems like you're sitting on some serious money."

"It's high end." Mitch sniffed. "Orders fulfilled to specification."

"And if I have someone in mind. Someone not in the shoe box?"

"Had an order like that myself just this morning." Mitch grinned. "Sent a friend to make the retrieval."

Yeah, Isaac wasn't touching the sandwich. And if this went on much longer, Edith would make her way over to ask what was wrong. Not that Mitch had a clue that Isaac disliked every part of this conversation.

"I'll think on that." Isaac tapped the card on the table, then pocketed it.

This was the kind of man the world wanted to believe he was. Considering Lana raised him as part of a private security group who did what she asked, what else they would think? Her methods were about the greater good, not who was destroyed along the way. That left a lasting impression on people she ripped off or outright obliterated.

People like Lyric.

He was in the same camp as her, wondering why he couldn't seem to forgive his mom even if he knew in his head that it was the right thing to do. The thing that might actually set him free. Wasn't it enough to leave that life behind? To live the way he wanted, do right by people—and the law —for once. Protect Lyric. Bring down Mitch and those he worked with.

Mitch finished his burger.

Before he could decide it was a good time to leave, Isaac said, "And if I'd like to get in on the 'retrieval' side of things? I mean, you probably know what I can do." He'd likely done background and found out Isaac worked for Chevalier Protection Specialists before he went to federal prison.

Being exonerated didn't mean much to a guy like Mitch, except that Isaac had skated out from under charges and was now free to break the law again. Until he was caught.

"Let's say I have some marketable skills in that arena," Isaac said.

The FBI guy, Kyle, had coached him to try to get in any way he could and see what was going on with Lyric. If Mitch had his attention to Clara in the hospital—and whether he would try and tie up that loose end.

Mitch nodded a couple of times. "Okay, good point. I can keep that in mind. You dealt with Adam. Maybe not the way I'd have done it, but you did as asked. That can't be discounted."

Depended on whether Mitch wanted yes-men, guys who just did what he said with no questions, or if he wanted to pay freethinkers who had creative ways of solving problems that could end up being better in the end for Mitch. And the business bottom line.

"Thanks," Isaac said. "I appreciate it." Since he needed intel, he continued, "You the boss? Or there is someone higher on the food chain?"

Mitch might need to keep that to himself, like Isaac was an asset he cultivated independently. Or he could be obligated to make an introduction. Of course, it was also possible Mitch was the boss. But the more he got into this, he wasn't entirely sure. It seemed like this man was more a head-of-security type. The one who got his hands dirty for someone else.

Because Mitch liked it.

"I could introduce you"—Mitch slid to the edge of the seat—"when you're ready."

"I should know who I'm meeting." Isaac was pushing it, trying to get a name. Worth the risk, though. "I need to do my homework, same as him."

Mitch gave him a chin lift. "See you at work tomorrow." Then he walked away.

Isaac grabbed his sandwich, taking two bites before Edith slid into the seat across from him.

"Want to tell me who that was?" she said.

He glanced at her table and saw the cop grandson was absent. In the bathroom. "No."

She tipped her head back and laughed.

Isaac motioned with one finger to his ear and mouthed, *Wire.*

Her white eyebrows rose to two peaks. "I'll need a hand later. I need to move a recliner into the other room. If you're available."

"Sure. I'll come across the hall and knock when I'm home." If Kyle still cared enough to listen, rather than follow wherever Mitch had gone, he'd have just put it together that Edith was Isaac's neighbor.

His phone started to vibrate in his pocket. He dug it out.

Edith knocked twice on the tabletop and slid to the end of the seat, though it took some doing. "We will be talking about this."

"I know." He wondered if he should help her up. Then he saw it was Addie calling and answered, "Yes?"

"I'm about to tell you something. But tell me first, can Kyle hear me?"

"No." He had the phone to his other ear than the mic'd one. "What's up?"

"Okay." She sounded out of breath. "Listen carefully. Stella is incommunicado. She's transferring Clara to a safe house so she can recover and we can convince her to tell us everything."

Isaac didn't know what else to say, so he settled on, "Yeah, that sounds fine."

"I lost contact with her." Addie exhaled sharply. "I need you to tell me where Lyric is, but don't let on to Kyle that anything is wrong. When he hears about Stella, he's going to lose it. Bigtime."

"Lyric was at the cabins with Russ, but I know she also wanted to check on Clara."

She'd promised not to go anywhere without sending him a text. He was supposed to go over there for dinner so he could do more work on the renovation while they figured out the next steps. After he'd dropped her off, the FBI had called to say Mitch was here and they wanted him to go in, wired up.

"Head out to the van. Tell Kyle what happened and get him to the hospital in case something is going down. I'm on my way, but it'll take me half an hour to get there. I need a sitrep as soon as he arrives."

"Copy that." Isaac hung up and saw she'd texted him to say she had gone to the hospital.

She's there.

He left a wad of twenties on the table and headed outside, already dialing Lyric's number. "Come on. Come on. Pick up. Where are you?"

27

"Let's just take the stairs. It's only a couple of floors." Stella strode ahead of them, her neck tight beneath her pixie cut. The rest of her was as trim as her hair, making Lyric wonder if she ever ate something without counting or measuring it.

Lyric held onto Clara's elbow. The hospital had offered them a wheelchair, but they were leaving the way people usually did—out the front doors to the curb where discharged patients were picked up.

Instead, Stella asked Clara if she could walk so they could make a less noticeable exit.

A security alert had gone off through the hospital, for whatever reason. Lyric had no idea what that code meant. Maybe Stella did, but she wasn't sure.

The elevators were overcrowded now and running slowly.

"I still can't believe you found me." Clara had been repeating this mantra ever since Lyric got to the hospital.

Lyric squeezed her arm. "Let's get you to the car so you can sit."

Clara hadn't talked to the police yet. So far she'd declined the conversation, which Lyric knew Stella hoped to turn around when Clara was settled in the safe house. Because Stella had told her several times. As though helping Clara feel safe, she gave Stella what the FBI wanted—information in the form of an official statement—was doing the right thing.

At least Stella felt the need to make amends. She was just going about it completely wrong.

All Stella seemed to want to do was order them around. Because she was worried they might not get to the safehouse in one piece? Since Addie and Kyle were busy, the FBI agent opted to have Russ drive them to the safe house. Which meant Lyric was going for now, too.

Stella held the door to the stairs open. As they passed, she whispered, "You could get her to talk about it."

The implication was that Lyric didn't want to. She shot the FBI agent a look.

Stella had lied to her. She'd pretended to be a guest at the cabins so she could find out if Lyric was a criminal.

"Pay your final invoice," Lyric said, "and maybe I will."

As if this had anything to do with the money. But still, Lyric didn't appreciate people who refused to follow through on their obligations. Stella had signed the booking contract stating she would make the final payment when she checked out.

Had she?

No.

Of course, not. Because Stella seemed to think the fact she'd arrested Lyric meant she didn't have to.

If Stella thought all Lyric worried about was money, who cared?

It was decently close to the truth, and Stella's reaction told Lyric what she needed to know about the woman.

"I know you've got to be something other than a regular person." Clara eased down the stairs slowly. But not in a way that worried Lyric. She was sore, dehydrated, and covered with abrasions and bruises. But most of all, she needed time to heal from the emotional and mental anguish she'd been under.

"What makes you say that?" Lyric asked.

"Why else would you have come and found me?"

"I'm glad I did." Lyric took the opening to jab at Stella. "After all, it might've been too late if I'd waited for the police or FBI to do it."

She wanted to feel pleasure at the barb. Instead, only frustration rolled through her. They still had no idea who was at the head of this. Lyric had no idea if that was even on Stella's radar. Seemed like the FBI way was to slow-roll everything. Gather statements. Proceed only when they were completely sure who was behind something.

Maybe it was better, as she figured that meant they probably got more convictions. Kept the people they worked with —and for—happier because they had a higher success rate.

But what happened to good old-fashioned "kick the door down, shoot first, and ask questions later" police work? It seemed as though some people could use a dose of that. Like people who thought anyone who didn't share their skin color wasn't worth consideration. Who denied historical events. Who thought *they* were God's chosen people.

"And here, I thought you were just another customer." Clara smiled, but for some reason it stung.

"I didn't deceive you." Not the way Stella had done to her. "I might've saved your life."

Behind her, Lyric heard Stella snort.

Like Lyric was trying to be petty. Was that really what the agent thought?

"In the past, that was exactly my role." The fact she could do it now for someone she cared about gave Lyric back a little of what the CIA had taken when they left her for dead. "I don't get to do it much these days," she told Clara. "So maybe I should thank you."

Clara's eyes glinted for the first time since Lyric showed up at the hospital. She hadn't even done it at the prospect of getting released. "You're welcome?"

Lyric chuckled. Who even cared what Stella thought now? It wasn't like she would be friends with the woman. Stella ruined any chance of that by lying about who she was.

Lyric didn't even care much about the arrest, or the questioning. Or the accusations.

What she wanted was the truth from people she knew.

It was part of why she loved Isaac, and never compared him to other men she'd met. He was honest about how he felt. How she affected him. What he wanted.

There was a lot to respect there…and be interested in.

On the next floor, the door had a sign that read Lobby. In the middle was a tiny window with those wires crisscrossed over it, for stability. Or security.

"Let me go first." Stella shifted around them and drew her weapon.

"Was that alert for us?" Lyric asked.

Stella frowned. "Why do you think that?"

Lyric wondered when this woman was going to give of herself anything without Lyric having to pry it out. To make her point, she gave Stella no answer.

"I'm in danger," Clara said. "That's why you're taking me to a safe house."

Lyric glanced at her. "It's because they haven't found

who took you, and since you were abducted from your house, it isn't safe for you to be alone." She paused. "I think you should come and stay with me. Stella already has a cabin out there she likes."

Before Clara could answer, the federal agent said, "Let's head out. But I go first and check it's clear."

Lyric said, "Russ should be making circles, watching for us."

She had told him to park illegally out front, but he said he didn't want to draw his attention, which was fair enough. Why they couldn't leave from the pickup lane was a mystery to Lyric, but Stella had insisted they switch it up from expected protocol. Because she was operating under the assumption someone would try and capture Clara? Or hurt her, the way a handful of others had been killed lately.

Since Isaac was currently meeting with Mitch—or so his text had said—she didn't figure they needed to worry about that. Not that she'd assume they were perfectly safe, either.

Was there something Stella wasn't telling them?

"You can call him when we get out there, right? Get him to pull around." When Lyric nodded, Stella pulled the door open. "Hang here a second." She stepped through the door.

The minute it closed, Clara said, "You aren't going to forgive her, are you?"

Lyric shrugged. "I'm not going to hold on to it for long."

She figured the irritation would wane, and they'd get to a place where they could tolerate each other. Or it was all on Lyric and she had to figure out on her own how to get over it. Either way it wasn't going to be an issue forever. And not just because Lyric didn't plan on having to see the woman all that much. Especially if Stella never came out to the cabins…after she paid her bill.

Lyric said, "I'll be—"

Two shots erupted behind the door in the lobby. The window shattered at the same time the muted blast sounded.

Clara's body jerked. Red blossomed on her chest, and she started to fall.

Lyric launched forward and caught Clara before she hit the ground, her legs bent awkwardly under her, then lowered her back to the cold concrete.

More gunfire erupted in the lobby.

"Hold on. Hold on." *This is a hospital. Clara can get help. I could…*

Her mind blanked.

"Just hold on." Lyric reached for her phone.

There was only one bar in the concrete stairwell.

Two missed calls from Isaac. How hadn't she heard he was calling? Was her volume down? Where was Russ?

She tried Russ's number since he was outside and armed. He had to know what was going on.

Lyric only got an angry dial tone.

Clara gasped and shifted, as though her mind finally caught up to what happened. Lyric set the phone down and pressed against the wound on Clara's chest. Each inhale was nothing but a wet-sounding gasp.

Not good.

Lyric snatched up her phone. It slipped from her wet, bloody fingers.

She tugged off her jacket, wiped off her hands. Balled it up. With her left hand she pressed it to Clara's chest. She thumbed to an emergency call with her other and prayed it would go through.

Nothing.

She had to get her and Clara out of this stairwell. They were inches from death and help. Lyric wanted one for them, but not the other. Whether or not Clara knew who was behind the abductions, or if she could help provide intel for any of it, didn't matter a bit. What mattered was that they live.

You're too invested.

Lyric winced. She grasped Clara under the arms and dragged her to the other side of the door. That put her halfway on Lyric's lap.

She moved out from under Clara and reached for the handle. Would they die as soon as she opened the door?

The gunfire was still going, every few seconds a shot rang out.

When it comes down to win or lose, you care too much. She could see her mentor's face in her mind. Her memories.

Too much heart.

Maybe in the CIA that was a bad thing. It might even be why Lyric opted for solitude at her cabins. Because deep down she'd absorbed their criticism. Believed it.

Turned out she didn't know how to turn it off. For good or bad, she cared what happened to people.

Lyric turned the handle enough the door could ease open, then let go of it. She pulled on the edge of the door from her seated position. Minimal coverage behind the wall beside the door. Anyone who tried to fire at her wouldn't hit Clara. She'd suffered enough already.

Lyric caught sight of a grief-stricken woman holding an older man across the lobby. Tears gathered in her eyes. "Stella!"

"Stay where you are!"

She kept peering around, far enough she saw Stella crouched by a sofa in the waiting area. Two men patrolled the lobby, waving guns around. Full face masks on. One was six five at least. The one who'd managed to hit her friend in the chest?

If they thought they'd killed Clara already, that wasn't their only goal because they hadn't just run off.

What did they want?

"Bring her out and no one else dies!"

Lyric winced.

Stella lifted from her crouch, her pistol dangling from one hand. "I'll go instead."

Lyric sucked in a breath. "No. Don't—"

She was too late.

28

Kyle hit the brakes and jerked the wheel into a space. Isaac shoved the door open with barely enough room to get out. Of course Kyle had plenty enough room between him and the car next to him on his side.

Isaac gritted his teeth and eased out without scratching paint on the truck beside him. It probably wasn't intentional that Kyle parked this way.

The guy was half out of his mind not knowing if his partner was all right.

A crowd had gathered away from the front doors of the hospital. Security guards held the people back. Some wore hospital gowns and slippers. Others wore regular clothes.

Kyle pulled on a bulletproof vest, then jogged over. Isaac kept pace right behind him. He didn't bother asking the fed for a gun. That wasn't going to happen, given the way Kyle reacted to news of Stella being out of contact. But dragging Isaac bodily from the van would have taken more time than Kyle wanted to waste getting here, so he'd drawn the line.

The lobby doors opened, and Stella came out. The pinched look on her face didn't read right, until Isaac realized the guy right behind her had a gun to the back of her head. He pulled her close, giving Kyle no shot at his center mass.

"Everyone out of my way!"

Stella's teeth flashed, and she walked forward with jerky movements.

"Put the gun down and let her go!" Kyle held aim with his weapon, but there wasn't a spot to point it that didn't mean he'd clip Stella first.

Isaac tried to get a read on their silent communication. As far as Isaac could tell, Kyle might be half in love with her, but this was about business. Their personal life was something they kept out of work.

"Everyone get out of my way or she's dead!" the guy yelled.

Kyle didn't back down or lower his gun. "Drop the weapon and let her go. That is a federal agent!"

Given the shift of her gaze, Isaac decided Stella wouldn't object to the guy behind her being shot. Through her. In fact, she seemed to be indicating Kyle should have done it already.

The male FBI agent flicked two fingers on his free hand.

Stella shook her head, a barely visible movement. Her gaze shifted to Isaac, then the people watching. Seemed like to her the fact this was all being observed, making her the center of attention, was the worst part. Not having a gun to the back of her head.

"Everyone stay calm!" She lifted both hands, fingers splayed so Isaac noticed she'd broken the index finger on her left hand at some point.

"Back up," the guy said. "You heard the lady. I don't want no trouble." He inched her to the left, his right.

So he could get away?

Across by the first row of parked cars a matte black van waited with its lights on.

Isaac broke off from the two agents' standoff with the gunman and raced to the van. Before he got five feet, the van engine roared and it sped toward him.

Isaac started to pull up short.

The van kept coming.

He stumbled and decided to dive, shifted his body, and flipped onto his shoulder. He tucked and rolled, building momentum as he went.

The van thundered past with a rush of hot diesel air.

Isaac shifted and sat up. His hands moved, a reflex, but he still had no gun. No way to do anything. Because he'd been a criminal, the FBI didn't trust him or consider him one of the "good guys."

He wasn't trying to make friends, but it seemed like Addie at least appreciated what he could do for them.

"You've got nowhere to go, so drop the weapon and let her go!" Kyle yelled. "You've got no play here. No leverage."

"I kill her, that's leverage!" the guy shouted back.

Kyle jerked his head in a shake. "You get a deal if you let her go. Kill her and you get *nothing*."

Isaac climbed to his feet. He realized the head shake wasn't for the gunman.

Stella shifted fast. In one move she twisted, ducked, and kicked the guy's shin. Uppercut.

He doubled over. The gun went off.

She grabbed it, clocked him with her free hand, and stood over him while he slumped to the ground.

Kyle moved up beside her. "You good?"

She held her gun aimed. "Tell me not to shoot him."

Isaac jogged over. "He could give us intel."

Kyle knelt by the guy and pulled cuffs off the back of his belt.

Stella said, "You get a plate from that van?"

Isaac gritted his teeth. "No."

It hadn't had a plate on the front, and he'd been too busy surviving when it drove away.

"We don't need your help, Isaac." Kyle clicked the cuffs into place.

Isaac didn't need to stay out here. "Where's Lyric?"

"Stairwell door. She's with Clara." Stella turned back to Kyle. "The other one is dead inside."

The guy on the ground with his hands cuffed behind his back yelled, "You killed Simon! You're dead. I'm gonna kill you!"

Stella leaned down a fraction. "You should save some of that survival energy for prison. Right, Isaac?"

His jaw flexed. No way was he going to rise to her bait.

Instead, he jogged through the lobby doors into the chaos of screams. Shouted orders from medical personnel. Two people in scrubs pushed a gurney toward the elevator bay.

"Hold up!" A security guard got in front of him. "If you aren't a cop or staff or in need of medical treatment, you should leave."

"My friend is in here. She might be hurt." He glanced around, found the downed gunman, and said, "Where's the stairs?"

"You aren't going upstairs, buddy. Not without a badge." The guy held up a hand. "And you won't get one of those until at least tomorrow. Everyone is busy and the receptionist just got shot." Grief filled his eyes.

"I understand. I just need to know if my friend is okay," he said. "She was with a patient."

So many times he and his friends had talked their way

into situations. Used fake IDs or told elaborate lies. He'd worked undercover for his mom.

Now he had none of that, for good or ill, and it felt like being a second-class citizen. No trust. No leverage. No access.

He wanted to yell so loud Lyric would hear him from wherever she was. But the noise level here was so high that he'd have to reach crazy decibels just to get her attention.

The security guard's attention shifted over Isaac's shoulder. *Please be Addie.*

He twisted and saw Stella stride in, gun still in her hand. "Let's get this place cleared out."

The security guard nodded. "Yes, ma'am."

"We need to find Lyric and Clara."

She strode right past him, pretty much ignoring Isaac. "Where's Kyle?"

"Where do you think?" Stella scanned the lobby. "Questioning that guy to find out who sent him."

Isaac wanted to know who the target was. Probably because he already knew who sent the man.

Stella's gaze narrowed on him. "Talk."

"We need to find Lyric."

Her lips thinned as she pressed them together. "You mean, Clara. The target."

"I said what I said."

"Who do the two of you think you are?"

"We're not FBI agents, that's for sure," Isaac said. "Because we don't have a high enough opinion of ourselves for that."

"Yeah, neither of you would qualify." Stella lifted her chin. "Agents have to follow the rules. Bring justice the *right* way. Not by lying, stealing, doing whatever you want and getting away with it. We're the good guys."

Isaac held back what he wanted to say. There was no winning with Stella. Whatever was in her gave her a low opinion of people who skirted the law—or confidential informants—and his words weren't going to change what experience had taught her.

"You heard what Kyle said to that guy about him having no leverage." She left that statement hanging.

"I don't care about leverage or what happens later," Isaac told her. They could arrest him, and it didn't even matter. *Been there. Done that.* "We just need to find them."

Stella strode across the lobby.

He jogged after her to a door marked Stairs. The tiny window had shattered. "Lyric!" he called as loudly as he could.

"Isaac!" she called back, a tremor in her voice.

He pushed the door open to the concrete landing between flights of stairs, where Lyric sat on the floor, Clara pulled across her lap.

Blood everywhere.

Clara's eyes stared, unseeing, at the ceiling.

Isaac crouched. He touched a hand to Lyric's cheek. "Are you hurt?"

She gave him a slight shake of her head. "Clara." Her voice broke saying the woman's name.

"I know."

Stella let out a long breath. "Kyle had better get something from that guy. Otherwise we have nothing."

Isaac gritted his teeth as a shadow shuttered down over the light in Lyric's eyes. He gathered Clara into his arms but paused before he lifted out of his crouch. "Let's get her taken care of. Okay?"

Lyric's eyes closed for a second. It was a measure of acknowledgement.

Isaac stood with Clara's body in his arms. "Where's Russ?"

Stella shifted around. "Good question."

Lyric said nothing.

"I'll go find out." Stella let herself out.

Isaac had to catch the door with his foot. Lyric touched the back of his shoulder, but not to get his attention. At least, he didn't figure she wanted to drag this out. Just let him know she was here with him.

A doctor spotted him and jogged over.

Isaac shook his head.

The doctor pulled up short. "Let's get her on a bed."

He figured there was still paperwork to do, even if Clara was no longer breathing. After he'd laid her on the bed, he turned to Lyric.

"The window just exploded."

Isaac nodded. "There was nothing you could've done."

"Sure there was. I just didn't bother because I was following Stella's lead."

The FBI agent heard Lyric's comment and frowned, her attention shifting from her phone call to them.

"Now Clara is dead. And for what?"

"Not for nothing." He touched her elbow.

Lyric frowned.

Stella strode over. "What do you know?"

She really thought he'd just hand that information to her? He'd been raised with more skill than that. "Where's Special Agent Franklin?" Isaac asked.

"Backing up her uncle. He was in the parking lot, but he followed in his truck." Stella shrugged. "So I guess you're stuck with me. Which means you answer questions, or I place a couple of phone calls and all those charges you got off with scot-free somehow will come back and bite you." She folded her arms. "And then where will you be?"

Threatening him with jail time?

As if it was a first.

Stella had no idea what he'd faced over the years.

She shifted and set her hand on the butt of her holstered weapon. "Turn around. Hands behind your head." She paused barely enough time for his brain to catch up with what was happening, then said, "You can answer my questions in an interrogation room."

"You're not arresting him." Kyle strode over. "We're taking the other guy to the office. We can sweat him. Get real answers."

Stella shifted her stance, her face tight.

Isaac wanted to grin. Too bad nothing about this was amusing.

"Let's go, Special Agent Meister." Kyle said it like it was a special club they belonged to.

Isaac figured it was, but being excluded never felt good.

They trailed away to the lobby doors.

"You guys need to clear out." The security guard rocked back and forth on the balls of his feet.

"Come on." Isaac tugged on Lyric's hand.

She slid hers free but walked with him.

Isaac held the door for her. "Are you okay?"

She only nodded.

"Why are you lying?" It was him. Why couldn't she just tell the truth?

Lyric stopped short. "I'm not like you. Don't try to make me like you."

29

I saac pulled into the club parking lot. Lyric realized she hadn't said a word since they left the hospital. Too many emotions warred inside her. She looked down at her hands.

Blood had dried in the creases of her fingers. She had a lot of it on her lap, and the liquid had dried the material, so it felt stiff. Because Clara had been shot through her chest.

Crack.

The glass shattered, and Clara's expression shifted. Froze. Then she fell to the ground.

Lyric sucked in a shuddering breath.

Isaac reached in front of her and flipped the glove box. It bounced open to reveal a gun among a stack of papers and napkins. She flinched. He bypassed both and pulled out a packet of disinfecting hand wipes.

He tugged one out and took her hand. Dabbed at it with strong fingers, while his other hand held hers as he cleaned off the dry blood.

She wanted to grab it from him and scrub. At the same time, it seemed like maybe it should be there. That when she looked down she should see the blood she had shed in some *Lady Macbeth*-level mental break.

"I need to go inside for a minute," Isaac said. "Are you going to be okay out here?"

"You're leaving me?" He'd done that before. Everyone she cared about did that.

Lyric would find herself alone, yet again.

A tear rolled down her cheek. Isaac groaned and dropped the wipe to thumb it away. "I'm not going anywhere. I said I loved you, remember?"

"That means you're *going* to leave." She could almost guarantee it. Not like some kind of self-fulfilling prophecy. It was just that life had taught her it was the way things went.

People left.

Or gave her up. Handed her off. Traded. Left for dead. Disposed of.

The Accountant's Office—or Isaac, more like it—had saved her life. Given her a new place to thrive. But had she? It seemed like nothing changed except the location. Certainly not her and the faults she had that inevitably led to it all falling apart.

Trying to distance herself from people hadn't worked. Neither had caring.

Clara was dead.

Isaac would leave. If anything happened to him, what would she do?

He frowned. "Is anything I say going to change your mind right now? I think you might be in shock."

She wanted to cling to him and cry for days. She hadn't even known Clara that well but tell that to her feelings. It was just that it happened right in front of her in a way that was shocking. Or she'd been out of the game too long and lost her tolerance. She'd been desensitized to terror and violence for years—pain hadn't really factored. Now she couldn't figure out how to get that back.

She wanted to be empty.

Uncaring.

"It hurts." Lyric closed her eyes. Instead of nothing, that blessed blank that should be behind her lids, she saw her dad in his recliner. The gun loose in his lap.

The pain, gone.

For him.

Isaac groaned. He leaned his head back on the seat. "I can't take the pain away. But I need to get inside so I can make the rest of it be over." He stared out the front window. "Can you please let me do this myself? Just stay here, where I know you're safe, and I can finish this."

"I don't need to be managed." She'd worked long and hard for years to take care of herself. Just because she was grieving and in shock didn't mean she'd forgotten everything. "I need a shirt to cover the blood, and I'm good to go."

"Maybe I don't want you to *have* to push it down. I want you to have peace." It sounded like he didn't believe it was something for him, but she deserved a life of ease for some reason. As if that was even a thing.

"It's the job." Surely he knew that. "That's how it works. You push everything aside, get it done, and then go home." Where she would cry in the bathtub.

He shook his head. "I'll do it."

The tone of his voice made her want to cry, where she hadn't yet shed more than a single tear for Clara.

Isaac was the one who broke down all her walls. Who cut through every piece of self-preservation she'd always had. From the beginning he'd been the one who cared for her, who understood her. Life had taken them in two different directions, but the connection had always been there—and always would.

There had never been anyone else.

The problem was that to build something, they had to get past the roadblocks and hurdles on the way.

She'd never done this with anyone else. Lyric didn't know what to expect.

She also didn't know how to win.

"Because you think I should be able to have peace, but you don't deserve it?" Lyric said. She'd heard it in his tone. She'd given up fighting four years ago when forced out of the CIA. That didn't mean part of her wouldn't always be the officer they'd trained.

"You're a different kind of person than I am."

She continued, "I'm not even supposed to be alive. They thought I would die in that foreign prison, some nameless inmate who wouldn't last a month. Like I was a dirty secret they could get rid of. Forget about."

"I got you out." He shook his head. "I wasn't going to leave you there to die."

"And you think that means you're not qualified to have a life of peace of your own?"

Isaac said nothing.

"As far as I'm concerned, you're a hero." He had to be able to see that. And yeah, she was so wound up and exhausted and frustrated she might've shouted it like an accusation.

"If I'm such a hero, why are you yelling at me?"

"Because maybe if I do, you'll believe it." She yelled that at him as well, for good measure. Then she let out a long breath. "You really think you have all this stuff to make up for? Or you're trying to prove something."

She'd given up trying to do that when the CIA cut her

loose. Who was he trying to impress? Surely not her, or anyone else she knew here. No one had demanding expectations. Least of all her.

As far as she was concerned, Isaac was already everything he needed to be.

"Everyone else thinks I have to make up for what I've done." He fisted his hands on the legs of his jeans, his body tight but not with aggression. "They look at me like I'm still in prison. Like I deserve what happens to me. Or I'm an asset, like I can be traded around and used as a commodity."

Her heart squeezed in her chest. She knew exactly what that felt like. "Apparently, isolating yourself isn't the answer. Because when you reengage with people, all your buried issues resurface, and things go back to exactly the way they were when it all went wrong."

"Clara's death is not on you." He sounded so certain.

The fact was, she'd been standing there. It could easily have been Lyric, or Stella. "If I didn't care about her, maybe it wouldn't hurt so bad."

He nodded. "That's true, but it means something in the world that when a person dies, there's someone left behind to care that they're not here. It means she made an impact."

And for years Lyric had made no impact. Because no one, except maybe Isaac—out of whatever obligation to her drove him—would've cared if anything happened to her.

No one else would have.

Then there was Stella, trying to make an impact by throwing her federal weight around. Yet another tactic to not connect. Keep herself emotionally separate from the people around her who could be bad guys. Bring justice and not have to deal with the feelings associated with it. Victims got hurt. Stella didn't want the disappointment of realizing a friend broke the law and she had to arrest them.

She would rather believe the worst about people who weren't victims or innocent bystanders. That there was a clean line between good and evil.

For years Lyric had believed the worst about Isaac. She didn't want to be like everyone else in his life now.

"I have to go in," he said.

Lyric held out her hand. "In that case, give me your shirt." He had a T-shirt under his plaid shirt, which would hang low enough maybe no one would see the blood all down her front.

Isaac let out a long sigh.

"You've been protecting me for years. You think leaving me alone in the car now is a good idea?"

"Are you going to follow me in anyway?"

"Yes." Because she didn't need him to feel obligated to protect her, and that was what was happening here. Maybe it had been love at one time. Now it was too wrapped up in his drive to do the right thing. To prove himself.

He sighed again.

"Turns out I'm in the market for a partner. Even if you like to be the boss way too much."

His lips twitched. There was enough light from street-lamps to see, and she liked it. "That's not going to stop."

She figured that much was true. For the first time in years, she was thinking about the future. But what kind of life would they have if no one figured out who was behind the abductions? "Tell me why you drove here."

"The two gunmen from the hospital work for the guy who owns this club."

She thought about the man who'd come out the day Sasha's body was found. In the trash behind this building. Her car was disposed of here. "Let's go see what he has to say about that."

Isaac unbuttoned his shirt and handed it to her. Not a great look, but it covered the blood. Along with the club lights, she'd be okay.

They crossed the parking lot, Isaac holding her hand. It felt way too good. She couldn't rely on it, or she would become accustomed to him being there. When it inevitably ended, the way everything always did, she would be so much more devastated than before.

And yet, she was the one who'd mentioned them being partners.

So strange how much her life had changed in such a short time. But it was Isaac.

It had always been Isaac.

Tell him.

When they got a moment together later, she would give up the whole of how she felt. What she wanted. It would be the best moment of her life. And she'd get to watch his face while she told him all of it. Seeing his reaction to realizing she felt the same would be the best part.

He slowed at the door and dropped her hand. "Sorry. Habit."

She frowned and started to shake her head.

"Partners. Though, pretending to be a couple isn't a bad play." He picked the lock on the side door. "I know you don't feel the same way. I'll try to check my attraction. You don't need to dance around it."

Before she could ask him what he was talking about, he ducked inside.

"Isaac—"

"You don't need to let me down gently." He didn't turn back. "I won't ever be good enough for you."

She had to hurry up or she was going to lose him, he was

moving so fast. Her jeans were so tough and dry it chafed. "Hey—"

Arms banded around her.

A hand over her mouth.

Lyric bit the skin. Hard.

He hissed but didn't quit dragging her backward. Out of sight. Into a side hall. "Scream and I'll kill you."

Mitch.

30

I saac got to the interior door. Something had happened behind him, but he couldn't let on that he knew.

Instead of grabbing the handle, he spun around.

The hallway was empty. Whoever snatched Lyric had gotten her outside already.

That was fast.

Isaac jogged down the hall.

Someone stepped out of a side door. Everything in him screamed *threat* a second before he felt the presence of a deadly weapon. Instinct flared. He spun to find the barrel of a gun pointed at his face.

"I'm leaving." They weren't going to stop him.

"Don't move or I put you down." The voice sounded like two packs a day and diesel engines.

"Someone just took my girl." He waved at the door, shifted an inch, and felt another person enter the hallway. Both underlings. Security for Salvatore. "I don't want trouble. I just need you to let me go."

A thousand questions raced through his mind. A thousand fears.

He'd worked intense jobs for decades, it never felt like this.

Lyric.

She would pray. Isaac couldn't even form the words.

"I have to *go!*" He screamed the words.

"Search him." Salvatore stood at the end of the hall.

One of the men grabbed him. Isaac fought it, running on pure instinct. He was slammed up against the wall, his legs kicked apart.

"I will shoot you."

The guy patted him down.

Isaac held it together, but barely. "Someone just took my girlfriend!" He figured that was close enough and didn't want to give away more than he had to. "I need to go!"

The guy grabbed the back of Isaac's jacket and turned him to Salvatore. "He's clean."

"So you come into my club, and you aren't armed." Salvatore's brows rose. "Interesting."

"Let me go."

"No, I think we'll chat first." He motioned with his head to the hall behind him.

Isaac wanted to kick off a fight here, but he would get shot. And then where would she be? "Lyric—"

"Ah, yes," Salvatore said. "That's some kind of woman you've got there. But I believe she can take care of herself, no?"

"She shouldn't have to." Whatever this guy thought he knew about Lyric, it couldn't be the truth. Maybe he'd heard back from the guy who broke into her house. The one she ran off. Isaac had thought it might've been Adam, but then there were others in this mix with a broken nose. Like the guy Adam had been fighting with the night Mitch had Isaac pick him up so Mitch could kill him.

Was that who took Lyric?

It didn't make sense to him that Mitch would do that. But if it was true, it wouldn't bode well for Lyric.

Mitch had killed multiple people in the last few days.

But before Isaac could get her back from whoever took her, he had to get out of here. Which meant following Salvatore through the club to his office—something Isaac had intended to do before but had no interest in now.

Not without Lyric.

His stomach churned as he walked into Salvatore's office and checked the guys behind him. Still holding their guns pointed at Isaac. There was nothing he could do. They were out of reach and if he even tried taking them down, he'd get shot for it. These guys likely didn't care if he lived or died here.

They only cared about what they wanted.

Isaac only cared about Lyric. Which didn't make him that different to their single-minded pursuit of money. Or status. Or both. But Isaac cared about a life. A human. Every person in the world was precious, a soul. Lyric was different.

She meant more. To him.

Even if she didn't consider him worthy anymore, because of his mom and the things he'd done. The man he had become.

He still loved her.

It was mildly tragic, knowing he would for the rest of his life. But he couldn't change how he felt.

And he would save her whether she loved him back, or not.

The office door was shut.

Isaac glanced again at the two guys with guns, then turned back to Salvatore. "I'm surprised you've got the full complement here, considering one of your guys is dead in the hospital lobby and another got arrested by the feds."

"Ah, yes. The feds." Salvatore lit a cigar.

"Seems like your men are dropping like flies." As far as Isaac could see, Mitch's business was tangled up in the abductions.

"And yet you remain unscathed." Salvatore took a puff. "Which makes me wonder if you don't have some kind of deal going with the feds." He grinned. "Planning on working both sides? Get your payday, and make it look legit."

"If you say so."

Salvatore chuckled. "Clever. You get paid and you get immunity. That the deal?"

"I need to leave. I think Mitch took her."

He didn't want to stand here and talk about double-crossing good cops. Working the system. Getting whatever he wanted because he was too selfish to do it in a way that could be considered honorable and worthy of respect.

Oh, no. Salvatore had drawn his own conclusion of what Isaac was up to.

Nothing good. He'd looked at what everyone knew of Isaac, what had been reported in the media, and assumed the kind of man Isaac would always be.

Except that wasn't what Isaac chose.

Whether he would have to fight this the rest of his life, or not, Isaac wanted to be someone others considered worthy.

"Yes, Mitch is in some trouble, isn't he?" Salvatore grinned.

"You know about that?" Isaac couldn't leave if there was a chance Salvatore would give him intel he could hand to Addie.

God, keep her safe until I get there. Give her strength.

She had training. He had to trust her, trust God had her

back. That He would protect her.

Otherwise, all that hope Isaac had for a future was nothing.

Sure, he might've just about convinced himself she didn't want him back. But a tiny part of him seemed to refuse to give up the what-ifs—the dream of what could be.

He hadn't asked to come to Benson.

What if it was God's plan?

What if *she* was God's plan?

Isaac said, "Why would Mitch take Lyric?"

"How should I know?" Salvatore sucked on the cigar. "Not like I'm the boss of anything other than this club."

"Is that how you play it?" Though he was careful not to move wrong, Isaac shifted his stance and wind up a target because they thought he acted threateningly. These guys would shoot first and clean it up later. No questions. "I don't buy it. Guy like you?"

"Why not?" Salvatore shrugged.

"You expect me to think you aren't the one in charge. Meanwhile you pretend you don't know exactly what's going on. Like someone else is the boss, and you just take your cut. Keep the cops clear of you because they think you're some underling. I'm surprised they haven't tried to flip you for your own name."

Salvatore's eyes gleamed with humor. "Everyone else believes it."

Isaac said, "I'm not everyone else."

He figured with Orlando's father's name on the building mortgage, the son painted himself as the partier. The trust fund kid who disliked responsibility—not someone who ran a criminal enterprise.

"Who broke into Lyric's house to hurt her?"

Salvatore took another puff. "Why would I care?"

"Do you know?"

"Adam was bragging about it before he got into that fight. Maybe it was him." Salvatore shrugged. "Now I have a question for you. What use to me is a guy with a recognizable face?"

"I came to give you a heads-up that the cops are onto you."

"So you're about favors?"

Isaac shrugged. "It's how the world works. You barter for what you want, and if no one will give it to you, you take it."

Which would mean he was like Mitch. Someone who would abduct another person because they wanted to, even if he thought he *needed* to do it didn't matter.

What did he want with Lyric?

Isaac said, "I might need help sometime, and you'll owe me."

"Hmm." Salvatore quieted for a moment. "Except I already know about the cops."

Isaac figured that was likely, since he'd sent two men to kill Clara and probably Stella as well. Then one tried to kidnap the fed. Now there were multiple dead bodies. The whole thing was a mess.

"Your guy got arrested," Isaac pointed out.

"You can't fix that faster than I can."

So the order to kill him had already gone out? "They'll be expecting that since Brandon Jones was also killed in county lockup."

Salvatore flashed his teeth. "They have no idea."

"I believe that. And it's none of my business." Isaac felt the need to rush out the door surge again. Maybe they wouldn't kill him. "I need to go take care of what *is* my business."

"Mitch is making moves to take over." Salvatore

smoothed down the buttons of his shirt. "Start his own thing elsewhere. So let's talk about that favor." He slid his finger across the mouse pad of his laptop.

"What do you want from me?"

"Take care of Mitch. No questions. No blowbacks. No cops."

"Done."

He motioned to one of the guys with his cigar. "Glen will go with you."

Isaac opened his mouth to object, then caught himself. "Fine." The quicker he was out of here, the better.

"Here." Salvatore spun the laptop so Isaac could see the screen.

Surveillance footage of an exterior door showed him and Lyric approaching and him picking the lock, after which they headed inside and the door closed.

He could hear their conversation in his head. The words he'd fired off at her, born of his fear and insecurity. The belief she didn't consider him any differently than anyone else did. He wanted to take those comments back. Plead with her instead.

He was a mess, and he felt kind of pathetic. But that was what love did to a guy. It made him stupid—until he knew he was loved back. Then it made him better.

Isaac wanted to be better.

Lyric would tell him it was God's love he needed to accept first. Isaac didn't know how to do that other than say a prayer, but right now he had to know she was still alive first.

On screen the door opened.

Mitch exited, Lyric in his grasp. An arm around her neck and a gun pointed at her head.

She shifted. Tried to get away.

Mitch hit her over the head with his gun.

Isaac hissed.

"Also got this." Salvatore clicked the mouse pad. The view changed to a wider angle of the parking lot.

Mitch dragged Lyric to a car. He opened the trunk, dumped her inside, then ducked his head and did something to her. Tie her up?

Isaac's jaw locked he tensed it so hard. "Where did they go?"

"Got LoJack on the car, since Mitch is gunning for my business. I'll send you the link."

"And I'm supposed to say thanks?" Isaac didn't like how this had turned out. The last thing he really wanted was to owe Salvatore anything. A guy like this? Addie would want the operation to continue, and Isaac would have to rub elbows all the way up the chain. Get the name of Salvatore's drug supplier from Juarez, or wherever.

"Take Glen." Salvatore glanced at his guy. "I want confirmation Mitch is dead."

That wasn't Isaac's priority. He only cared about Lyric. If that meant killing Mitch, then so be it. But he could just as easily subdue the guy and hand him over to the feds.

Whatever it took to get her back.

Salvatore turned to Isaac. "Kill him for me. I'll owe you."

Isaac nodded and headed for the door. Glen, whoever he was, followed right behind him until Isaac pushed the door open in full view of the same camera that caught him breaking into the club. His phone buzzed. The GPS for Mitch's car.

Two steps out the door, he spun back. Elbow first.

Glen went down.

Isaac took his gun but not the guy's phone, headed for his own car.

And went after her.

31

———

The car under her rumbled along the road. Every time Mitch turned a corner, Lyric rolled over in the trunk. Hands tied in front of her. Breathing fast, bruises all over from being manhandled—and everything else in the last few days. Or weeks. Or her whole life.

She was tired. So tired of trying so hard to get it right when God was supposed to have done that work Himself. Why did it seem so difficult? Lyric sighed and pushed away those thoughts. They wouldn't get her out of here.

Mitch had driven at least two miles. She had a reasonable idea of where they were, given their direction starting at the club. The turns Mitch made. The noises around them. Mitch's apparent propensity for making friends with the floor under the gas pedal.

The engine roared as he accelerated along a straight stretch of road.

Lyric felt the zip ties. As soon as she'd realized he intended to tie her up, she'd ensured the outcome would be in her favor. She'd managed to keep a tiny gap between her wrists. Hands facing each other.

She lifted her knee, raised her hands to the inside roof of the trunk, and brought them down fast and hard. Teeth gritted.

She grunted. The plastic snapped, leaving her hands free.

"Ouch." Lyric made sure to whisper, even if she didn't think Mitch would be able to hear her.

Before she could feel around her, the car swerved to the right and she rolled. Lyric's face smashed the seat back separating the interior from the trunk. She pushed off with her hands and scooted back, then turned over and felt around where the taillights were. It was sometimes possible to kick the taillights out and get someone's attention in older car models. Maybe new ones, too.

If there was anyone behind her whose attention she could get.

Nothing. Just carpet, no seams. Nothing to pry loose. No way to get out.

Where was the latch? There should've been one.

She felt around some more.

No latch to lower the backseat. There is no way to get into the car from here and get the jump on Mitch.

A lump clogged her throat. Lyric swallowed it back down. She couldn't let her feelings overwhelm her. She had to push out the emotional reaction and work the problem. How many times had she faced a situation like this, with no backup and seemingly no way out?

More than she could count, that was for sure.

It wasn't like this was any worse than any other situation she'd been in. It certainly wasn't worse than being locked in a Syrian prison—or any of the other missions that had gone horribly wrong. And yet, she couldn't hold back the tears that threatened. The ones that trailed from the corners of her eyes no matter what she did to fight it.

You've gone soft.

She swiped away the tears. This was ridiculous. She'd never cried, not even on her worst day. Lyric wasn't the kind of agent who broke. The fact that she was doing it now meant the last four years had given her too much distance from her efficiency and skill. Going to church, becoming a believer.

Allowing God to sway her with His heart.

Working a job that had nothing to do with everything she'd learned how to do as a CIA agent. Letting Isaac in so that he could stomp all over her feelings and tell her he thought she didn't love him the way he loved her. How ridiculous was that?

About as ridiculous as a trained CIA agent letting some local dirt bag get the jump on her.

Twice.

Lyric brushed her cheeks. She had to sniff back the tears and sighed out all her frustration. As soon as the trunk opened, he would find out fast how she felt about all this.

Even if the Bible taught otherwise.

Lyric winced. Was Mitch her neighbor? It depended on how she looked at it. And while her instinct wasn't to turn the other cheek, that likely meant she was probably supposed to. It seemed so at odds with what she wanted. The fight for freedom, the fact she should be all ooh-rah about standing up for her rights.

The truth was, she needed to yield to what the Bible said. Not become the aggressor for the sake of her own wants.

Everything she'd learned the last three or four years was about trusting God for the outcome. If He asked her in the moment to fight, she would. But He might stay silent and ask her to submit to a plan that didn't involve her taking control and trying to fix it herself.

As much as that might chafe.

She'd learned that the thing that seemed so foreign to her flesh was usually the right thing according to God.

There might not be much time to mull it over, as things like this usually kicked off fast. So fast she'd been snatched without realizing what was happening. But God could over-come that issue.

I trust You.

She had to. After all, she could no longer trust her own skills. She'd lost so many walking away from everything she'd been. Determined to leave it all behind.

Then Clara had disappeared. Isaac turned up. That man broke into her house.

All the time she'd spent pretending the person she had been didn't exist, trying desperately to be a new creation because that was what she wanted. Even if she'd forgotten the finer skills, the trained agent was still there.

Maybe she shouldn't have just tried to forget who she was and pretend that person didn't exist. The moment she had been put in a situation like her past life, all that stuff rushed back as though she'd never dealt with it enough not to affect her. The person she'd been wasn't anyone she wanted anything to do with.

She wasn't proud of anything she'd done with the CIA.

As much good as she might've done in the world, what was the point when the whole agency was like a bad stain? They were hardly the Boy Scouts of the world. She'd been part of that. For all the good it did.

Pretending that person didn't exist hadn't worked. Not to heal her, and not to save her life when it counted.

The Bible said she was supposed to be new. That the old had been washed away. But that wasn't how she felt. Instead, that old life lay dormant—like a specter that never went away—and she'd just ignored it. Now she was being bitten by that ghost of the past. Whether it made sense or not, that's what it felt like.

Lyric let out a long sigh that shuddered and broke at the end.

God had moved in her life. He had softened her and shown her how to live. And yet, it seemed like there was something she'd never managed to figure out. Her old life had no business here with her new life, the one He had blessed. He'd kept her safe and continued to do it even now.

On her own, she couldn't make that part of her perish the way she wanted it to. It would always be with her. But if the Bible was right, it should be gone. Spiritually. Maybe that could mean she also felt more distant from it than this.

She didn't want to react to a threat like an untrained civilian, but she had no business acting like the worst kind of agent—one who got the job done with no regard for human lives made in God's image.

I want You to do the work in me, Lord. It hasn't worked with me trying it.

Her past was supposed to be as dead as Jesus had been for those three days before His power brought about a resurrection. She was supposed to have died with Him and been raised new.

I want to feel that today, and every day.

A relationship with Isaac wasn't going to work unless it was God who did it.

She believed God had brought them together, so why would He do so if He was only going to leave them to make a mess of things when they tried to work it all out on their own? That didn't make any sense. And it didn't show His love. The kind of love that saw only righteousness in her because of the blood of Jesus, and yet had the wisdom to lead her to be sanctified more and more every day.

Lyric had a lot to work out, but didn't everyone?

First of all, she had to get Mitch to let her go. That might involve capturing him the way he'd captured her, but she could deal with it.

Show me what to do, Lord.

She was done trying to figure it all out herself.

If the woman she was now had any hope of getting free, of surviving, then she needed to trust God.

That was what people like Lyric Thompson did.

Not the way a CIA agent would solve things—at least, not the kind she'd been.

Mitch hit the brakes. Lyric's stomach clenched. He'd know she was crying, alone in the trunk. He'd either not care, or think it was amusing. Or both. His superiority would cause him to underestimate the creative way spies could solve problems.

Lyric realized her old way of doing things wanted to get back in the driver's seat, but it was only the fear of what might happen.

The engine shut off. She heard a car door slam, signaling Mitch was outside.

He spoke, his voice muffled as though far away. Alongside the car. "Yeah, I'm all set. Ready to meet up." He paused. "Of course I have her. That was our agreement, right?" Another pause. "I'll meet you there soon."

Was it the club owner, Salvatore, that he spoke to? That was who Isaac thought was running the whole operation. *Isaac.* Maybe he was right behind them, ready to rescue her. That could be God's plan.

Or she had to follow His lead and get herself out of here.

God's heart was forgiveness. Maybe the end would come

when she offered it to Mitch for what he was doing. After all, she'd had to forgive herself the things she had done when she accepted God's forgiveness. She just hadn't been living her life as though He'd washed it away. The chains had been there because she refused to let God break them, believing the outcome would be the same if she just ignored it.

The trunk flipped open. Mitch stood, backlit by street-lights. Outside there was only silence and the rustle of trees.

"I forgive you."

It sounded strange to her own ears to say the words. She would likely get used to it, someday. Now was as good a time to start as any.

Mitch reached in. "Whatever."

"Who are you taking me to?" She wanted to know the name of the boss. Isaac could give it to the FBI. Some good would come of this. Like her chance to figure things out with God.

He grabbed her elbow and dragged her out.

She clasped her fingers together, so he might not notice she was untied. "You don't have to do this. Just let me go."

"It's not personal." His hot breath wafted over her face. "Just business."

"It's personal to me. I'm sorry your conscience is so seared you can't see that." She lifted her gaze and stared at his face. "But no one is past being forgiven. I know that more than most."

"Are you hoping to irritate me into killing you, or is this a stall?" His hand on her arm gripped tighter.

Lyric didn't let on that it hurt.

"Time to go." He dragged her away from the car, toward a mansion at the end of this quiet street in the middle of nowhere.

With no one around to help.

32

I saac barely got the car parked before Special Agent Franklin—Addie—spoke through his car speakers.

"Don't engage before we get there."

"How long?" As if Isaac was going to wait even a second.

"We're two minutes out. Isaac, wait for—"

He was out the door and running before she finished. He headed toward the car, where Mitch stood with Lyric, down the lane that led to a mansion.

He'd followed them all the way across town to this suburban neighborhood. The FBI had tracked Mitch's phone as soon as Isaac called them to say he'd taken her. Isaac's insides had been cold since he saw that video. Since Salvatore had asked him to kill Mitch, like he was no better than any common criminal who would take money to end someone's life.

The delay while he waited for the feds might've cost Lyric her life, but she was alive right now. He had been delayed long enough after Salvatore had him strong-armed into the office to make that offer.

Whether Lyric was unhurt? That was a different question.

He'd seen Mitch drag her from that trunk and saw their conversation. What had she said to him? He shook his head and skidded up to them. Didn't matter.

The only thing that mattered was getting her away from Mitch.

Before Mitch could even spin around, Isaac said, "Let her go and throw your weapon down."

Mitch dragged Lyric in front of him and pointed the gun at the side of her neck, just below her ear. "Think you can play hero? Unlikely."

"You're not going to kill her," Isaac said. "You're going to let her go." He could see the tears on Lyric's cheeks. The fear in her eyes. Yet she held still and didn't fight back. She ran the risk of the gun going off against her head if she did, but he'd seen trained agents take the chance at life and come out with their hearts beating and everything intact.

She seemed content to be still.

It was a peace he envied.

Mitch inched toward the house.

Isaac stared at him down the barrel of his gun.

"Like I said"—Mitch barked a laugh that sounded hollow—"you're no kind of hero."

"You're right. I'm nothing."

Isaac was never going to change everyone's mind. People would think what they wanted about him. It didn't matter that he'd tried to do the right thing and be a man he and his friends could be proud of. No one saw a person's intentions —their heart.

All the trying he'd done since he got here had amounted to nothing.

He was a criminal. No matter what, some people would always consider him that.

Lyric would never see him as a hero. She was probably just waiting for the right time to solve this herself, or she could see the FBI approaching from somewhere he couldn't. She would never anticipate that he'd be the hero in any scenario.

Even though that was exactly what he wanted to be for her.

So he moved forward. "Put down the gun."

All the training he had? There were shots he could take here that minimized the risk to her. Where he could hit Mitch and the danger of the shot going wide and hitting her instead was minimal.

Worth the risk.

Lyric shifted. The move caused Mitch's body to turn.

Isaac wasn't going to kill him. "I said put it down!" He screamed the words, tears filling his eyes. He blinked those away, but it made Mitch think he was losing it.

Lyric moved another fraction. Blinked.

Isaac squeezed off a shot. The bullet grazed the back of Mitch's shoulder, from his arm toward his spine in an almost straight line, and embedded in a tree behind him.

Mitch cried out and arched his back.

Lyric slipped out of his grasp.

Isaac slammed the guy in the head with the butt of his gun, then grasped Mitch's gun hand. The weapon clattered to the ground.

Isaac flipped him onto his front and tugged his arms behind him. "You okay, Lyric?"

"You saved my life."

"With your help." He wanted to look at her but couldn't take his focus from Mitch. The guy squirmed under him, hard enough he would flip off Isaac—if Isaac wasn't so stubborn.

"Isaac!"

The thunder of federal boots raced toward them.

"You're with the cops?!" Mitch screamed against the asphalt.

"And you murdered a man in front of me." If he thought he was getting a deal, he could think again. This guy was a stone-cold killer. Even if they needed the name of everyone involved so they could shut down the entire operation.

"Isaac!"

Right. Addie was trying to get his attention as she ran over. He yelled back, "Got any cuffs?"

"Is he bleeding?" She stopped beside him. Special Agent Franklin right now. She would have no loyalty to him as a client of her uncle's company. This was about doing right by the law.

Isaac wondered exactly how much trouble he was in.

"Ma'am? Are you hurt?" That was the male agent, Kyle. The guy spoke to Lyric like she was another innocent victim.

"She's good." Isaac figured Kyle didn't need the wrong impression about Lyric's ability to withstand whatever life threw at her. "She's strong."

She was probably the strongest person he knew.

If only so much of the stuff she'd gone through hadn't been down to him and his family. Isaac winced. Sometimes he hated his mom. And that was the problem, wasn't it? He only hated her *sometimes*. The rest of the time he loved her. The whole thing was completely messed up in his head.

Stella patted Isaac on the shoulder. "Let me, yeah?"

He didn't want to hear a comment about how she had a badge and he didn't, so Isaac stood. "I grazed his shoulder."

"We'll get him medical attention." Stella already had him

cuffed. She rolled Mitch, then lifted his shoulders so he was sitting.

Mitch grunted and glared, as if he wanted to spit on the agent.

"Oh, I'm sorry." Stella's voice held not one ounce of guilt. "You don't like being manhandled against your will? That's a shame."

She backed up, left him sitting there, and pulled her weapon out again. Stella might not do things in ways he or Lyric would appreciate, but she was a solid agent. It was clear to him she had her heart in the right place, even if life had tried to trample it.

He couldn't say that about himself or Lyric. They hadn't lived right lives and sought justice every time. Not the way Stella probably had. Still, he figured the agent had a story of her own to tell.

Isaac put his gun out of sight in the back of his belt. He didn't want to give it up. No point putting Addie on the spot to make the call either. Not when she would likely side with her badge—and her coworkers. That meant Isaac didn't keep hold of his gun.

When was he going to quit thinking the worst of people?

Except for Russ and his elderly neighbor, Edith, everyone he met just didn't measure up. He assumed the worst of them. Didn't trust them. He concluded before they did or said anything that they wouldn't measure up to the friends he'd had before. Brothers. Teammates.

And that, in return, they would consider Isaac not to measure up.

He blew out a breath, paced away a few steps, and tried to get a handle on himself.

"Hey." Lyric touched his arm.

Isaac didn't know what his deal was. She would probably

see right through him, and maybe even know what was up with him, but he wasn't sure he wanted to unpack it. Likely it would only leave him lacking—and her all the more aware of it.

She squeezed his arm. "Hey."

He lifted his head and saw the concern on her face. Only he could do nothing about it, not when she would never feel about him the way he knew he felt about her. Always had. She would feel for him as a friend, connected to him because their lives had intertwined over the years.

Not because they were ever supposed to be together.

That was nothing but a fanciful dream. One that meant he'd have to ask Russ for a reassignment. He couldn't stay here in the friend zone, tortured because he wanted so much more.

He was going to have to let her go.

Lyric shook her head. "Isaac, listen to me. You saved my life just now. All I had to do was surrender."

"You gave up?" He couldn't believe it. Seriously? "This is unbelievable."

She'd actually surrendered? Like she gave up, as though the best thing was for her to die? He couldn't even breathe with the idea he might have to bury her.

It made his chest clench. His heart thump harder, struggling to keep up.

"I had to surrender to what God wanted. Which is something I don't think I've ever done." She shook her head. Her expression was probably meant to be self-effacing but ended up seriously cut.

He was always struggling to keep from passing out at the idea she might've not fought back. That she'd have wound up dead.

"I guess there's a first time for everything," Lyric said.

"I don't know what you're talking about." She was alive, safe. That was the only thing that mattered. They could figure out this whole giving-up business, and he would leave after they got it squared away that she would stay alive. No matter what.

Isaac tugged her to him and gave her a hug. Not what he wanted to do, but three feds and Mitch weren't too far away.

"The grace of God."

Isaac shook his head, his cheek against her hair. "I don't know what that is."

"The reason I could stand down, as it were, and you could be the hero I know you are."

Isaac started to object again.

Lyric leaned back before he could speak. Probably to give him the brush-off. She touched his cheeks with her hands, her fingers cold. She needed a blanket. "I love you."

Isaac frowned. "You don't need to—"

"Isaac." She cut him off. "I *love you.*" Her tone sounded like she wanted to call him a big idiot.

He frowned.

"I'm serious. I really do."

He studied her face.

"You need to believe it."

He wouldn't have her saying whatever this was just to make him feel better. He shook his head and started to object.

Lyric covered his lips with hers.

Isaac turned them so all anyone would see was his back. Lyric's arms behind his neck. He tilted his head to the side and shut out all errant thoughts. Let her tell him exactly how she felt. It swept him away. A tidal wave he couldn't fight any longer. Nothing could withstand the force of what she communicated with that kiss.

Her love for him.

Lyric pulled back, and he touched her forehead with his.

"I love you, too."

She grinned. "Isaac, you're *always* going to be a hero to me. Even if I don't appreciate it all the time."

He frowned.

"I still want you to be that in my life." She squeezed with her arms, bringing him closer. "No one else ever was. Not even my dad. Not one single mentor I ever had. It was only you that protected me. Ever."

"That's all I want to do."

Her eyes drifted closed, and he pressed a kiss to each eyelid.

33

───────

As they turned back to the three FBI agents and the man who'd abducted her, Lyric couldn't help thinking she had everything she'd lost in the palm of her hand. Literally since Isaac took her hand in his and stood right beside her.

Everything that'd gone wrong started when he and his mom left their house in the middle of the night. Now it was as though it had all been restored to her.

She knew it wasn't fair to blame him for that, since he'd been as much of a child as her at the time. If she met his mom now, Lyric hoped she would be able to let go and let God take the reins of her feelings, and the words that came out of her mouth. She didn't want to react the way her humanness wanted to. Rather, she wanted to be able to figure out in all the parts of her life how to be a new creation.

Isaac tugged on her hand, and she leaned on the outside of his shoulder. He kissed her forehead.

Lyric let out a long sigh.

Mitch was in cuffs. She was safe. Isaac was here.

Things weren't perfect, but they just might be better than they'd ever been before.

Addie paced back to Mitch. "Stay silent all you want. We have plenty to charge you with, which means you won't see the outside of a prison until you're past your sell-by date. I'd think you would be interested in another option, though?"

Lyric frowned. She couldn't possibly be talking about offering Mitch a deal, could she? The guy had committed more than one murder, among a number of other serious crimes. There was no way he should be able to—

Isaac squeezed her hand.

Lyric realized she'd stepped forward to strain against his hold on her. She took a step back and glanced at him. Isaac shook his head. He didn't want her to interject herself into the questioning? That was probably the right point to take, considering she was the victim in this particular crime. Nor was it a good idea to object to an FBI agent's line of questioning when she had no idea what Addie's thought process was.

Addie was up to something. At least, Lyric hoped so.

Kyle and Stella stood off to the side, both looking at the screen of Mitch's phone. Trying to gather evidence from it. Figure out Mitch's overall plan here from his messages and call history.

Mitch slumped on the ground but still managed to seem defiant. Like he had no intention of backing down or admitting to anything. "What do I care about other options? Do whatever you're gonna do. My lawyer will have me out in the morning."

Addie said, "Is that right?"

Lyric looked at the house at the end of the lane in the middle of nowhere, a mansion with the exterior lit up in order to showcase its grandeur. Was that where Mitch had been taking her? Or was this simply a spot to leave the car where it might not be found for days, or even weeks? She didn't like the idea she'd have disappeared with no trace, but it did happen.

Some people were never found.

Surely the house had something to do with this. It couldn't be a random place to pull off, and there was no sign of a secondary vehicle if this was where Mitch intended to switch cars.

"Whose house is that?" Lyric asked.

Isaac shrugged. The FBI agents didn't seem to know either.

She held out her hand. "Can I borrow your phone?"

One eyebrow rose, but he entered his password and handed it over.

She looked up their location, then put the address into the county website.

Addie said, "I'm thinking your lawyer might have a hard time explaining away the witness I have to two murders you committed in the last few days."

Mitch's attention whipped around to Isaac.

Lyric went back to the phone, trusting that they had it handled. That all this was under God's sovereignty.

"That guy?" Mitch said. "A known terrorist?"

"He was exonerated," Addie replied.

"You think my lawyer isn't going to *tear* him apart?"

Lyric felt Isaac stiffen beside her, and her heart squeezed. She didn't like anyone talking badly about Isaac. Even if she'd believed so much of it herself that didn't mean she was right any more than they were.

"Evidence is evidence," Addie said. "You think I can't prove you guilty beyond a reasonable doubt even without witness testimony? You've just strengthened my case, because now I know what your tactic will be. And it's nothing but a smoke screen designed to deflect away from the fact I can prove you're the kind of man who abducts and sells women. Deals drugs. And if you think I can't prove you're the one who fired the guns that killed two people in the last few days —if not more, and I'll find them, too—then you don't understand the FBI well."

Lyric pulled up the information for the house. "Whoa."

Kyle moved toward her. "What is it?"

"The house at the end of the street belongs to Jeremy Allerton Senior."

Kyle's eyebrows rose. He turned to Mitch. "Friend of yours?"

Lyric said, "I'm surprised Mitch hasn't killed him already. Which means the guy is likely his ticket out of here." She addressed Mitch, saying, "The question is, do you work for him or does he work for you?"

"Neither." He grinned a flash of white teeth in the dark.

Her eyes had adjusted to the night and the twin beams of all the car headlights. She could even see into the trees now, though that would be better if they turned off that yellow glow.

Addie took over the questioning. "Give us information on Allerton and what he's up to, and it could put you in better standing with the US attorney. Get you a cell with a bigger window. Or more TV time."

At least they weren't offering him a way out of the mess he was in.

"Like tell you Allerton is the mastermind of all this?" Mitch said. "He's the one giving orders, the one who told me to bring her to him." He motioned with his chin in Lyric's direction. "Because he's the boss."

She turned to Isaac and whispered, "Does he really think we'll believe that?"

Isaac shrugged with a slight smile that was just for her.

Stella handed Addie the phone. "Kyle and I will check out the house. See what Allerton Senior has to say for himself about Mitch. I figure there's a chance we can find the truth for ourselves regardless of what these two say."

Addie nodded. "The evidence will speak for itself."

The two feds strode off down the lane toward the house.

Lyric had no desire to be there with them. Not because she didn't like the person she'd been as a CIA agent, or even before that. Pushing her emotions down and getting the job done with cold efficiency all to keep from caring too much about the people who were hurt—the innocents caught up in collateral damage.

Isaac moved forward a step toward Mitch, still holding her hand. "We know you're cutting out Salvatore and starting your own business. That's what all this is about."

Mitch said nothing.

"If you're working with Allerton, it's because he's betraying whatever agreement he also has with Salvatore, or he's your payday so you can get the funds to make a run for it. Start over somewhere else."

Lyric nodded. "We know you've been cleaning house, making a move. It's obvious to everyone, so don't bother pretending. You're not that good."

Mitch spat in her direction.

"And as for witnesses?" She paused. "There's always me."

He blinked.

Isaac let out a low chuckle that sounded satisfied.

She resisted the urge to grin in triumph. "Local business owner. One of your victims." She turned to Isaac. "Of course, we'll have to explain why we came to be at the building supply yard where we witnessed the murder."

She gasped and turned back to Mitch. "Oh, but that's right. He isn't dead."

Mitch didn't move. Didn't speak.

"So I guess *he* can be a witness that you tried to murder him."

"Attempted murder." Mitch scoffed. "Or so you say."

"Yeah. But I don't really care," she said. "That's the thing. You and your future don't mean anything to me. At all."

It wasn't her job to be invested in everything that went wrong in the world. She had tried her best to save Clara, and things had turned out badly but not because of her lack of trying. If she'd prayed, she figured she'd have done the same thing. Though, she might've had Isaac go with her. That could've meant he was the one who caught the bullet—or it could easily have been her.

Who knew how things would turn out except for the One who held everything in the palm of His hand?

She trusted Him.

After all, He had given her a future intertwined with Isaac's. A thought that had her turning to him.

He frowned. "What is it?"

She wanted peace, and him. How did she tell him that? She had a million things to figure out, like deciding if she wanted to keep trying with her cabins. Would she want to live in the city if she gave up her business? "Maybe the whole thing with Allerton wanting my land was about Mitch and whatever they had going on." She frowned. "I don't know."

"Or that's what their company does, and then you caught his eye."

She winced. "When I went to see him?"

"Maybe." Isaac shrugged. "But it's over now, and they're all going down. No one will be trying to take your business from you or abducting you."

"Sounds good." She managed to smile. "Some peace and quiet sounds really, really good."

"We could go on a date."

Her smile turned to a grin. "I like the sound of that."

"You could wear—"

"Absolutely not." She knew he was talking about the dress she'd worn to get Allerton's attention—which evidently might have worked *too* well. "I'm burning that thing."

Isaac chuckled.

"Is there anyone else in the house apart from Allerton?" Addie stood over Mitch. "Well?"

Isaac let go of her hand and strode to the guy. "Was it Allerton you were supposed to meet?"

Mitch turned his head away. "I'm not talking to you."

"You might not have a choice." Isaac folded his arms across his chest. Protecting her. Saving her.

Mitch scoffed. "Do I look like I care?"

Lyric bit her lip, ready to go. She'd been rescued, and as soon as they were allowed to leave, she and Isaac could get out of here.

Gunshots sounded in the direction of the house.

Lyric whirled around and reached for a weapon she didn't have. She would have to rely on God to keep her safe, because she couldn't defend herself if anything happened. The others might not be available to help her in the heat of a dangerous moment.

Don't let me fail.

She didn't plan on losing her resolve when she'd just learned how to put things in the right order.

Addie twisted around, moving so she could see Mitch and look at the house where the shots had come from.

Lyric spotted her lips moving silently and realized the agent was praying. She immediately did the same in her heart, asking for safety and protection for the two FBI agents who'd gone in to get Allerton.

In the distance, through the trees, Lyric spotted a figure on the move. Running fast.

Allerton was getting away.

"Hey!" Lyric tore off in that direction.

34

———

I saac sprinted right after Lyric as she tore down a narrow path through the forest. It took him a couple of steps, but he figured out what triggered her to run.

A dark figure sprinted through the woods. One arm straightened, the muzzle of a gun in their hand went off, and a gunshot echoed through the night.

"Lyric!" Isaac tried not to shout too loudly. Did they need to take cover? He didn't want to sideline her, but he wouldn't allow her to get hit.

She slowed a fraction, and he caught up.

He picked up his pace and ran slightly in front of her.

"Don't tell me to go back." Her voice was breathy, but he could hear her determination.

"Just stay behind me."

If anyone was going to get shot here, it was him. That was for sure. After finally reaching a great place—a place he wanted to hang out before they took the next step—he wasn't about to lose Lyric. She had to do what she thought she should, which meant he was with her—guarding her the way he'd wanted to do every day of his life.

The way he would for the rest of their lives if she let him.

She said nothing, so he kept running toward the fleeing man. Whoever it was.

Isaac pumped his arms and legs, determined to take the guy down. This had to be over tonight. Something in him said they couldn't let anyone get away or they would never be safe.

Lyric would never be safe.

For some reason, Mitch's words rolled through his mind. Even though that was the last thing he needed, Isaac couldn't spend the energy fighting errant thoughts. He couldn't deny Mitch's words hadn't hurt. And he didn't want to be that guy they all thought he was—not now, and not ever.

Nearby, Addie prayed.

That kind of faith wasn't something he found himself comfortable with yet, but it would be a good idea to get comfortable with it.

He could believe in a God who had given him back Lyric like He had.

She was the only person who knew everything and saw him the way he wanted to be seen. Even his former teammates from Chevalier Protection Specialists hadn't understood when he did what he did. They'd called it betrayal at first. Then things had been strained—to say the least.

Lyric had hurts of her own, but she had given him a grace he didn't deserve. Because she knew God. Like the pastor had explained, she could give away His gifts to others.

He could *not* lose her now. And he didn't want her anywhere else but with him.

Thank You.

Lyric in his life, both of them loving each other, was a grace he hadn't done anything to earn. She was a gift, plain and simple.

Stella appeared to his left, running full out. "FBI! Freeze!" She chased down the suspect with an impressive determination.

Isaac did the same, picking up his speed, and found the two paths joined together.

Stella glanced once at him.

Isaac said, "Kyle?"

"Behind me."

Isaac didn't have time to look. He'd have to hope the fed didn't shoot him in the back by accident. "Stop! It's over!" he yelled. "Give it up." Mostly just so Kyle would know he was on their side.

They chased down the man ahead of them, Lyric right there with them. Was it Allerton? Surely an older man couldn't run this well. But he hadn't seemed frail or overweight. Maybe he kept his figure trim because he worked out.

Stella yelled, "FBI! Stop!"

The man ahead of them swung his arm around and fired another shot.

They all split apart and ducked. Isaac slowed enough to check Lyric was good. Stella got off a shot. She missed. Isaac planted a knee, aimed, and squeezed the trigger like he'd done a thousand times. Now he was doing it to keep Lyric safe, and there was something so right about that.

The man ahead of them spun from the force and fell to the ground, crying out. Isaac had winged him.

Not dead.

They raced over to him. Stella kicked the gun away from his hand. "Don't move."

The guy clutched his shoulder and glared up at them. Not the older Allerton. Isaac frowned. "Steve?"

Stella said, "Hands on your head."

There was such authority in her voice Isaac almost lifted his own hands. He opened his phone and flipped on the camera flashlight. He was right about the man's identity.

"You know this guy?" Stella shifted a fraction. Barely.

"Works for Mitch."

She said, "You okay, partner?"

Kyle had jogged up to them. The male agent said, "Yep." Also clutching his shoulder.

Isaac asked him, "You were shot?"

Kyle winced. "Just a scratch."

"I'm not so sure about that." Lyric moved around him. "I'm going to look, okay?"

Isaac didn't like her being so far from him, but the threat had been neutralized. He figured now was as good a time as any to trust God had them all in His hands. To Stella he said, "And Allerton Senior?"

Kyle hissed.

"Sorry," Lyric muttered. "You're right though. It's not deep, but you still need it looked at. Bullets are dirty, and that will get infected even if you don't need stitches."

Stella frowned. "How do you know that?"

"I didn't always run a resort of cabins."

"You told me you were a travel agent."

Lyric shrugged. "It was a good lie."

Steven lay on the ground, clutching his shoulder, narrowed his eyes at Lyric with a menace Isaac didn't like at all. Not on a night like this when all his instincts fired.

Isaac could read plenty into his expression, regardless of whether he said anything. "Don't even think about it."

"Allerton is inside the house," Stella said. "Dead."

"So Mitch was here to meet you?"

Steve scoffed. "As if I was going to let them make the

deal behind my back? I'm not losing money. And I'm *not* being cut out of anything."

"Right." Isaac figured the guy was entitled enough to get his back up that Mitch was making a run for it. And yet, Salvatore was the one who oversaw the whole operation. When he found out everyone was in this for themselves, things would get ugly. "Wanna tell me why you've got a broken nose?"

Lyric sucked in a breath.

Now that Isaac thought about it, he hadn't seen Steve at work since Lyric was attacked. Because he was her assailant?

Salvatore had told him Adam bragged about doing it. But he could've been lying, spreading a rumor. Who knew what the truth was?

Steve and Allerton either got protective custody in prison —which involved being in solitary confinement twenty-three hours a day—or Salvatore would send a killer and they would find themselves shanked in a dark corner of the prison.

Stella said, "Let's get this guy up and back to Addie."

Isaac told her, "You keep your gun aimed," then moved to Steve. As long as she didn't shoot, he'd take control of the suspect who'd shot at them. "I got him."

"Thanks."

He frowned at her. "You're welcome." Why Stella was suddenly grateful, he didn't know. He wasn't going to discount it. They were only three agents in Benson. Backup came in all shapes and sizes, but he'd worked private security most of his life. Never anything official, even if so many people believed he'd been CIA.

Maybe it wasn't normal for cops to ask civilians to give them a hand.

Or accept help.

Still, the FBI agent handed Isaac a set of cuffs. He then secured Steve's injured arm to his belt, leaving him to hold his shoulder with the other hand, and patted him down for any hidden weapons. He found a small amount of coke in his pants pocket in a clear baggie and gave that to Stella. No weapons.

Isaac turned. "Lyric?"

"Right here." She moved to his side, and they walked as a group toward Addie and Mitch. Kyle up front on point, since he was injured. Stella at the back, able to protect them all at their most vulnerable side.

"Is it over?"

Isaac considered Lyric's question and the fact her instincts remained. She might be rustier than him, as she'd been out of the game for four years now. But she was right. "Keep your eyes peeled."

Kyle picked up his pace slightly. "We got them both. We get them back to lockup and we go home." The guy shrugged, but he still scanned the area as he walked.

Stella said, "Burgers at O'Callaghan's."

"Addie is never gonna go for that," Lyric said. "Russ hates that place so much."

Kyle chuckled. "True. I was thinking Café Fiesta."

Stella sighed. "Fine."

When Addie was in sight, she called out, "You guys good?"

Kyle yelled back. "Senior is dead in the house. We need PD and the crime lab there. But we also need to get these two and the civilians out of here."

"Ambulances?"

"We can take them to the hospital. Then jail," Kyle said. "I vote everyone gets checked out."

"Good," Addie said. "If we get this done fast, I should be

good to pick up Jake from the airport tomorrow night."

Isaac said, "Paperwork seriously takes you that long?"

Lyric chuckled. "There's a reason why we did the jobs we did."

He grinned at her. "You're right about that."

Stella took hold of Steve from him. "What jobs? Who are you guys?"

"You don't know about me?"

Stella said, "Okay, fine. Maybe you didn't have paperwork, but what was Lyric?"

"She could tell you," Isaac said. "But then she'd have to kill you."

Lyric shoved his shoulder playfully, chuckling. "He's joking."

"Am I?"

Stella said, "My security clearance is pretty high. I worked with the military once finding a missing stealth plane."

"Huh."

"You'd be surprised." Stella wandered off with her suspect.

Lyric rode with him. The feds doubled up, Kyle and Stella taking the two prisoners so Addie could take point here at the house with the cops.

Isaac figured that was a good idea. Still, he said, "I'm not sure about the hospital."

Addie shrugged. "We can get your statements tomorrow at the office."

"Sounds good." Isaac held Lyric's door for her and closed it when she'd settled.

When he got in her side, she said, "Is this how it's going to be?"

"How about not being shot for a while?" he suggested.

"Some peace and quiet sounds good."

"I was talking about you holding the door for me."

"Yes, that's *exactly* how it's going to be." He checked he was behind Stella and Kyle and glanced over at her. "You okay with that?"

"Would you be okay if I kept my cabins and tried to make them work?"

"If that's what you want."

"What if I closed down the business and we just lived on the land?" Her voice had softened.

"I can do construction jobs. Might be a gap in the market now half the guys in the city got arrested or died." He might even be able to clean house at Mitch's business and start his own. "I can help you if you want to change up anything around the resort. Fix up the house and make an addition. Renovate a bit."

"That's not going to bring in money."

"Hmm. Guess we will need income," he said. "No burning desire to write a tell-all memoir about your life as a spy and how the government betrayed you?"

"That sounds much too much like paperwork." She squeezed his hand.

Isaac laughed.

Up ahead he spotted an SUV on the left side of the road brake hard and stop in the middle of the street. A guy jumped from the back.

Before Isaac could do anything, the man lifted an RPG-7 from the backseat and fired it at the car in front of them.

The FBI vehicle exploded. The front end lifted into the air, and the whole thing flipped over. Isaac hit the brakes and Lyric screamed.

The car landed on the asphalt in front of them, flames everywhere.

35

L yric took another breath but forced her body to stop before she screamed again. She gasped a couple of times. "Isaac."

In front of them the car lay upside down. Flames licked the undercarriage. The SUV that had stopped on the other side of the road was still there. The guy who fired the RPG stood where he was to survey his handiwork. All pleased with himself.

She wanted to punch his smug face—if that wouldn't end up with her getting shot.

Isaac pushed out a breath. "We need to see if they're alive."

She'd never been more grateful not to be alone. It was just that Lyric couldn't vocalize it.

Two FBI agents and two criminals. "I hope someone is."

She heard the words as though another person said them. Shock. She was in shock.

The likelihood of survival for the occupants in the car in front wasn't high, though. She thought that as she stared at the damage in front of them and tried to get a handle on the surprise of seeing it happen right in front of them.

Process. Move on. Work the problem.

She pushed her door open and moved to get out. Get to the FBI agents. Get help.

"Lyric." Isaac barked her name.

She didn't have time to turn back and see what it was before Isaac climbed over the center console. "Go. Go." He shoved her out the door.

She landed on the asphalt and heard the telltale launch of an RPG. Isaac covered her with his body.

"No." Everything in her mind screamed. He would let himself die to protect her. She knew he would. He wanted to be the one who got hurt rather than allow her to be injured or killed. It was what he wanted. "*No.*"

"Hold still."

The car exploded behind them.

"Don't." She couldn't formulate more words than that, and it didn't matter. The word was lost in the fireball blast of heat and flames that rippled over them. She hissed a breath out in defiance of him and the attack.

Isaac cried out, the sound ringing in her ears. As though he was all around her. Covering her.

Lyric felt the burn of tears, as hot as the flames surrounding them.

"Here." He shifted and put a gun in her hand, then lifted his weight off her.

Lyric winced at the pain points where he'd pressed her against the asphalt but clambered to her hands and knees, adjusted her grip on the gun, and moved to the car's front end. Theirs hadn't flipped over like the car in front.

As she watched, men poured out of the car with guns.

There were three of them, followed by the RPG guy who ditched it to grab a pistol. "Salvatore."

They headed for the car in front, determined to finish the job they'd started. Ensure everyone was dead.

Lyric planted a knee and took out the first guy.

Isaac lifted up beside her, fired two shots of his own over the hood of their car, and downed the second one. That took care of half the men.

One remaining man ran for the car they'd taken out first. The other hunkered down behind an open door.

She had to get to the car in front before they did.

Otherwise they'd won.

She said, "Cover."

Isaac disagreed, but said, "Go."

She ran flat out for the car ahead of them. It was still burning. The man who had hunkered down fired at her, and she fired back as she ran. Arm outstretched. She didn't even look, just fired blindly to the side and pumped her legs and free arm as hard as possible. Not her finest moment.

Isaac squeezed off shots to pin him down.

Salvatore. The one responsible for this.

But she wasn't going to go after him. That would only be revenge. She needed to check for survivors and see if anyone needed help she could give immediately. If Isaac wanted to take care of the culprit, that was fine by her.

She ducked to a crouch behind the front of the car, now pointed toward theirs. The first man, who'd come over to the same car, emerged around the front. She fired at him, and he went down.

Isaac would take care of the man behind cover. She needed to check for survivors.

Lyric dipped her head and looked in the front.

Two shots. She heard a man fall.

Isaac raced up behind her. "How bad is it?"

"We need fire and police and an ambulance." Best to cover all their bases. It seemed wrong to worry about the heat on her face, to feel its effects when both men in the back were gone. Kyle had been seated in the passenger seat.

"Go check on Kyle."

She opened the driver's door, fought the straining metal, and managed to get it wide enough she could crouch between the door and frame. "Stella? Stella, can you hear me?" There was a lot of blood. Stella had fallen out of her seatbelt and lay twisted on the roof of the car. She pressed two fingers against the female agent's neck.

"Kyle is DOA."

Lyric winced. "I've got a pulse." She turned so she could get a good grip on Stella. Lyric slid her from the car and laid her out on the asphalt. "Hey, girl. You with me?"

Above them, the underside of the car flickered with flames. Would it blow?

Isaac knelt by her.

"Do we need to move away from the car?"

"Fire will be here in a few minutes. They can take care of it." He squeezed her shoulder.

She was so grateful to him for being here with her she almost slumped onto the ground, but Stella needed help. "She's bleeding on her leg."

Isaac said, "I see it," and unbuckled his belt. It took her a second to figure out what he was doing, but she put it together when he fastened it tight. High on Stella's leg.

She was going to bleed out if she didn't get help.

Lyric's head swam. She planted a hand on the gritty asphalt and took a moment just to breathe.

"You good?" Isaac said.

She shook her head. Three people were dead, and Stella could lose her life. So much destruction.

Lord, help us.

She didn't want Stella to die. But if the FBI agent woke up right now, she might want to. Her partner was dead. She would be in immense pain. Maybe it was for the best.

Lyric cared about her, even though Stella hadn't done right by her. She didn't want the agent to have to suffer. "There's no one else we have to be worried about, right?"

"Unless Salvatore sends more guys, we're good."

She pushed out a breath and looked around. The street was empty. She could hear distant sirens, but they weren't in view yet. "Hurry up. Hurry up." She'd never been so invested in first responders in her life. Never saw a need for them. Now it felt like a lifeline, as much as having Isaac here with her. "Thank you."

He touched her cheek. "You don't even have to ask."

"I know."

"I want to be at the cabins, even if it's just us and no guests. There's something about it that's just…peaceful."

She wondered if really anything would feel peaceful surrounded by burning cars and sirens. But she knew what he meant. She nodded, too overwhelmed with emotion to speak without breaking down.

Lyric sniffed back a tear and looked down at Stella. "We need to call Addie."

A fire truck pulled up, and first responders spilled out like worker bees. All she could see was black and yellow as they rushed around, then lifted her to stand and led her away from Stella.

Lyric turned to look at them, now surrounding the agent. "She's FBI!"

"We have her, okay?" His grip was firm, his voice gruff. "Then we'll get you checked out."

Lyric shook her head. "I'm fine."

Then Isaac was there. Surrounding her with the strength of his arms.

She slid hers around his waist and found shreds of clothing. Hot edges, as though his jacket had been burned. She ran her hands up and down and found hot skin on the back of his neck. Singed hair. "Isaac—"

He shook his head and kept holding her. "I'm good. Just hang on to me."

She buried her face in his neck, and they stood together while the world erupted around them in chaos. Shouted orders. The spray of water hoses. An ambulance siren.

Cops.

Just hang on to me.

Lyric held tight to him, and his words. "Don't let go."

"I won't."

Her next inhale shuddered through her, and tears gathered. They were okay. Stella wasn't, and Kyle had lost his life. But they were okay.

In a way it felt like a hollow victory. There was plenty to be thankful for. Plenty to entreat God about, like asking for Stella's quick recovery or that she wouldn't lose her life later because her body succumbed to the injuries.

And yet, even with all that she could be grateful they'd survived.

36

"What's the prognosis?"

Isaac blinked and realized Russ stood in front of him. He stood up from the waiting room chair and stretched his arms. "Nothing new, but they did say she's stable."

Lyric sat on the chair beside him. Her head against the wall, as if fast asleep. Beyond her sat Edith, who'd been driven here by her grandson Eric. The older woman had sat with them, beside Lyric, watching over her now as she slept. As for the cop, Eric wore a worried look on his face and paced the waiting room for news about Stella. Something Isaac and Edith both found interesting.

He ushered Russ away a couple of steps and said, "She has broken bones and a concussion. They're patching up the cuts. She was bleeding a lot."

Isaac had no idea if he was even making sense.

Russ squeezed his shoulder. "You did good."

He felt his chest expand to its full size for the first time since they saw the car explode in front of him. Of all the things he'd seen and done in his life, for some reason that one stopped him in his tracks. Probably because Lyric had been in danger again.

He looked back at her. Still sleeping.

"She okay?"

Isaac nodded. "I think so. Maybe better than me, considering she seems to have taken all this in stride."

"Addie will be here soon. She met with the police securing both scenes—the house and the street—and she wanted to be there when Kyle's body was removed from the car."

Isaac said, "That's good." He didn't envy what it would feel like when Stella woke and discovered her partner was dead. Or Addie, losing a friend. Kyle's family and friends would be burying him in the next few days.

"Need anything else from me? The Accountant's Office is happy to provide whatever it is. You've done a service to this community."

Isaac didn't want to have earned kudos or favors. All he wanted was peace and time to spend with Lyric. He could ask for bookings at her cabins, but did she want to be a host right now? Then there were his own needs. Or wants. Or things he simply needed to get past so he could live his life.

"What is it, Son?"

"My mom is a client, right?" He didn't want to mention the Accountant's Office when it might be overheard.

He'd also believed—for several weeks—that she was dead. Even if history suggested it might not be true, Isaac had acted as though it was.

His biological father had been supposedly dead for years, only to die for real in front of a former friend of Isaac's. For a while Isaac had considered that to be yet another faked death, considering he'd lived with the man for years—been raised by him—while the world believed he was dead.

It was hard to know what to believe, and easier to put all of it out of his mind. Especially when he'd discovered Lyric was here.

"It's under consideration," Russ said. "That's part of why I mentioned her to you."

"Because she wants to talk with me?"

"Your reaction to that request told me a lot of what I was looking for, what I needed to know, in order to proceed with her case." Russ shifted his shoulders in the chambray shirt. "You won't see her unless you want to."

"I don't think she should live in Benson."

"Okay." Russ nodded.

"But maybe I want to talk to her. See what she has to say." Isaac hesitated, wondering if that was even a good idea.

The conversation could go several ways given it was his mom they were talking about. She might want to apologize, or blame him, or commiserate in a totally passive-aggressive way. Or she could believe they were the victims.

Isaac had no clue until he spoke with Lana. It didn't mean Lyric had to establish a relationship with her, but he figured he could do with the closure for himself.

"I'll let her know. See when we can set it up."

"You can just give her my number."

Russ nodded. "Will do."

Isaac glanced over at Lyric and Edith. The older woman had her hand over Lyric's, her lips moving while Lyric slept. Praying, the way Addie had.

Surrounding them both with prayer.

Isaac figured it was why things came out the way they had, even if no one could discern why Kyle still lost his life. Victory didn't mean everyone survived. It didn't even mean the mission turned out the way it had been planned.

God knew what the future held. He knew the why.

As Lyric would've told him, Isaac just needed to trust Him. And given all the grace he'd been shown so far, in his friends and his victories—his survival—and the hope of life he had in front of him? Isaac couldn't do anything else.

"Is there any way for me to contact my former teammates? Maybe get them a message that I'm okay." He was more than okay, but that would be enough.

"You think they don't know you're doing just fine here?" Russ's bushy white brows lifted. "Your old boss, Zander something, has been hounding me since you showed up. My inbox is full." Russ grinned. Before he said anything else, he twisted around and lifted a hand.

Addie was here.

But Isaac couldn't focus on this. He was too caught up in the idea that his former boss—a friend and brother at one time—even cared about him.

Yet more grace.

37

L yric woke to the murmur of voices.

"Hey, there."

She twisted and saw Edith still beside her. After believing the older woman didn't like her at first, Lyric thought it strange she was so supportive now, but maybe not so strange. It had been a crazy day, following a crazy few weeks.

Lyric realized Edith was waiting for a response. "Hey."

Addie crossed the waiting area to them.

Eric, Edith's cop grandson, met them. Russ sat by Addie. Then Isaac took his chair by Lyric, and her hand.

"I called Kyle's supervisor in Seattle," Addie began. "They're driving to his parents' house to inform them what happened." No one said much. "Salvatore is dead, along with everyone else involved. The police department executed search warrants on Mitch's house, Allerton's place, and their businesses, including the club. There's a lot to clean up, but it seems they were all involved in Salvatore's abduction and auction business."

Eric's jaw flexed.

Russ squeezed his shoulder.

Addie continued, "I'm coordinating with the police department. We're going to get a list of everyone they're connected to, and not one person related to this will get out from this unscathed. Heads are going to roll."

"Good." Edith sounded so determined, Lyric wondered what the woman got up to in her younger days. She lived on the same floor as Isaac, but that couldn't mean she had anything to do with the Accountant's Office. Did it?

Maybe it was need to know—or Edith would tell her one day.

Addie said, "Thank you for all your help, Lyric. And Isaac. Both of you saved the day as far as I'm concerned."

Eric nodded. "Me, too. You probably saved Stella's life."

Lyric figured there was likely no "probably." They had saved her, considering Salvatore and his men had hung around to finish the job.

"Any other time, I'd recommend you both for medals." Addie shrugged. "But…"

Lyric nodded.

Eric frowned. He was about to speak, probably to ask what they were talking about. Edith shook her head, and he said nothing.

Isaac squeezed Lyric's hand. To Addie he said, "You're welcome."

"Come by my office on Monday. We can talk about how you get a cut of all seized illegal assets or a percentage of their monetary value."

Lyric blinked.

"As a confidential informant, it's part of the deal," Addie said. "And given the operation you took down, this could be serious money."

"Uh…thanks," Isaac said, as if unsure what to make of

it. A little hope, a little caution—the result of being burned so many times.

"Anything else?" Lyric was ready to get out of here as soon as they got word that Stella had woken.

Addie shook her head.

Isaac squeezed Lyric's hand. "Let's go get coffee for everyone."

Edith said, "Tea for me."

"Yes, ma'am."

They headed down the hall, still holding her hand. Isaac jabbed the button for the elevator, then turned to her. "Doing okay?"

"With you here? How could I not be?"

His face softened. Still, underneath she could see his exhaustion. Lyric touched her hands to his cheeks and kissed him. "It starts now."

"What does?"

"Forever."

Three weeks later

Isaac stepped into Lyric's main cabin. A guest stood at the desk, checking out. The guy, fiftysomething and about as benign as a loan officer, handed her a key.

"Thank you. I hope you enjoyed your stay." She gave the guy a perfunctory smile, glanced once at Isaac, and turned to her computer.

"We did," the guest said. "Thanks." He hesitated, then continued, "I saw that you're closing down for a while on your website."

"That's right." Lyric nodded. "Likely for a few months, though I haven't completely decided yet if or when I'll reopen."

Isaac had also persuaded Addie to write Lyric's name down as a confidential informant. That way she'd been officially given half what he made from the recovery of all the illegal assets. She now had the money to do whatever she wanted with the cabins.

He'd already started his new construction business, and now Lyric got to decide what was next for her.

"Have a good one." The guy headed out.

Isaac waited until the door shut, then moved into her space. "Hey."

Lips twitching, she lifted her gaze to his. "Hey, yourself."

Isaac had bought a ring the day before. The urge to get on one knee burned in his gut like a gas station corn dog, but he wanted to wait for the right time.

He lowered his face to kiss her when the phone in his pocket buzzed.

Isaac groaned and moved away, pulled it out, and looked at the screen. He didn't recognize the number.

"I should go check on the slow cooker," Lyric said. "Make sure it's not boiling over."

Isaac nodded. He vaguely heard her head upstairs. Instead of wondering who it was and missing the call, he slid his thumb across the screen. He'd learned a lot about grace the last three weeks, talking for hours with Lyric. Coffee with Russ. He'd even met with the church pastor and got enrolled in a new believers' class.

"Hello?"

There was a beat of silence, then he heard, "Isaac?"

"Yeah, Mom. It's me." She'd finally called. Lana, a woman who didn't have much maternal instinct that he'd been able to find in her. As for operating, she was the best there ever was. No joke.

"It's good to hear your voice." She sounded sad almost.

"How are you?" Isaac didn't want to get into how he'd turned her down if she wanted to live in Benson. He didn't mind getting to know each other now that they were free to live different lives, but he didn't need her in his and Lyric's faces. Things would take time, and he had to protect what God was building here until then.

"I'm good. Things are…quiet." She spoke softly, in a way he'd never heard from her before. "I've had a lot of time to think since I got hurt before Christmas. Time to reflect and figure some things out."

"Can I ask you something?"

"Sure, honey."

Isaac found himself frowning at that. "Is my father alive, or is he dead?"

"As far as I've been able to figure out, he really did die in Africa with Judah."

Not that Isaac doubted his friend, but he needed to know. And yet, he found he still wasn't completely convinced. "It's only been a few weeks, but it feels like a lifetime I've been out of everything I knew. So much has happened. Things are good."

"It's okay if you don't want to rock that boat."

That was pretty accurate for how he felt.

"I'm glad things are good."

"Thanks, Mom." He'd always called her Lana on missions, or around others. "We could talk regularly, if you want."

"I'd like that." She went quiet for a second.

He wondered briefly if she would apologize to him. For any of it.

"I love you." Before he could respond, she said, "Take care of Lyric."

The line beeped.

Isaac stared at the phone.

"She hung up?"

He turned to Lyric and nodded.

"Everything okay?" She slid her arms around his middle.

Isaac touched his lips to hers. "Best it's ever been."

"Yeah?"

"Although," he said, "maybe it could be better."

"How's that?" The brightness of her smile glinted like the sun reflected there.

"Marry me."

"Was that a question?"

Not really. "Sure."

Lyric chuckled. "Then I guess your answer is, 'Sure.'"

He frowned.

"Why not?"

He deserved that. "Yes. Why not?"

The humor on her lips tasted like the promise of a future he couldn't wait to experience.

And forever started right now.

I hope you enjoyed *Hard Target*, please consider leaving a review, it really helps others find their next read!

The series continues in *Hollow Point*, coming May 2022.

ALSO BY LISA PHILLIPS

The whole Last Chance Downrange series:

Point of Impact

Hard Target

Hollow Point

Terminal Velocity

Find more stories based in Last Chance County at:

www.lastchancecounty.com

Find out about Lisa's other series and stand-alone books at her website:

authorlisaphillips.com

Other series by Lisa:

Chevalier Protection Specialists

Last Chance County

Northwest Counter-Terrorism Taskforce

Double Down

WITSEC Town (Sanctuary)

Love Inspired Suspense titles

ABOUT THE AUTHOR

Find out more about Lisa Phillips, and other books she has written, by visiting her website: https://authorlisaphillips.com

Would you also share about the book on Social Media, leave a review on Lisa's page and share about your experience? Your review will help others find great clean fiction and decide what to read next!

Visit https://authorlisaphillips.com/subscribe where you can sign up for my NEWSLETTER and get free books!